SACRIFICED

A KIERAN YEATS MYSTERY

LINDA J WRIGHT

Published 2019
Printed in the United States of America

First Edition
ISBN 978-1-7323593-2-1
E-ISBN 978-1-7323593-3-8
Library of Congress Control Number: 2019907799

Cover Design by Bianca Gill
Cats Paw Books

Book layout by ebooklaunch.com

For information, contact:

Cats Paw Books
630 Hickory Street NW
Suite 120-119
Albany, OR 97321
catspawbooks@mail.com

PRAISE FOR
STOLEN: A KIERAN YEATS MYSTERY

"A superb series kickoff. Wright, who has been involved in animal advocacy for over 30 years, combines her passionate commitment to animal rights with a riveting whodunit that's not dependent on murder to sustain interest."

Publishers Weekly (Starred Review)

"One of the best-reviewed books of 2018."

Booklife

"A powerful tale of the rescue of pets stolen from an upscale Victoria, British Columbia, neighborhood . . . the best animal book of this or any other year. A terrific rescue story!"

Safe Haven Humane Society, Albany, Oregon

"*Stolen* is a mystery that explores animal rights and welfare by giving an honest look at the abuse animals often endure for profit. While containing some hard moments, the story is uplifting, has a terrific ending, and is told through Kieran Yeats's clear, passionate voice - that of investigator who fights to save animals."

Liz Konkel, Readers' Favorite Book Reviewer

"If you have any interest in animals, or are just a mystery buff, you have got to read Linda J Wright's newest novel, *Stolen*. All the characters in this book are well-developed, and the story will keep your interest. A great read!"

Kathe Stander, Past President, Central Coast Humane Society, Newport, Oregon

"*Stolen: A Kieran Yeats Mystery* was one I quickly got caught up in. The characters were all sharply defined and it was easy to identify, to empathize, and to root for all of them. The author used the story to raise awareness of the need for more protection for animals under the law, and I am always impressed, as a reader, when social issues are able to be promoted in fiction, without taking away from the enjoyment of the story, and this author does it extremely well."

Grant Leishman, Readers' Favorite Book Reviewer

"Linda J Wright has written an exciting mystery that will appeal to animal lovers and mystery lovers from young adults on upwards. Readers are introduced to some of the issues involved in using animals as research subjects, and the heartbreak owners face when their pets are stolen for such research. I look forward to reading more of Wright's books."

Sandy Calkins, Librarian, Yachats, OR

"Wright's plot is taut and well-constructed. The story's bucolic setting on Vancouver Island had me wistfully considering relocation. I'm looking forward to reading about Kieran Yeats's future cases. *Stolen: A Kieran Yeats Mystery* is most highly recommended."

Jack Magnus, Readers' Favorite Book Reviewer

"We need another and a wiser and perhaps a more mystical concept of animals. In a world older and more complete than ours they move finished and complete, gifted with extensions of the senses we have lost or never attained, living by voices we shall never hear. They are not brethren, they are not underlings; they are other nations, caught with ourselves in the net of life and time, fellow prisoners of the splendour and travail of the earth."

Henry Beston, "The Outermost House", 1928

For Sheila Crandles

ACKNOWLEDGMENTS

Many people helped to bring this book into being. If I've neglected to mention anyone, I'm truly sorry.

Thanks to my editor Christi Cassidy for being a spelling, grammar, and usage maven, and for saving me from falling down embarrassing rabbit holes. Thanks to my development editor Nancy Fay who told me what worked, what didn't work, and where to put those bagpipes. Thanks to my beta reader Jac Lambert who told me honestly what was *meh*, what she liked, and what she *really* liked. And thanks to my smart and long-suffering partner Martha, for reading and commenting on individual chapters as the book grew. These women are worth their weight in chocolate.

Thanks again to some of the poets and writers whose work continues to enrich my life: Mary Oliver, William Stafford, Gerard Manley Hopkins, and the mad medieval genius Christopher Smart. Thanks also to Henry Purcell, whose odd opera "Dido and Aeneas" continues to delight and perplex me, and to writer and psychiatrist Willard Gaylin, whose book "Feelings", is well worth an annual re-read.

And thanks to the people at Cats Paw Books for believing that light needs to be shed on injustices done to animals and that I might be one who could shed such light.

ABOUT THE AUTHOR

Linda J Wright is a Canadian citizen. Born in Ontario, she grew up in a military family, and spent part of her childhood in France. She lived in Victoria, British Columbia, before moving to Oregon, where she now lives with her partner and their spoiled rotten cat. In the 90s, she was awarded three California Arts Council Artist-in-Residence grants to teach fiction-writing to GATE high school students and won a California Association of Teachers of English Excellence Award for those classes. She is the author of eleven novels, and in 2019 was a finalist for the Lambda Literary Award for Best Mystery for the first book in her mystery series, "Stolen: A Kieran Yeats Mystery".

An animal rights advocate, Linda has been involved in animal welfare for over 30 years. In 1990, she founded the rescue organization The Cat People, and served as its first president. Since then, she has served on the boards of several animal welfare organizations and has been a consultant to hundreds of animal rescue/welfare groups. In 1999 she was part of the team that rescued Keiko the orca (the real Free Willy) and rehabilitated him in Newport, Oregon, setting him free off Iceland. She continues to advocate for animals through her writing.

MONDAY

CHAPTER 1

M IDNIGHT.
I sank a little lower in the front seat of my Karmann Ghia and sipped the last of my coffee. Parked here in the shadows of Murphy's Auto Repairs, the Karmann Ghia lined up with a dozen wounded road warriors, I was all but invisible. And bored. I had nothing to do but listen to the creak of Murphy's sign as it swayed in the wind and watch the occasional pair of headlights go past on the highway leading to the ferry docks. And wait. I am not a patient waiter.

A particularly icy gust of wind swept across the highway from the ocean, and I shivered, zipping my windbreaker higher and jamming my hands into my pockets. Why hadn't I remembered my gloves? Late October on Vancouver Island is definitely gloves weather. I wiggled my fingers and found my phone — the phone on which only several hours before I had received the cryptic text that had brought me here to this desolate stretch of highway. The text read:

Please help me. I can pay you $500. I have a package I need you to take. Meet me at the Donut Stop on Saanich Highway about midnight.

Shrew

I'd texted Shrew back immediately but she hadn't replied. High melodrama indeed! Ordinarily I might have ignored such a strange proposition — after all, I'm an animal crimes investigator, not a parcel retrieval service — but October had been a rough month. Not to put too fine a point on it, but I hadn't seen hide nor hair of a paying job in thirty days. So I made an exception to my own First Commandment (Thou Shalt Take No Off-The-Wall Clients) and agreed to this nocturnal rendezvous. Just to be on the safe side, however, I parked one establishment down from the Donut Stop at Murphy's. Caution is one of my middle names. When Shrew drove up to the Donut Stop, I'd assess things, then decide if I wanted to take this mysterious package.

"C'mon, Shrew," I muttered. "It's past midnight. I'm freezing my hindquarters off and missing my sleep. Let's get on with it."

But nothing happened. The wind moaned a little louder in the branches of the Garry oaks, Murphy's sign creaked even more ominously, and a tangle of paper cups, hamburger wrappers, and newspapers went scudding across the Donut Stop's parking lot in a crazy tarantella. Somewhere nearby an owl hooted, a mournful, tremulous sound. I turned, checking out the shadows for gremlins, and saw the bulk of Mount Douglas looming like a hulking beast against the night sky. Suddenly I remembered — in a few days it would be Halloween, the night when ghouls and witches were abroad, speeding along the roads on their errands of mischief. I snorted.

In North America, Halloween has become nothing more than a children's celebration, a meaningless night of freeloading and silly costumes. But Halloween has its origins in a solemn Celtic celebration. It marked the end of the bright season and the beginning of the dark, and on the Yeats farm in Ireland, huge bonfires called *Samhnagen* had been built year after year for centuries to call the shivering ghosts of our family's dead in from their wanderings.

Although I had never seen such a bonfire, the idea was oddly appealing. My grandmother Aoife had explained it all to me when I was very young. If farmers took pains to move cows and sheep from the summer pastures into the barns where they could be cared for during the winter, would they do any less for the spirits of their beloved departed? She assured me that farmers always lit bonfires on the hills to call the newly dead home for one last evening of warmth and hospitality before they went on their way to the spirit world. I knew Aoife was disappointed that we couldn't have a *Samhnagen* in the little bungalow where we lived in Ottawa, but life in the modern world of Canada proved a constant disappointment to her.

As did I, I reflected. The night she died, she took my hands in hers and made me promise to build her a *Samhnagan*. Faithless grandchild that I was, I never had.

While I brooded, watching the night sky, a silver fingernail paring of moon pushed its way out from behind Mount Doug, casting an unhelpfully wan light over Murphy's and the Donut Stop. I was getting morose, thinking of my grandmother and my childhood, and I resolved to put such thoughts aside. Where the hell was Shrew anyhow? I peeled back my sleeve and looked at my watch. Twenty-five after twelve. Five more minutes, then I was heading home to a hot bath and my bed.

A pair of headlights turned into the little Donut Stop parking lot and I sat up straight. At last. With a protesting squeal of tires, a red VW Bug roared into the lot and made a pass around the garbage dumpster, where something was tossed in. Something in a medium-sized white bag. Then the VW stopped, motor idling.

The VW's driver rolled down the window and a woman's sandy, spiky-haired head emerged. If this was Shrew, she was clearly taking a good look around.

As I approached through the shadows to the driver's side of the VW, she turned in my direction, and called to me over the sound of the idling motor. The voice belonged to a young woman. A frightened young woman.

"Are you Kieran Yeats?"

"Yeah," I called back. "And you are . . ."

"Shrew." She looked back nervously over her shoulder. "Thank God you're here. I didn't know if you'd show. So I tossed the things I had for you in the dumpster."

Frightened? Amend that to terrified.

"I'll call you later. Don't come after me. And, God, don't leave the others behind. They only have until Saturday. Oh shit! He's right behind me."

"But — "

The screech of tires cut me off. Fairly leaping off the pavement, the little Bug went careening out of the parking lot. For my part, I decided to beat a hasty retreat back to Murphy's. As I crouched down behind a battered Corolla, a big white SUV — a Sequoia maybe — rocketed into the Donut Stop lot, slowed for a moment, then hurtled toward the exit in pursuit of the VW. I had one fleeting glimpse of a bearded male profile as the car shot past. I cursed the feeble light of the new moon, which made it impossible to make out any of the letters or numbers on the license plate. All I registered was that there seemed to be something unusual about it. Then, with a shower of sparks from a low-slung muffler, the SUV disappeared south into the darkness after Shrew's car, toward Victoria.

I dithered for a moment, tempted to walk away from this, but recalled the terror on the young woman's face. All right, all right, I'd go fetch the damned package. As for the gibberish about "the others", well, who knew? Maybe she'd make that clear when she called me.

Still crouching behind the Corolla in the shadows, I hesitated. Even though no one had popped out of the bushes, I didn't like this one bit. Packages that can't be delivered in the light of day, by UPS or FedEx or Canada Post, usually have nasty, embarrassing, or incriminating contents. I had already decided that if the package contained drugs or money, this was a game I did not want to play. Frightened or not, Shrew would just have to find someone else.

Hurrying to my car, I took a flashlight out of the glove compartment, and headed over to the Donut Stop lot. A cold finger of wind found its way down my collar, and my teeth began to chatter.

Grabbing the edge of the dumpster and hoisting myself up onto my elbows, I shone my light into its depths. It was far from empty.

"Great," I muttered.

A layer of garbage, bagged and unbagged, lay two feet deep on the floor. I clamped my nostrils shut and tried to breathe through my mouth. Then, before I had a chance to change my mind, I heaved myself up and over and dropped down into the smelly depths. Things I refused to imagine squished underfoot, and I resolutely told myself not to think about maggots. Or rats. The package Shrew had tossed in lay in the far corner and seemed to be a coarsely woven white sack. I bent and picked it up with my free hand, and as my fingers closed over the drawstring, something inside seemed to squirm.

"Shit!" I exclaimed, dropping the drawstring and stumbling backward. Shining the flashlight on the sack, I saw that it was indeed squirming.

Now what? I swallowed, gingerly reached for the drawstring, and pulled the sack toward me. It was heavier than I expected, maybe five or six pounds. And now I had no choice but to pick it up. Holding the sack at arm's length, I waded through the garbage back the way I'd come and tossed my load over the side of the dumpster. Jumping out, I landed on the asphalt beside the sack. Fortunately it wasn't squirming now. I felt encouraged. Maybe it hadn't squirmed at all. Maybe it had been my imagination. I shone my light on the sack and, to my dismay, it gave a convulsive heave.

"No, no, no, no, no," I moaned.

Grabbing the drawstring, I held the sack as far away from my body as I could. Then I hustled over to my car, fishing the keys out of my pocket as I went. I opened the trunk, intending to heave the sack inside, and was just preparing to do so when I heard a sound. From the sack.

"*Mair,*" a voice said mournfully, hopelessly.

"What?" I said in amazement.

"*Meeair,*" it reiterated, with a great deal more feeling this time.

"No," I said, my numb fingers wrestling with the sack's drawstring. "It can't be what I think it is."

But it was. As soon as I had loosened the drawstring, a head popped out. A cat's head. A small, striped tabby head, which swiveled in the direction of my voice. But there was something terribly wrong. I shone my light on the sack and bent closer, an atavistic dread gripping me. What in hell had happened to its eyes? Instead of being yellow or green or golden, they were . . . bloody. A fiery red, the fur around them coated with some yellow substance that I didn't want to think about. And they evidently hurt him a great deal because after one look at me, he squinted them shut. With a cry of horror, I stuffed the cat back into the sack, then stood there in the parking lot for a moment, the small weight clasped in my arms.

Hugging the cat closer to my chest, I closed the trunk, then opened the passenger side door and placed the sack gently on the seat.

"No wiggling, guy," I whispered as I got into the driver's seat and started the car. As I put one hand on the sack, I felt the cat begin to purr. My heart broke a little here, because I knew he was purring from pain, not from pleasure. "Son of a bitch," I said helplessly.

Easing the Karmann Ghia into gear, I drove slowly out onto the highway, trying to cushion the inevitable bump where the parking lot met the street. The cat gave a soft cry and my heart contracted a little.

Eyes wet with tears, fury in my heart, I thought of Shrew speeding in terror through the night, the big SUV pursuing her.

"I've got him now, Shrew," I said. "I've got him."

TUESDAY

CHAPTER 2

I STOOD IN the cold wind, pounding on my friend veterinarian Zaira Lau's door. I'd called ahead, explaining as much of the situation as I knew, and she assured me she'd be ready for me and the cat. Her daughter — my goddaughter, thirteen-year-old Jen — met me at the front door, short, dark hair standing up in tufts. She was clad in pink-and-green checkered flannel pajama pants and a black sweatshirt that proclaimed in red MEAT IS MURDER. I winced. Jen had recently become a vegan and was unabashedly evangelical about it.

"I didn't mean to wake you up, too, kiddo," I apologized. It was two a.m. for cripe's sake.

She shook her head. "It's no problem. Mom says go on into the clinic." Jen looked anxiously at the sack in my arms, her brown eyes worried. "Is that the cat?"

"Yeah." I clasped the warm living weight of the little tabby to my chest.

"I'm supposed to be in charge of making tea," she said quietly. "But I wanted to know —"

"Jen!" Zaira called from the hall. "Have you — "

"— put the kettle on? Yeah, but can I come into the clinic with you and Kieran? I could help."

Zaira, or Zee, as most people called her, gave me an appraising look, clearly wanting me to make the call. I shrugged. I was sure Zee could use Jen's offer of assistance. The kid was calm and cool-headed in emergencies. I, on the other hand, was not at my best tonight. Waiting for Shrew, wading through the garbage, discovering the maimed cat, racing through the dark . . . I really was a wreck. So I nodded.

"All right," Zee said. She pushed the sleeves of her navy turtleneck up above her elbows. "Go ahead in and get things ready for an exam, Jen."

Jen hurried away down the hall and Zee glanced meaningfully at me. A small, slight woman of Asian descent, perhaps forty, she was one of my best friends. I'd known her and Jen for all of Jen's thirteen years, ever since I'd come to Vancouver Island from the east. She'd known me in my previous incarnation as attorney in the Crown Counsel's office and had held my hand as I made the scary transition from real person to private investigator. Hers was the doorstep I usually ended up on when things got rough. Like tonight. Sometimes I thought I was too hot-natured for this business, but Zee assured me my psychological temperature was just right. She raised an eyebrow but said nothing. However, I got it. Zee's eyebrows spoke volumes. Tonight they said: *"What on earth?"*

"A frantic two a.m. phone call," she remarked, "and a cat in a cloth bag. Life as your friend is never dull, Kieran."

"Yeah, well," I equivocated. "I couldn't think of where else to bring this guy."

"You did the right thing," she said. "Let's go take a look." She held open the swinging door to the exam room.

"How will we do this?" I asked, edging through the door, blinking in the bright overhead light. Strangely, I found I was reluctant to let the cat out of my arms.

Zee smiled. "Well, for starters you could put him down on the table," she said, washing her hands at a little sink set into the counter. "He's safe now."

I did as she asked, setting him down gently on the stainless steel exam table. But now I found that I couldn't take my hands off the sack.

"Kieran, do you want me to unfasten the drawstring?" Jen asked, evidently puzzled by my paralysis. "Or do you want to do it yourself?"

"Kieran," Zee said, quirking her mouth in a smile, "we'll take good care of him. Why don't you go into the kitchen and make tea?"

"Erm, all right," I said, realizing that I was a liability in the exam room. I'd grown fiercely protective of the cat in the sack. Oh brother, how had that happened? I'd known him for maybe two hours, tops. And all I'd seen of him had been his head.

I went through Zee's little kitchen to the front entryway where I removed my smelly shoes. Ugh. Nothing like a midnight scamper through a garbage dumpster to ruin a good pair of sneakers. I wondered if they could be saved. With my shoes off, I realized that my socks were dismayingly damp and, reluctantly, I shed them, too.

Padding barefoot into the kitchen, I rummaged in a cupboard beside the stove and found Zee's favorite blue teapot, some loose Dragonwell green tea that she was particularly fond of, and three white mugs. I took the kettle off the heat, made tea, and while it steeped, I sat at the table and tried to make sense of this case. Because a case it evidently was. I had a client, albeit with an odd name, who had hired me to perform a service, which I had done. But what about "the others" Shrew had mentioned and the "behind" where she had enjoined me not to leave them. Too many questions. Well, she said she'd call me. Okay. I checked my phone. Yup, it was on. So, I'd wait. She'd call eventually.

I heard the door to the exam room open and close, and Jen came to join me at the table. She poured tea for herself and me and took a sip, looking at me over the rim of the mug, eyes filled with concern.

"What happened to him, Kieran?"

I shook my head. "I don't know, kiddo. I was just hired to pick him up."

"Mom got all tight-lipped when she saw his eyes," Jen said. "She actually *hissed*."

"Shit," I muttered.

"She gave him a shot of painkiller and a sedative. She says she'll work on him tomorrow. He's sleeping now. His eyes look terrible. All red and goopy. Like he has URI, but ten times worse. And there's some yellow stuff on his face. Mom says that before you got him, his eyes had been clipped open," she said in a small voice. Then, "I don't know what that means? Do you?"

"No, I don't," I said, feeling helpless.

Jen sniffled a little and wiped her nose surreptitiously on the sleeve of her sweatshirt.

I held out my hand and she took it. Who was comforting whom, I wondered? We said nothing, sitting at the table together, my thirteen-year-old goddaughter and I, united in our sorrow for an animal we didn't even know.

"You're a good kid, Jen," I said.

She sniffled again, then drained her mug. "I'd better go to bed. I don't want Mom to have to remind me."

"How's that playing at school?" I asked her, motioning to her MEAT IS MURDER sweatshirt, trying to lighten the mood.

"What? Oh, this." She grinned. "My billboard. Better than you might think. We have a vegan club now. My friend Charlie and I started it. We have ten members already."

"Charlie?" I didn't want to pry, but the last time Jen and I had talked about friendships, she had forthrightly quizzed me about being gay, asking when I'd known about myself, and whether she was too young to know. I assured her she wasn't. So I wondered about Charlie. Kids change their minds and feelings as often as they change their socks. Maybe not their feelings about their gender identity . . . but I wanted to get things straight, so to speak. I wanted to be on the same page as Jen insofar as the important people in her life were concerned.

She blushed furiously. "Charlie's not a boy in case you were worried about *that*," she said disdainfully. "She's Charlotte. A friend at school."

"Ah," I said. "Is she the friend you were talking about that day in the car? The day we saw the geese?"

If it were possible, Jen blushed even more deeply. "Well . . . yeah."

I squeezed her hand. "It's okay, kiddo. Thanks for telling me." Then I changed the subject. "It's good that you've got a vegan club. Ten is a good number. You guys can support each other."

Serious, Jen informed me, "People need to know about meat. And other things."

I smothered a smile. "Indeed they do, sweetie. And I can imagine you're just the person to tell them."

"Maybe," she said thoughtfully. "Anyhow, Mom says she'll be out in a minute. Night, Kieran."

"Night, Jen."

Jen got up to rinse her mug at the sink. As she put it in the dish drain, she turned to me. "Um, one thing."

"Uh-huh?"

"Tris and Aliya were over here on Saturday and we were talking about the sweatshirts. I'd just picked them up. I explained they were for the vegan club."

"Oh, no," I said in dismay, willing to bet I knew what was coming next. Tris was Tristan, my eight-year-old adopted daughter, and Aliya was Tristan's nanny, tutor, and much-loved guardian angel.

"Oh yes," Jen said breezily. "I gave her a sweatshirt. We talked a little about it. About meat being murder."

"Ai yi," I said, imagining how veganism would play at Tristan's school where I was sure they ate chicken nuggets for lunch.

"Well, why not?" Jen asked defensively. "It's the truth. And it's never too early to be thinking about our relationship with animals, is it?"

"Well, in Tris's case it might be a smidge too early," I suggested. "She's only eight."

"Well, anyhow," Jen said with a yawn, "I'm off to bed. I just thought I'd let you know. In case Tris wants to wear the sweatshirt to school."

I wondered briefly if Zee had anything stronger than tea in the cupboard. Meat is murder, midnight assignations, maimed cats. If I were honest with myself, what I really wanted was to go home, quaff a dram or two of something alcoholic, and pull the covers up over my head.

"He's resting now," Zee said, coming from the hall into the kitchen. She took a seat across from me at the table. "Do you have any idea what happened to this cat?"

"Not a clue," I said. "My client tossed him into a dumpster. I retrieved him."

Zee poured herself some of the now-lukewarm tea and shook her head. "I really won't be able to tell how badly his eyes are injured until I can wash them out. I'll know more tomorrow. Speaking of tomorrow, will I see you then?" she asked, changing the subject.

"Tomorrow?"

"Today actually. Later. You have an appointment for Trey."

I groaned. "I do, don't I? Thanks for reminding me. Tris wants to come along. She's pretty worried about him." Trey was my portly gray cat, and he'd been behaving oddly this last little while. His appetite had vanished and he'd taken to hiding in odd places: a box of rags on the back porch, behind the toilet, in the pantry. Time for a visit to his favorite vet. "I'd better go home and get some sleep."

I left Zee in the kitchen and made my way to the front door. Donning my soggy socks and smelly shoes, I hurried out to my car, started it up, and pointed it down the highway in the direction of home, heater switched to high. It was that odd hour of the night when darkness had almost trickled away, but morning had not yet arrived. The ancient Romans called this time the hour of the wolf. They believed it to be the time when demons had heightened power and vitality, when nightmares occurred, when most people died.

Hmmf. Such silly nonsense. Still, I came from a line of mystical Irish poets, and I found the idea oddly appealing. What had my famous forbear written?

> And what rough beast, its hour come round at last
> Slouches toward Bethlehem to be born?

Of course what great-uncle William Butler Yeats had meant by those oft-quoted lines had no relevance to what had happened tonight, I told myself. But the lines had occurred to me for some reason. I shivered. Something — the lateness of the hour, the strangeness of my errand, the horror of the tortured cat — had certainly laid its hands on me. What rough beast did I see in the shadows?

I was halfway home, thinking with one part of my brain about the hot bath I craved and with another part about Shrew's cryptic instructions, when it hit me. What she had said. *All* of what she had said. I'd been so horrified by the injured tabby cat that I'd temporarily forgotten. Wasn't it: "the things I had for you"? *Things,* Kieran, *things.* Plural. More than one thing. Worse yet, was that what she had meant by "the others"? Was the dumpster teeming with maimed cats that I had somehow overlooked? Or . . .

Fanciful thoughts of wolves and slouching beasts vanished from my mind. With a yell, I drove onto the shoulder of the road and turned my car around. So much for the hot bath. It seemed as though another trip to the dumpster was in my future.

CHAPTER 3

T HANKFULLY, THERE WASN'T a gaggle of maimed cats waiting for me in the dumpster. Apart from bagged garbage and loose trash, the only thing I could find of interest was a sealed brown envelope with my name on it. Shrew must have thrown it into the dumpster along with the cat but, due to the poor lighting, I hadn't noticed it. It felt lumpy, and I put it on the seat beside me as I headed finally for home.

Still no phone call from Shrew. I had passed from being irked to being worried as hell. *C'mon, Shrew*, I broadcast mentally to the universe.

I let myself into my house through the back door, closing it softly behind me. It was odd not seeing my big black feral, Vlad, up in the rafters of the little enclosed porch, but Vlad had moved on to better things. My friend Miranda Blake ran an animal sanctuary up-island

and had started a Rodent Ranger program for the unadoptable felines in her care. As her program literature described them, these were the hissers, the pissers, the litterpan-missers; the growlers, the howlers, the midnight prowlers; the biters, the fighters, the up-all-nighters. No manners? No problem. Working in a barn, a warehouse, a factory, or a stable didn't require manners. The cats were neutered, vaccinated, microchipped, and provided at no charge. Kind of a green pest control. Miranda had graciously extended the program to Vlad, who now worked in a wildflower seed warehouse that had previously been overrun with mice growing fat and insolent from feasting on all those tasty seeds. No longer. The warehouse manager said that when Vlad arrived for his "interview", he'd made one pass through the warehouse and about 1,000 mice fled squealing for the exits. Needless to say, Vlad was hired on the spot. He got two square meals a day and, in exchange, presented his employer with at least one rodent daily. A card-carrying touch-me-not when he had lived with me, Vlad's new profession — and the attendant praise — had mellowed him. He now had a cushy bed in the manager's office, a spiffy red collar, and a bowl with his name on it. Warehouse personnel vied with each other to see who could bring him the tastiest treats. The merely-tolerated human supplicants received a slit-eyed squint of recognition from Vlad; the favored ones, an approving lick.

Snapping on the kitchen light, I draped my windbreaker over a chair and laid the brown envelope on the table. I tiptoed over to the door leading to the living room and closed it. Aliya was probably asleep on the sofa — it was now well after three in the morning — and I didn't want to wake her. I thought about coffee then decided, nah, too much trouble. Rootling around in my kitchen drawer of odd things, I found a pair of scissors and cut open the envelope, emptying it onto the table. Out tumbled one cell phone, one key card and lanyard, one computer flash drive, and five one-hundred-dollar bills. I took the phone in my hands and tried to turn it on. Nothing. Either it was dead or locked. Was this the reason Shrew hadn't called me — because she couldn't? But surely there were other phones in the world.

A tentative knock sounded on the kitchen door. "Kieran?" a voice called quietly.

I smiled. "Yeah, come in, Aliya."

A small woman with short, curly, dark hair and dark brown eyes, Aliya came in and closed the door behind her, pulling on a red hoodie with the name CAMOSUN on it in white. "You're so late," she said, brows drawn together in worry, straightening her sweatshirt. "Did everything go all right?"

I'd told Aliya only that I was off to a midnight rendezvous when I asked her to stay with Tris. She knew what I did for a living and was used to the strange hours and errands of my profession.

"Not exactly," I sighed.

She nodded. "I thought as much. Can you tell me . . ." She let the question hang.

I thought about the maimed tabby cat now sleeping in a cage in Zee's clinic and shook my head. No need to share those facts.

"I had to pick up some things a client left for me." I gestured to the phone, key card, and flash drive. "But I can't get the phone to work."

"May I?" Aliya asked, motioning to the phone.

"Sure," I said. "In fact I was hoping you'd ask."

She shot me a quick smile. In addition to the roles she filled for Tris, Aliya was a computer sciences student at Camosun College. A few years ago, when I'd met her at my friend Lawrence's photography shop, she'd been a twenty-year-old newly arrived in Victoria with her parents from Lebanon, the ink barely dry on her degree in humanities from the American University of Beirut. Now, in addition to working for Lawrence, she was finishing another college degree, and morphing into a tekkie.

"It's the new Samsung," she said. "Nice. It needs to be charged, though. Maybe that's all that's wrong with it. If not, then it's locked."

"Huh. Can you unlock it?"

She shrugged. "Well, maybe. But let's charge it first. My charger's in the next room. I'll just get it."

"How's Sprout?" I asked her when she returned, plugging the phone into the charger and the charger into a power outlet by the coffeemaker. Sprout was my nickname for Tristan, a name I'd given her six months earlier when I'd met her as a boy named Trouble.

Then he was an abandoned kid who lived in the woods with a neglectful grandfather, an abusive drug-dealing uncle named Connor, and Con's two hangers-on friends, Peter and Stephanie. Trouble and I had had quite an adventure, and together we ended up saving each other's lives as well as the lives of twenty-six pets that Con, Peter, and Stephanie had stolen in order to sell to underwrite their drug habit. I'm not quite sure how the nickname Sprout had come into existence, but it had stuck. We both liked it. Tris grinned every time I used it, and when she did, I felt a kind of blossoming in that region of my metaphorical anatomy called the heart.

"Homework all done with no problem," Aliya reported. "I've never seen a kid so eager to do homework, if you can imagine such a thing. I used to race through mine on the bus going home from school so I could spend the evening watching music videos. I had a misspent youth," she said confidentially.

"Hey, how misspent could it have been?" I asked her. "You ended up in college. You studied humanities. You graduated. And now you're becoming a tech guru."

"Well, maybe not a guru," she said. "But I sure do like what I'm doing. Anyhow, Sprout. She's doing well."

I'd shared Tristan's history with Aliya when I asked her to be the kid's tutor, and she understood the reasons for the appalling state of Tris's education. If ever there was someone who'd had, as the orphans said in the movie *Annie*, a hard-knock life, it was Tristan.

The kid's father, Canadian Armed Forces Sergeant Andrew Malvern, had died a war hero in Afghanistan when she was just a baby; her mother had been killed in a car wreck not too many years later; and her grandmother, in whose care Tris had been placed, had keeled over dead one day from a heart attack. All this before Tris was six. The only good thing that had happened to her, it seemed was that her grandmother had taught her to read and write. Reading is an amazing gift: it's an escape hatch. If you can read, you can fly away. To anywhere — the Orient, the high seas, and, in Tris's case, the Amazon jungle, the location of her favorite series of books. There, a boy named Bomba had animal friends, met kindly explorers, and searched for his parents, who had unaccountedly misplaced him in the jungle after a plane crash.

After her grandmother's death, when the legal dust had settled, Tris had found herself packed off to the home of her only remaining relative, with her stuffed cat, a garbage bag of clothes, and only one of her Bomba books. Thomas Malvern, her grandfather on her father's side, was a despicable old guy — an animal thief called a buncher — to whom Tris, not realizing she was related, had come to refer to contemptuously as "the old dog man."

To be fair to Malvern, he hadn't always been an animal thief. He'd operated a legitimate kennel business that unfortunately came to an end when he fell off the roof one day fixing something. He wrecked his back and began taking opiates to kill the pain, which never relented. Soon his other son, the only occasionally employed Con, and the low-life hangers-on who lived with him, began helping themselves to Dad's drugs, and everyone ended up hooked. All thoughts of the little six-year-old girl who had been placed in his care apparently vanished from Malvern's head. After Con's pal, the dogfighter Peter, burned her arm with his lighter when Tris asked if she could have one of the stolen dogs as a pet, she assumed the persona of a boy. She decided to live up to, or down to, the name those brave men gave her: Trouble. If they messed with her, she was going to give them trouble all right. She bought an air pistol from Amazon, dressed in Con's cast-off camo clothing, tried not to come within six feet of anyone, and kept her head down. Life with her grandfather and the guys must have been a succession of horrors.

I smiled at a memory. Tris had come to me with literally just the clothes on her back. So we needed to go on a shopping expedition, right? Something every kid would enjoy. Tris confided in me that she would never wear anything pink, or anything with a unicorn or a rainbow or a fluffy bunny on it. I thought I'd listened, but still I found a way to step in the, er, crap with her. I remembered ruefully the day of our shopping trip when we stood in the girls' T-shirts' section of that huge superstore that we all love to hate. Thinking I might help Tris with her rehabilitation, I held up a Wonder Woman T-shirt.

"How about this, Sprout?" I suggested. "She's a kick-butt super-hero. She doesn't take any nonsense from anybody. Kind of like you."

Tris looked at the T-shirt carefully then, clearly puzzled, up at me. "Why is she in her underwear, Kieran?"

Oops. I put the T-shirt back on the stack and we went home to cyber shop. There were fewer pitfalls there, and I let Tris tell me what she might feel comfortable wearing. She now owned a dizzying array of bird and animal-themed T-shirts and sweatshirts, none of them pink, and none of them featuring women in their underwear.

I loved Tris immoderately, and as far as I could tell, so did Aliya. Indeed, her devotion to Tris was one of the reasons she was moving into my remodeled basement. She liked her job as Tris's tutor and worried, as did I, about the irregular hours I kept. So as well as tutor, she'd taken on the job of nanny. Tris was delirious with happiness. Especially since today was the longed-for day, the day Aliya was due to move in.

"Say, Aliya," I said, just checking. "Are we still on for today? Reilly and sons are coming in —" I looked at my watch and groaned "— three short hours. Some carpeting, a little vinyl in the bathroom, and then the downstairs suite will be yours. No second thoughts?"

Aliya grinned. "Not a single one." When she'd needed to move, apparently she did a fair amount of looking around and found the rents to be pretty astronomical here in Victoria. Which is why I offered her the downstairs suite. "You're a life-saver!"

"Yeah, well," I said. "I had ulterior motives. I didn't want Tris's nanny and tutor driving around Victoria in the wee hours. Some of those new intersections are murder, even at night. There's so much traffic." Victoria sure wasn't the sleepy little backwater it once was. It had become a mini-metropolis. "I'm afraid we've been discovered."

Aliya yawned. It was contagious. I did the same, looking at my watch again. Almost four.

"I'll get Tris off to school in the morning," she told me. "Then I'll go over to Lawrence's shop for a while. I'm working on a couple of projects for him and I need to finish up. After all, he's letting me borrow the shop's van to move my things. My brother doesn't know it, but I'm going to borrow him, too. I have some computer stuff, a work table, bookcases, a futon, boxes of books, clothes on hangers . . . that sort of thing. I thought I'd bring everything in the early afternoon if that's okay? Then I'll just . . . stay."

"Sounds good," I said. Tris and I were going to take Trey to visit his vet, just before four.

"I'll pick Tris up at school," I said. "And by the way, any sign of Trey?"

She shook her head. "No. But I noticed he hasn't eaten any kibble."

"Fooey," I said. "Well, I'm hoping Zee can sort him out. Let's get some sleep."

Aliya gestured to the phone still charging on the kitchen counter. "You could try the phone later. It ought to be charged by breakfast."

"Yeah, okay," I said. "I need to find out who the owner is. She said she'd call me later, but I can't think how she'd do that when I have her phone. Well, she could borrow one, but still. No one throws their phone away."

Aliya frowned. "Not willingly. And it's too expensive to be a burner."

"It's beyond me," I said. "I'd just like her to damned well phone me. I'm worried as hell about her. Anyhow, my brain is fried. I can't think about this case anymore tonight."

CHAPTER 4

S O THE HOT bath didn't happen. Neither did clothes-doffing or pajama-donning. I guess I just collapsed on my bed, smelly sneakers, damp socks, and all, wrapped in my comforter, because, before I knew it, my clock radio began warbling: the oldies station, which I usually enjoy waking up to, but not this morning.

"*Gaak,*" I said, not certain if I were alive or dead. When a bouncy tenor assured me that my kiss was on his list of the best things in life, I thought briefly about thwacking the radio but realized I hadn't the energy. Besides, someone was shaking my foot. I opened one eye. A small person was standing at the bottom of the bed. Curly blond hair, bright blue eyes, it was Tristan, looking scrubbed and combed.

Today she sported one of her animal T-shirts, a tough black one with a toothy, pointy-nosed, buff-colored, catlike creature on it. KEEP CALM AND HUG YOUR MEERKAT, the shirt read. A little peculiar, but thank heavens it wasn't Jen's MEAT IS MURDER sweatshirt. It was much too early in the day for an ethical debate.

"Are you all right, Kieran?" Tris asked, frowning. "You still have your shoes on. I have coffee. Aliya says it's the heart-starting special."

"Am I all right? Hmm. When I escape from the anaconda-like coils of this comforter, I'll let you know. In the meantime, how about handing over that coffee? My heart could sure use a little starting."

Tristan giggled, as I knew she would, and carefully handed me the mug of coffee, taking a seat in the rocking chair in the corner of my bedroom.

"Mr. Reilly's downstairs," she said, eyes sparkling.

"He is?" I said, feigning ignorance. "What can he be up to at, what, eight in the morning? Do we have burst pipes, a clogged toilet, a rodent in the drywall?"

"*Kierannn,*" Tristan said, "he has *carpet*. For the floor in the suite. Remember?"

I smote myself theatrically on the forehead, careful not to spill the coffee, which was indeed a heart-starter. "Oh, yeah, I remember now. We're getting a tenant. But I forget. Is it Samir, Alexa's brother? I know I rented the suite to one of the twins."

"No! It's Aliya!" Tristan said, laughing. "You're just being silly. She's moving in this afternoon."

"So she is," I said. "I remember now. Thank heavens I have you around to keep things straight for me."

"Breakfast!" Aliya called from the kitchen. "It's just Egg McMuffins from McDonald's, but there's one for you, too, if you want it, Kieran."

"Gotta go," Tris said, wiggling out of the rocking chair.

"I might skip breakfast right now," I told her as she was vanishing out the door of my bedroom. "Don't you eat mine though, you ravening beast. I'll probably want it later. Just ask Aliya to leave it in the microwave. I don't want Trey nibbling on it. And don't forget . . . I'll see you after school. Three-thirtyish. Trey and I are picking you up."

"Uh-huh. I remember," Tris said. "Trey has to go to Zee's. I'm going, too. I'll see you outside the school. At the big door. Bye, Kieran."

I closed my bedroom door on the sounds of happy kitchen domesticity and lay back down on my bed with a groan. When had late nights gotten to be such a trial? As my dreaded fortieth birthday edged ever closer, I guessed. I felt as though I had been beaten up and cast away for dead. Well, a shower ought to improve things. I bent to remove my sneakers (no, they couldn't be saved, I decided) and was just untying the laces when the traffic report came on the radio. The morning show hosts, Buzz and Mandy, decried the latest in an all too familiar string of traffic mishaps on Victoria's streets.

"Another accident at Ravine Road and the Pat Bay Highway, Mandy," Buzz said. "It seems that every other morning we report an accident there, and this morning, tragically, it's a one-car accident, but a fatality."

"Yes, Buzz," Mandy said. "So unfortunate. According to Provincial Police, about four a.m., a red VW Bug crossed over the median between the east and westbound lanes of the highway and just . . . fell into oncoming traffic. Now I know that spot well — I pass it every day — and it sure isn't easy to just jump the median. It's a raised grassy bank. You have to wonder how that happened."

Buzz continued. "BCPP asks anyone having information about this accident, anyone who saw anything, to please call. A young woman died, Mandy. If we had better lights at Ravine Road to slow down traffic, well, maybe we wouldn't be reporting a fatality this morning. I don't know about you, but I'm very upset about our continuing traffic mess here in Victoria. How many deaths will it take . . ."

I stopped listening, a wretched sense of foreboding descending upon me. C'mon, Kieran, I told myself, there must be hundreds of red VW Bugs in Victoria. Well, scores. Right? Right.

I tossed my sneakers into the corner, thought about a shower, then thought, oh to hell with it. I knew what I needed to do. I needed to make a phone call. To someone who could answer a question for me. And I needed to make the call now.

CHAPTER 5

I MADE AN end run around the electronic limbo of the Victoria Coroner's Office phone system and dialed Suzanne Paulsen's private number directly. A grizzled-haired, no-nonsense type who described herself as a harpy, Dr. Paulsen was, in my experience, every bit of that. But for some reason we'd hit it off. Perhaps it was our shared macabre sense of humor. I'd not only laughed appreciatively at the sign on the wall behind her desk that said I SEE DEAD PEOPLE but tried a *bon mot* of my own. One day when I was forced to cool my heels in her office for what I thought was an unconscionably long time, I opined that that scores of people must be dying to see her. She briefly glared at me, suddenly got the joke, then uttered one approving bark of laughter. On my way out of her office, she presented me with her business card with her private phone number written on the back.

"I actually answer this one," she said.

I called the number now.

"Paulsen," a terse voice answered.

"Hey, Suzanne, it's Kieran Yeats."

"Morning, Kieran," she said, her voice becoming as warm as it ever got, which was a few degrees north of absolute zero. "It's awfully early to be interested in the dead."

"Yeah, well," I said. "I need to ask you a question. There was an accident on the Pat Bay Highway this morning about four. A young woman was killed. I'm hoping you'll tell me her name."

"Yes, I could do that," she said. "They brought her in first thing. Very unfortunate. I'll get the name . . . just a minute." Silence, then: "Julia Stevens. I'm reading this off her driver's license. Do you need her address?"

Did I? "Well, sure," I said. "In fact, could you fax me her license? I'd like to take a look at the photo." I realized I was harboring a fatuous hope that the dead woman wasn't Shrew. And who knew, maybe it wasn't. Could I identify her if I saw her driver's license photo? After all, I'd seen her for all of fifteen seconds. Hmm. Yeah, I thought I could.

"I'll have Trilby do it."

Trilby was Suzanne's extremely weird assistant. I guessed the dead, as well as Suzanne, didn't mind piercings, tattoos, and fuschia hair. Oh well.

"Any particular reason you want to look at the photo?" Suzanne asked, plainly curious.

"I might know her. From a case I'm working on. That is . . . well . . . um, I think I might."

"Might, schmight," Suzanne said, clearly critical of my uncertainty. "Oh, what the hell. I'll have Trilby fax it to you."

"Hey, thanks, Suzanne." I ended the call and headed for my office to wait for Trilby's fax.

On the way I did a cursory search for Trey — under Tris's and my beds, nope; in our closets, nope; in Tris's and my bathrooms, nope; in the pantry, nope. I was about to give up when a thought occurred to me: what about the back porch? Vlad's old kingdom? I opened the kitchen door and peered into the gloom. Sure enough — up in the rafters was Trey, a miserable-looking gray lump wedged under a ceiling beam.

"For heaven's sake." My exasperation turned to pity as I realized what might be going on. "Trey... you miss him," I said in astonishment. "Vlad, the alpha cat who terrorized you off and on ... you miss him. Is that what this is all about? You're pining? Grieving?"

"*Raff,*" muttered Trey.

"Oh, give me strength. Well, Zee can plumb the depths of your psyche. I'm sure it's beyond me. See you at three, big guy."

Just what I needed — a cat with a mood disorder.

While I waited for my fax, I stood in the kitchen looking out the window. The morning was a little foggy, but after peering at the sky, I concluded that this was the kind of fog that would burn off by midday. We would probably have a beautiful afternoon — a Technicolor sort of day that occurs only on the coast, a day when everything shines, and the sky is such an impossible shade of blue that you can hardly bear it.

Days like this bring out the gardener in all us Victorians, and even I vowed to go outside and commune with nature. Maybe I'd rake up the leaves in my side yard. The three massive Garry oaks — the site of Tris's colony of bird feeders — were already bare, but my maple, which had turned fiery red-gold at first frost weeks ago, still stood bearing its bounty of leaves like individual flames. And the apple tree, home to family after family of robins, bore a bumper crop of Macintoshes. I really should pick them, I thought. Tris and I could make a pie. Or some apple butter. I snorted. The Queen of Domesticity I was not. I'd be doing well to get the leaves raked.

My fax chirped and I went on into my office. Taking a deep breath, I held up the single piece of paper it had disgorged. Please, no, I prayed. But my prayer went unheard as do all atheists' entreaties. A serious-looking young face stared back at me — sandy spiky hair, pale eyes.

"Crap," I said.

Shrew.

∽

I wrestled with the idea of a shot or two of Method and Madness Irish Whiskey for about an hour as I lay on the living room couch in a funk. Then I got up, ate the Egg McMuffin that Aliya had left for me in the microwave, drank some more heart-starting coffee, paced around the living room, and asked myself what the hell was going on.

"He's right behind me," Julia had babbled in terror.

Who? The guy in the white Sequoia, who else. And why was he chasing her? I paced a little more. Had her car just taken a header off the eastbound lane of the highway, over the median, and onto the westboud lane all on its own? Had panic made her overcorrect as the Sequoia barreled down on her in pursuit? Had she simply missed a turn? Or had something else happened that made her car jump the median? I felt a spasm of guilt. Even though she'd told me not to follow her, why hadn't I? She was only a kid according to her license, and a terrified one at that. If I had fallen in behind the Sequoia, I could have . . . what? Prevented the accident? Possibly. Called 911? Definitely. I hadn't known then that there was a cat waiting for me in the dumpster, but he would have been okay for a while. I shook my head, disappointed in myself.

I felt too antsy to settle down, so I decided to go outside and apply myself to the leaves. Maybe a spate of raking would give me a clearer perspective on all this. I found my seldom-used rake in the garage, donned a pair of seldom-used gardening gloves, ventured out into the back yard, and started persuading the leaves into piles. In record time I found myself bored with the whole thing. At least I'd corralled the leaves into three humungous stacks against the garage, ready for bagging. But not by me, and not today. Enough was enough. I put my rake and gloves away, shut the garage door, and had to admit that fresh air and exercise were greatly overrated. I still hadn't convinced myself that Shrew's mishap was, as Buzz had asserted, a one-car accident. Fooey. Maybe I was just an overly suspicious broad. And maybe not. In any event, it was time to do some detecting.

CHAPTER 6

DETECTIVE SUPERINTENDANT ALEXANDER MacLeish of the Oak Bay Police Department was fortunately in his office and answering his phone. A burly, fair-haired Scot in his late fifties, Mac had been my friend for years. We'd helped each other out on many occasions, and I was hoping he could help me out now.

"A slow crime day, is it, Mac?" I said. "Why aren't you out there nabbing criminals instead of warming your office chair? My goodness, what *do* we pay you boys for, anyhow?"

"Good morning to you, too, Kieran," he said. "You're sounding a wee bit testy. And lest we forget, I'm management now. I get to spend a considerable part of each day warming my office chair. While crime-solving, of course."

"Of course," I said. "And yes, I'm testy. I'll admit it. My latest case has produced some niggling doubts in my mind and I'd like to settle them. So I have a favor to ask."

"Och, those niggling doubts," he said. "I'm guessing you want to be admitted into one of our inner sanctums."

"You guess correctly. I need to take a look at a VW Bug. It seems to have taken a header over the median on the Pat Bay Highway at Ravine Road last night."

"Well, it's probably in Forensic's lot, awaiting someone's pleasure. Hang on and I'll call over there."

I hung on, trying to convince myself that when I got in to take a look at the Bug, there would be nothing suspicious to see. Because if there were something, that would turn this case from a late-night misadventure into, well, something else. Something beyond my pay grade. Something I'd be happy to drop in Mac's lap.

"Kieran, it's in Forensic's lot out on Quadra." He sighed.

"You're sighing. That usually means there's going to be a problem. Will there be?"

"I called Forensics to find out who's on duty at the lot."

"And?"

"Today it's that brainless young twit Dermot. Fancies himself a ladies' man. Worse than that, if it's possible, I've been told he has a wee scam running. So . . ."

"Oh, c'mon, Mac. Dermot sounds like a pain in the ass. Why don't you get rid of him?"

"I entertain fantasies daily," Mac said tactfully. "But alas, he's a parolee and a pet project of the Chief."

"Oh, all right. I'll prepare to be ogled. And scammed."

"If all else fails, you can invoke my name," Mac said. "Being management ought to be good for *something*."

"Ladies' man indeed." I sighed. "I'll deal with him. Thanks, Mac."

The long-overdue shower felt wonderful, and as I wiped the condensation from my bathroom mirror I marveled that I didn't look as bad as I'd feared. True, I was on the cusp of middle age, but my wavy dark hair bore only a few wispy white interlopers; my teeth, with the exception of a few crowns, were my own; my pale Celtic complexion was mostly free from the warts and wens that presaged dotage; my gray eyes were still clear and guileless. About to be forty and holding. Hmmf. Who was I kidding? I hauled from my closet a pair of voluminous gray coveralls acquired from an earlier escapade, and struggled into them over jeans and a turtleneck. Also from the depths of my closet I plucked a Vancouver Canucks baseball cap, found a pair of mirrored sunglasses in my office, and prepared to match wits with Dermot.

ços

I parked outside the chain-link fence surrounding the Forensics lot on Quadra Street and strode confidently up to the little hut by the gate. In my baggy coveralls, baseball cap, and sunglasses, I was certain I had achieved androgyny. A skinny kid, dressed in a pair of baggy jeans and a navy jacket with FORENSICS stenciled in white on the front, came out to greet me. He was about twenty, with long, greasy brown hair, a nose that looked as if it had been broken in a fight, and a ferocious case of acne.

"Detective Superintendant MacLeish sent me," I announced, deciding to invoke Mac's name right off the bat and thereby short-circuit annoyances. "You Dermot?"

"Yup," he said, looking me up and down, grinning a male grin. Was he serious? I was old enough to be his aunt. Or his mother. I groaned. So much for my disguise. Perhaps a tight sweater and a zippered leather skirt might have gotten me more traction with Dermot.

"I need to take a look at the VW Bug over there," I said. "The red one by the fence."

"Department ID?" he said, raising an eyebrow at my rumpled disguise.

I shook my head. "Fooey. I must have left it in the car."

He shook his head. "Nope. No ID, no lookin'. All this here is evidence. I can't let civilians in."

"Oh, really?" I said. "And Superintendant MacLeish called Forensics just for me."

34

He shuffled his feet and looked at me uncertainly. Who knew? I might just be telling the truth. "No one told me," he said, aggrieved, moving a golf-ball-sized piece of gum from one side of his mouth to the other.

I shook my head in feigned commiseration. "That's always the way, isn't it? The big shots never tell us little guys anything. I run into that in my line of work, too."

"Oh yeah?" he asked. "So what's your line of work?"

"Insurance," I invented. "I'm just a grunt, though. I get called when people need a set of eyeballs to look at something they're too lazy to go look at themselves."

"Well, that Bug's a wreck," he said, looking through the fence at the red VW. "It's like, totaled. It must've rolled." He scratched his nose. "You just need to look?"

"Yeah. And I'm really going to be in trouble with my boss if I can't make a report," I said, manufacturing a worried tone.

He scratched his nose again, clearly monetizing my worry. Dollar signs might just as well have appeared in his eyes. "Trouble, huh? How much is it worth to you to stay out of trouble?"

I sighed. Dermot, Dermot. This is your bad-boy scam? Nitwit. This is the way you get to be an *ex*-parolee. Reaching into a pocket of my coveralls, I extracted a folded twenty and handed it over.

"What the fuck." He pocketed the twenty. "Lookin' won't hurt nuthin'. And MacLeish did clear it with the office, you said."

Fishing a key ring out of his pocket, he unlocked the gate, ushering me inside.

"It's a mess," he said, accompanying me over to the Bug. "Check out the inside. There's blood everywhere. No one could've walked away from that." I detected more than a hint of ghoulish enthusiasm.

"I'll just walk around the car," I said, hoping he'd go away so I could look for what I hoped I wouldn't find. "Blood makes me queasy."

Damn, but the Bug was a sorry sight. I didn't doubt that Julia had rolled it. There didn't seem to be one square foot of metal that was undented. Ominously, the front windshield was missing, as was one of the side windows. I walked around to the passenger side of the car and sighed. There it was — a long dented scrape. I squatted down, examining it closely. White paint. Quite a bit of it. White like the Sequoia that had chased Julia into the Donut Stop lot last night. I willed Dermot to go back to manning or personing the gate or whatever the hell he was supposed to be doing. Nope. He was sticking to me like a burr. This might've been the most excitement he'd had in days. Squatting down beside me, he ran a grubby finger over the scrape.

"Looks like it was sideswiped," he said.

"Yeah, it does, doesn't it," I agreed. Circling the car again, I stood looking at the white paint on the dented passenger side. Dermot, finally bored, went back to his post at the gate, jingling his keys. I shook my head. I had indeed seen what I needed to see. Damn.

"Done?" Dermot asked as I passed through the gate. "You know," he added slyly, "for another twenty, you could take pictures." When I said nothing, he clanged the gate shut behind me.

"I'll take a pass on the pictures," I told him, feeling bleak about what I'd just seen and grumpy about his ham-handed extortion attempts. "But here's a piece of advice. Superintendent MacLeish really does know I'm here. And I won't tell anyone about the twenty I gave you. But you might want to think twice about your scam. I might've called someone instead of paying up. And you might've found yourself out of a job."

For a moment, he looked guilty and miserable. Pulling an extortion scam on the police Forensics parking lot? He was ether very ballsy or very stupid. I voted for the stupid.

"What twenty?" he said, glowering. "Don't talk to me. Just go the fuck away."

❧

I sat in my car, depressed, thinking over what I had just learned.

Julia's car had been sideswiped all right. I tried to imagine what might have happened. Presumably the Bug had lurched sideways, driven onto the median, fallen into the westbound lane of traffic, and rolled over. And then? Had the Sequoia's driver fled in a panic?

Or circled around and come back? Why the hell was he chasing Shrew anyhow?

I imagined the crumpled VW lying on the pavement, tires spinning, glass from the smashed windows scattered around like confetti. Was Shrew dead at that point? Hard to imagine she wasn't. I had a ghoulish thought: had the Sequoia's driver stopped his car behind the wreck of the VW, gotten out, walked to the Bug, reached inside, and shoved the young woman's lifeless body out of the way as he looked for . . . what? What the hell was this all about, I asked myself.

I felt frustrated. Shrew's phone would certainly be charged by now. I wanted nothing more than to go home and take a look at it. It and the flash drive. But family business beckoned. Looking at my watch, I cursed. I was running late. If I hurried, I had just time enough to go home, shed my coveralls, corral Trey, and go pick up Tris at school. My melancholic cat had an appointment with his vet.

CHAPTER 7

TRIS WAS WAITING for me at the "big door" — the Oak Grove School's main entrance. An L-shaped cedar-shingled structure in a grove of, unsurprisingly, Garry oaks, the small private school was located not too far from my house in Oak Bay Village. Tris was standing with a little dark-haired girl in black leggings and a long green sweater, and the two of them were chatting with a woman I recognized as Tris's teacher, Marie Linley. A middle-aged, motherly redhead with gold-rimmed glasses, Marie was smart, funny, and thought outside the box. She seemed perfect for Tris. I'd visited three private schools and interviewed seven teachers in my search for a school and a teacher for Tris, and Marie and this school seemed the best match. I'd explained Tris's background, including the fact that the kid had literally been raised in the woods and hadn't spent a day inside a classroom, but Marie was unfazed. She'd put Tris in with other eight-to-ten-year-olds and so far, things were working out. Fortunately Tris could read and write at a level far beyond most eight-year-olds, and the adventure stories she wrote for English assignments, and read to her classmates, made her exceedingly popular. Everyone wanted to become a character in Tris's stories.

I think Tris's facility with language helped to disguise the enormous black holes in her education, but Marie Linley wasn't fooled. Tris still didn't know exactly where Labrador was, or which countries Queen Elizabeth ruled, or why we spoke both French and English in Canada . . . but she was cheerful about the things she didn't know. Which was fortunate, because they were myriad. The not-knowns were why I had hired Aliya to tutor Tris and they were gamely playing educational catch-up. The important thing was that Tris liked the school, liked her classmates, liked Marie. In fact I'd yet to find anything that Tris didn't like. Except green vegetables. I commiserated with her. I didn't much like them either.

"Hey, Sprout," I said as she climbed into the front seat and buckled her belt. Tris was very proud of the fact that she met the safety standards that allowed kids to sit in the front seat.

"Hey, Kieran," Tris said. She turned to look at Trey huddled in his carrier on the folded-down back seat. "He looks sad."

"Yeah, he is. But Zee will be able to fix him up."

She looked at me doubtfully. "Really? She can fix sad?"

"Probably," I said, mentally crossing my fingers. "That's what Zee does, remember? She's an animal fixer-upper."

Tris nodded. "Yeah, I know. She fixed up the spots."

The spots were eleven Bengal cats stolen last year during the case in which I'd met Tris. They'd developed URI from being out in the rain for far too many days, but URI is usually pretty easily cured. Everyone recovered.

"Who was the little girl with you and Miss Linley?" I asked.

"Daniela," Tris said. "Dani. She's eight, too. She's from Syria."

"Wow," I said. "Are her parents refugees?"

"Uh-huh," Tris nodded. "They lived in a refugee camp before they came here. I'm not exactly sure what that is. So I'm going to ask Aliya to help me find out during Google time." Google time was the half-hour after Tris's homework and remedial tutoring were finished, when she and Aliya used Google to investigate things on the Internet. I didn't allow Tris online without supervision, and she accepted that.

"Dani said her father was a tailor in someplace called Aleppo. Her mother helped in the business too. But they can't do that work here because they don't speak English well enough," Tris explained. "But Dani speaks English pretty well now. So she's helping them."

"That's great, Tris. She sounds like a nice little kid." Privately I wondered how a Syrian refugee kid's parents could afford a place like Tris's school, but reminded myself that the school offered scholarships. Tris's spot was paid for by her trust fund — she'd inherited five acres north of Sidney, on the water, from her dead grandfather, the despicable Thomas Malvern, the "old dog man." Her trustee and I had sold off an acre this summer, for what seemed to me to be a fabulous price. Tris still owned four acres and we'd decided to hang onto them. The little girl was never going to have to worry about affording education, or anything else that cost money, if I had anything to say about it.

I wondered if Tris had something else on her mind to tell me about Dani, apart from her and her parents' history, but apparently not. Ever mercurial, she grinned, and said, "I have jokes for you."

"Oho," I said, "so jokes are what you learned at school today, huh. Lay them on me. I'll see if I can do better than last time."

"Bet you don't get them," Tris said. "Okay. What did the owl do when she lost her voice?"

"Hmm," I said. "Beats me. What?"

"She didn't give a hoot." Giggles. Then, "I've got another one."

I groaned. "I'll bet you do. Okay."

"How can you tell which rabbit is the oldest?"

"How?"

"Look for the gray hares."

"Har, har. You're killing me, Sprout," I told her, enjoying this as much as she was. Since Tris had come to live with me, I'd discovered silliness. I had never been silly as a child, but I was discovering it now in my about-to-be forty senescence, and realized I liked it.

"One more. Then it's your turn. What's the difference between a fish and a piano?"

"No idea. What?"

Tris could hardly speak through her giggling fit. "You can't tune a fish."

"Huh?" I pretended to not get it.

"*Kierannn* . . . you know, tuna fish?"

"Ha ha. Pretty darned funny. So is it my turn now?"

"Yup."

"What's black and white and red all over?" I asked, embarrassed by the lameness of the one joke I remembered from my childhood.

Tris immediately became serious, closed her eyes, and screwed up her face, concentrating. "I've got it," she announced after a few seconds' intense thought.

"Yeah?"

"A blushing zebra!"

"Nope."

"Nope? Then what?"

"A newspaper."

"A . . . I don't get it. Newspapers aren't red."

"Not r-e-d red, but they're r-e-a-d read, aren't they? And everyone reads them, so they're — "

"Read all over. That was pretty good," she said generously.

Then we were driving through Zee's leafless hazelnut orchard, bouncing over the uneven road that led up to her rambling one-story house and clinic. Tris held the Karmann Ghia's passenger seat for me as I wrestled Trey's carrier out of the back.

"We may have to leave him overnight," I told Tris. She nodded solemnly. Trey often slept with Tris, and I just wanted to warn her that we might not be coming home with her sleeping companion. "Zee's going to give him a good exam, maybe draw some blood."

"Will it hurt him?"

"Maybe just a little," I reassured her. "But Zee knows how to be gentle."

"Okay." Tris glanced toward the door. "Can I go over to the barn? Jen said she'd be there. I'm meeting the pony today," she said eagerly.

"Oh yeah, the pony." Last night's activities and today's discoveries had driven most other thoughts out of my mind, but I did remember the pony. I told Tris several months ago that she could have anything she wanted (within reason) as an adoption present, and after thinking things over, she decided she wanted to learn how to ride. We talked to Zee and Jen about Tris learning on Jen's spotted pony, and here we were. Lesson Number One.

"Go ahead," I said. "I'm going to take Trey into the clinic. I'll come get you when we're through."

‌

Zee met Trey and me at the front door.

"Go on back to the first exam room," she said, taking off her lab coat and draping it over a chair in the kitchen. "Trey's my last patient today." I noticed the lab coat was speckled with blood.

"A disagreement with a patient?" I joked, indicating the bloody lab coat with my chin.

"No," Zee said, looking grim, and I realized that whatever had happened, it was no joking matter. "The blood is from the cat you brought in last night. I just finished what I thought would be a little procedure. It turned out to be bigger and, well, bloody."

I was instantly alarmed. "Bloody . . . is he okay?"

"Now he is," she said. "But let's take a look at Trey first. You can help me. Jen's my assistant today, but she's out in the barn with your daughter," she said with an amused smile. "Jen informed me they'll be talking horses."

"Apparently," I said, shaking my head. "Who would've thought Tris would want riding lessons as a present? What's next? Surely not a horse of her own."

Zee laughed. "Jen can tell her all about mucking out the stables, and curry-combing, and rubbing the pony down after rides, and checking his hooves for stones. That ought to take a bit of the romance out of prospective horse ownership."

"God, I hope."

"Let's see about this guy," Zee said, unloading a miserable-looking Trey onto her exam table. "Tell me what's going on with him."

I described his symptoms — spurning his food, even halibut from Willows Galley Fish And Chips; expressing no interest in things he previously enjoyed, like shredding the sofa or unrolling paper towels; squirreling himself away in the rafters of the back porch.

"I have a theory," I told Zee as she listened to Trey's heart and peered into his mouth, peeling back his lips to look at his teeth. "Could his problems be, well, psychological?"

"Hmm, maybe," Zee said, taking Trey's temperature, a job that would previously have required six people clad in Kevlar. Not today, though. Trey sat meekly as Zee inserted her thermometer into his nether regions. "What's changed in his life recently?"

"Well, Tris came to live with us. But Trey really likes her. They sleep together sometimes."

"Anything else?" Zee said, looking into his ears.

"Yeah. A couple weeks ago, Vlad, my feral, went off to be a Rodent Ranger. He's a working cat now, hunting mice in a wildflower seed warehouse."

"Hmm. And Trey's odd behavior started about then?"

"About then. You know, I think Trey misses him, screwy as it sounds." I told her about how Vlad made his life hell from time to time, asserting his right to Trey's food, booting him off the sofa, driving him away from the best sunning spots. Poor old Trey got accustomed to being undercat over the years. "But I don't quite get it. Shouldn't he be dancing a jig now that Vlad is gone and he has the sofa all to himself? Is this feline depression?"

"Depression." Zee scowled. "I don't even like to use that word in connection with humans, let alone animals. It's too fraught with connotations of disease. And disease needs to be medicated. With drugs. At least that's today's thinking. Psychiatrist Willard Gaylin, oh, way back in the days when psychiatrists actually talked to people — the good old pre-Prozac days — felt that most depression wasn't a disorder, or a disease, but a protracted form of grieving caused by what he called 'the loss of the loved object.'"

"That was pretty poetic for a shrink." I looked at Zee, curious. "I didn't know that you read psychiatry in your spare time."

She smiled. "It never hurts to read about the mind. Not that the mind is what psychiatrists today are concerned with. They're obsessed with brain chemistry. No, I prefer to read Willard Gaylin and Irvin Yalom — old-school psychiatrists. After all, animals come to my clinic with their owners. And it's *their* minds one often needs to know more about. Animals are easy; it's their owners who are difficult. Besides, Willard Gaylin was a wonderful writer." She added, "In my opinion, everyone could benefit from reading "Feelings", Gaylin's most accessible book."

"Right," I said, a little mystified. Oh well . . . what do we really know about our friends, anyhow?

"So, coming back to Trey," I said, "in this case the loved object was Vlad?"

"Maybe," she said. "Or maybe not. Maybe we need to interpret the loved object more loosely. Maybe it was Trey's routine and the familiarity of his place in your family. The loved object can be anything we value — or sometimes overvalue — a job, a person, a pet, our social standing, our children, our beauty, our memory."

"Huh," I said. "I can see how this might apply to Trey. He and Vlad certainly had a dysfunctional feline relationship, but now that Trey's lost it, he's kind of at sea."

Zee nodded. "They may not have been buddies, but Trey knew exactly where he stood in the household. He was second cat. Undercat, as you said. Now? There is no other cat. He's alone."

"Oh, crap," I said.

"Not to worry. We'll figure this out."

Zee picked Trey up and put him in a stainless steel cage at the end of the exam room. There was a furry leopard-print mat in it, plus a bowl of kibble and one of water. "I want to take an X-ray just to be sure all this lethargy isn't caused by something physical, like constipation, say," she said. "I didn't feel any fecal masses, but I want to be sure. Jen can help me later. I'll do a blood draw, too. And I think I'll give him 250 ccs of Ringer's. He feels a little dehydrated. You're okay leaving him?"

"Sure," I said. "We need to get to the bottom of what's wrong with him. I told Tris he might be spending the night."

"Then we'll leave him for a bit," she said. "Come on into the next exam room." As we left, she dimmed the lights. "Trey can snooze. Let's go next door and take a look at Shrew's cat."

"Zee, wait a minute," I told her bleakly. "He's not . . . well, I don't really know whose cat he is. He might have been Shrew's cat. But Shrew sure won't be coming for him." I took a deep breath. "Shrew's name was Julia Stevens. And Julia Stevens is dead."

CHAPTER 8

FOR THE SECOND time today we sat at Zee's scrubbed pine table in the kitchen, drinking Dragonwell green tea. Also for the second time, I longed for a slug of Method and Madness Irish Whiskey. Or two. When would that pass? I wondered. As Zee poured tea, I told her about my phone call to Suzanne Paulsen, the discovery of Shrew's identity, my trip to the Forensics impound lot, and my examination of the VW Bug.

"Dammit, Zee, I think Julia was driven off the road," I said. "I think it was deliberate. Whether the driver of the Sequoia intended to kill her, or whether that part of it was an unfortunate accident, I can't say. What the hell was so important that he had to chase her to Ravine Road? Was it for the things she left for me in the dumpster — a flash drive, her key card, her phone, the cat? Did he think she had them with her in the Bug? All I know is there's one wrecked car, one dead woman, and one tortured cat. I'll admit that I'm feeling more than a little guilt about all this. Yeah, Julia told me not to come after her, but if I had, I might have helped."

"Or you might have ended up in the middle of that little drama," Zee said. "At the very least I could have called nine-one-one," I said. "Or . . . ah, dammit, I don't know, Zee. I might have been able to do *something*."

"Or maybe not," Zee said. "Perhaps you're being too hard on yourself."

I said nothing for a moment. Then, "I'm feeling a little desperate. Julia asked me to do a couple of things besides pick up the cat and retrieve the envelope that I found in the dumpster with him."

"What things?" Zee asked.

"Not to leave 'the others' behind, whoever and wherever they are. Oh, and do it by Saturday. Zee, I don't have a clue what those things mean. And now she won't be able to explain them to me. I'm worried as hell that there may be more cats like the tabby somewhere."

Zee shook her head. "Julia can't explain those things to you in person, true. But I'll bet you find clues on the flash drive. Or her phone. Undoubtedly she left them for you for a reason."

"I'm counting on it."

"Come on," she said. "Let's take a look at the cat."

I followed her out of the kitchen and back into the little hallway that led to her clinic, and into the exam room. In a large stainless steel cage, on a piece of fake sheepskin, the tabby was lying asleep. He seemed to be a delicate little guy, about six months old, not yet full-grown, but judging by the size of his paws and ears, I didn't think he would be a big bruiser like Trey. I could see where patches of fur had been shaved off his sides in a regular pattern, and red splotches now blossomed on them. His eyes were closed, although above each eye was an angry-looking furless red welt.

"He's pretty well sedated," she said. "I cleaned the yellow substance away from his eyes, and from the sores on his sides. He was in a lot of pain. I took care of that. His eyesight though . . . well, I can't tell just yet, but there's a chance he'll never see again. I hope I'm wrong, but there's a lot of damage to his corneas."

I swallowed, appalled at what had been done to the little cat.

"What the hell do you think happened to him, Zee?"

She set her lips in a tight line. "I don't know, but whatever it was, it was no accident. At first, I thought he might have gotten into some sticky caustic substance, but I changed my mind once I started cleaning him up. The welts above his eyes, the pattern of shaved spots on his sides . . . no, someone applied this to his eyes and his sides deliberately."

"What?" I said. "I don't get this!"

"And look at his feet."

I bent closer. "He's . . . missing toenails. What happened?"

"I had to remove two," she said. "They seemed to have been partly ripped out. I think he got into one hell of a fight, struggling against what was being done to him. He must have hooked his back feet in something, or someone, and scratched like hell. I used surgical glue on the wounds. There are no sutures. But he's going to be limping for a while."

"Jesus, Zee," I whispered. "Who would do something like this?"

"Who? I can't imagine," she said. "I've not encountered anything like this before. But you have, haven't you?" She looked at me sadly. "This was torture, Kieran. Deliberate, intentional torture."

I closed my eyes. Animal torture. My *bête noir*. Against my will, I thought about the case that had driven me from the law, an animal torture case, and I shivered a little. Who would do something like this? I could answer my own question. Someone like Owen Mallory, a thoroughly reprehensible jerk who had tortured and killed his girlfriend's pets. It wasn't Mallory, of course. I'd kept half an eye on him since his parole — I wanted to be sure he didn't make a return visit to Gianna Brock, the girlfriend, and her remaining dog. But the cat torturer, the man who had done this to the little tabby, he was surely someone cut from the same cloth. These were particular kinds of sadists, men — and they were almost always men — who lived for *schadenfreude,* the malicious joy of causing pain to others, and in this case, to animals.

I looked at the little maimed tabby sleeping on his sheepskin and a baffled, helpless rage rose up in me. Gianna Brock had turned to the law, to me, for justice for her tortured and murdered pets. I fought for them in court, and in a landmark legal case, I did indeed get justice for them until, in a cruel and unexpected spate of legal maneuvering, Mallory's sentence was overturned. Nevertheless, Gianna's pets had had an advocate. Me. What advocate did the tabby have? Who would fight for justice for him? Tears welled up into my eyes and I wiped them away angrily with my sleeve.

"Let's leave him," Zee said, putting a hand on my shoulder, snapping off the light in the exam room and opening the door to the hall. "He's safe. He needs to sleep and heal now. I'll keep you posted on his progress. We'll hold a good thought for him."

✂

I walked slowly over to the barn, my thoughts turning from the tabby to Zee. I needed to see her more often, I realized. As I'd been busy absorbing Tris into my family, I'd neglected her. Heck, I missed her. As well, I was concerned. I wanted to inquire more closely into this newly disclosed penchant for reading psychiatry tomes. Surely there were writers other than long-dead psychiatrists whose prose could be appreciated. I wondered if there was a subtext there, something she was trying to tell me.

From inside the barn, voices drifted to me. Jen and Tris seemed to be done with the riding lesson. I stood outside the open barn door, listening, giving them some space. After all, I didn't know how experienced a riding teacher Jen actually was, and I didn't want to make her self-conscious. What I heard, however, riveted me to the spot.

"Tell me about Nigel," Jen said. "What exactly does he do to Dani?"

Dani . . . Tris's little school friend?

"He pokes her in the ribs when he thinks no one's looking," Tris said, angrily. "He steps on her feet and pretends it was an accident. But he smiles, so he knows he's doing it, and it isn't an accident. And he says mean things to her, Things that make her cry."

The situation sounded suspiciously like bullying. I felt a brief stab of disappointment that Tris had gone to Jen with this problem, and not to me, but shrugged mentally. I was just glad she was telling *someone* about it.

"Has she told anyone about this? Your teacher?" Jen asked.

"No. She's afraid to. She's afraid she'll get in trouble."

"She won't get in trouble," Jen told her. "But I get it that she doesn't want to tell your teacher. No one likes to be a tattletale. However, she can't let this go on."

I applauded Jen's common sense. That was exactly what I would have said. Bullying has to be squelched — if it isn't, it gets worse.

"What kinds of things does he say, Tris?" Jen continued.

"He says things like she should go back to Syria, like she doesn't belong here, like she's stupid because she can't speak English, and no one at school likes her. Which is not true," Tris said heatedly. "She can speak English. It's just not perfect. And everyone likes her. Except Nigel. I don't know why he acts so mean."

Tris was silent for a moment, and I thought sadly about the *danse macabre* Dani and Nigel were caught in. Why did Nigel act so mean? Because he could. Because there was something . . . off about him. Oh, there was a lot of psychological claptrap written these days about bullying in school and how we need to understand the needs of the poor bullies, but that didn't wash with me. I had my own theories about this. I'd had firsthand experience with bullies when I was a kid and later, as an attorney, when I'd prosecuted their grown-up ilk. Yup, I knew the *genus* well.

Bullies seem to have a sixth sense for the different, the shy, the weak. They're like cruising sharks, scenting blood in the water. And Jen was so right — they absolutely need to be stopped. Because on their own, they will not stop until the object of their bullying is destroyed. Just look at the heartbreaking rise of suicides among bullied school children. Henry Purcell, seventeenth century Baroque composer, put it perceptively in one of the lines from his opera *Dido and Aeneas* when the bad guys high-five each other in anticipation of their latest life-destroying scheme.

"From the ruin of others our pleasures we borrow," the bad guys chortled.

It's as simple as this: bullies do these awful things because it makes them feel good. I really don't give a rat's ass about the why of it, about why it makes them feel good. Cruelty to the helpless makes me come unglued. So I listened closely to what Tris was saying. Maybe I could help, if she wanted to confide in me.

Tris continued talking. "Dani told the class a great story about her parents. D'you know, they named her baby brother Justin Trudeau?"

Jen laughed. "That's so weird it's cool!"

"Everyone loved the story except Nigel," Tris said. "He laughed and made a burping noise. And Dani told us that her mom says Canada is a garden and the people are its flowers."

"Wow, Tris."

"Right after that, right after the story, we were in the cafeteria line and Nigel stood on Dani's foot so she couldn't move. He whispered that she and her parents should go back to Syria, that the Mounties will come and arrest them and deport them."

"That's cruel and dumb, Tris," Jen said hotly. "Mounties don't do things like that. And besides, Dani's family belongs here. They're refugees. We took them in. That's what Canada does. We help people."

"I got really mad at him," Tris said. "I told him that if he didn't leave Dani alone, I'd cut his nuts off."

For a moment, I thought I might faint. Oh, my fierce little adopted daughter! She went to DEFCON 1 right away. No half-measures for her. Undoubtedly Tris had heard Con and Peter threaten someone with a line like this during the time she lived with them in the woods.

But when I had recovered from the shock, I wasn't too surprised. She told me that the day Peter had set her arm on fire for asking to have one of the stolen animals as a pet, she ordered an air pistol from Amazon. No one was going to hurt her that way again. She couldn't save all the animals those two assholes had stolen, but she made up her mind that she would save the spots — the Bengal cats. And herself. And, touchingly, me. She protected the things that mattered to her. It didn't surprise me a bit that she was thinking of some way to protect Dani.

"Omigod, Tris. Did anyone hear you? Besides Nigel?"

"Nope. Well, Dani did."

"Did he get the message? Is he leaving Dani alone?"

"So far," Tris said. "I just wanted to know, though . . ."

"Oh, I get it," Jen said. "You want to know what to do if he goes back to being a jerk."

"Yeah. Because I can't cut his nuts off." Tris sounded wistful. "I probably should have told him I'd do something else. Something I could *really* do. Like fill his locker with horse poop. But that wouldn't have been scary enough."

"No, it wouldn't have been," Jen said. "I don't think horse poop would scare someone like Nigel."

She was quiet, and I listened, wondering what she might say to Tris. How would a thirteen-year-old advocate stepping up a threat beyond DEFCON 1?

"Sometimes," Jen began, "we have to, you know, consult people who know more than we do. I'll think some more about this, and I'll be happy to tell you if I think of anything good — maybe some dirty tricks — but I was thinking you might want to talk to Kieran. Remember how she handled Con and Peter? She kicked their butts. And when she was a lawyer she prosecuted bad guys all the time. I bet she'll have some ideas."

Thanks, Jen. But I was glad she'd tossed the ball to me. Indeed, I did have some ideas. I thought I'd wait for Tris to bring the subject up, but I wouldn't wait too long. It might be awkward, but I could always say I'd heard the girls discussing the matter, which was true.

"Yeah . . ." Tris said thoughtfully. "She might. Okay."

"Speaking of horse poop," Jen said. "When you come next week, you need to bring a helmet."

"All right," Tris said. "I'll have Kieran take me to a tack store, like you said."

Silence. Then Jen said, "Can I ask you something?"

"Uh-huh," Tris replied.

"Do you always call Kieran, well, Kieran?"

"Yeah."

"Not 'Mother'?"

"No." Tris sounded pretty matter-of-fact. I'd wondered about this myself, about what the kid might want to call me. We'd never really talked about it. I listened carefully in case there was something for me to learn here.

"Is it because, well, you had a mother, and Kieran isn't her?" Jen asked, plainly curious.

"No," Tris said, clearly not at all perturbed.

"Then . . ." Jen paused.

"Kieran can't be my mother," Tris explained patiently. "She's my hero."

CHAPTER 9

"ANY THOUGHTS ABOUT dinner?" I asked Tris as we pulled out of Zee's little road onto the highway leading back to town. "Aliya's probably exhausted after moving her stuff into her suite. I thought we'd ask her to join us."

"Well, it's Tuesday," Tris said a little tentatively. "Tuesday's my night to pick takeout. I usually pick pepperoni pizza."

"You sound a little uncertain there, kiddo," I said, looking over at her. "Is your enthusiasm for pizza waning?"

"Noooo, but . . ." She turned to me, a worried look on her face. "Kieran, eating meat, you know . . . eating animals . . . well, it's wrong, isn't it?" she asked. "Jen says so. She says we shouldn't eat things like pepperoni pizza."

Thanks a lot, Jen Meat-Is-Murder Lau. I was afraid this was coming. And here it was, appropriately, just before dinner.

"Well, that's a complicated question," I equivocated. "I don't think I can answer it right now. I need to think about it." Then I had an idea. "Say, why don't we call a halt to meat-eating for the time being? We could be bold. Strike out on a culinary adventure. Go meatless."

"Could we?" Tris asked.

"Well, sure," I said. "Do you want to stop by the health food store? I bet they have lots of meatless dishes in the café."

"Okay," Tris said, sounding a little more upbeat.

"Just a couple of things to think about, though," I said. "Apart from no pepperoni on pizza, going meatless means no bacon on Egg McMuffins." I didn't mention school lunches, which I could see would be an enormous problem. One thing at a time. We'd have to see how serious Tris was, and how long this meatless phase lasted.

Tris chewed her bottom lip. "Yeah."

I maneuvered the car onto Beach Drive, and we drove beside the ocean in the last of the late-afternoon sunshine, heading for Oak Bay. I looked over at Tris again. "Am I right that you've been worrying about this ever since Jen showed you her sweatshirt and talked about her school's vegan club?"

"Uh-huh," Tris answered in a small voice.

"Fret not, my sproutlet," I said, trying to lighten the mood. "We can figure this out."

She looked at me uncertainly, clearly wanting to believe.

"Really, we can," I told her, becoming serious. "You and Aliya can start investigating the problem during Google time if you like. I bet there's lots online about this. I'll do my own research and we'll put it all together. We'll make up our own minds. If we decide we shouldn't eat meat, well, we won't."

Oh, lordy, Kieran, what are you promising? I asked myself. Well, hadn't I told my upstairs tenant, Helen Mikita, six months ago that I was most of the way down the road to veganism? I had the sinking feeling that I'd be accelerating my trip.

"Okay," Tris said, smiling at last.

"Now . . . let's go investigate the health food store's lentil loaf," I told her. "I hear it's particularly irresistible with mushroom gravy."

While Tris perused the menu at the health food store's café, I nipped into the aisle that sold personal care items. We both needed toothpaste. I usually shopped for toothpaste and other toiletries at Shopper's Drug Mart, so I was pretty much at a loss here among the socially responsible brands. How in hell would I find toothpaste that hadn't been tested on animals. God, it was horrifying to contemplate that everything we rubbed on our skin, squirted in our hair, or squeezed into our mouths had been responsible for animals' deaths. I picked up a couple of possibilities — Dr. Bronner's, Tom's of Maine, Jason's — and stood there with them in my hands, paralyzed. Going meatless was one thing but toiletries choices was quite another.

"Look for the leaping bunny," said a young blond woman with a buzz cut who had come around a corner of the aisle. Her green apron, embroidered with **Oak Bay Natural Foods** and the logo of a leaf, identified her as an employee. Her name tag identified her as Daria. And her white smile and healthy-looking skin identified her as a likely consumer of the products she sold. Heck, she looked . . . natural. She carried a wicker basket containing tubes of toothpaste and was systematically restocking the shelves.

"Okay," I said. "And the leaping bunny is . . .?"

"I'm glad you asked me that," she said, smiling. "The leaping bunny logo is an internationally recognized symbol guaranteeing consumers that no animal tests were used in the development of any product displaying it. Companies are subject to independent audit of their entire supply chain to check they meet strict criteria. Its database is always up to date." She paused. "You can trust the bunny. Here, let's trade." She took my tubes of toothpaste from me and handed me one of hers. "This is a pretty good choice. Zesty Mint. Made by Island Naturals, a local company. They were one of the first cruelty-free cosmetic firms in the province. No animal testing. Guaranteed. And it tastes okay, too."

"Ah, but what does 'okay' really mean?" I asked. "I have an eight-year-old daughter. She's used to the, um, traditional brands." As was I.

"Well, it's minty, which she'll like. The sweetener is stevia, so that might take a little getting used to, though. And it doesn't contain sodium laurel sulfate, which is good. Of course SLS is the chemical that makes toothpaste foam, so going foamless may be a bit odd for you guys at first."

Meatless, sugarless, foamless. It was all a bit much. Still . . .

"Thanks," I told her.

"No problem. Say, are you interested in learning about product testing on animals? Why we started doing it, why we keep on doing it?"

"Sure," I said.

"Well, there's a Pub Talk on the subject tomorrow night. At U Vic. My partner's class is presenting the subject." She grinned. "I'm drumming up an audience for them. There's a flier on the bulletin board over there. Actually there are two fliers on cosmetics testing," she said. "One about the Pub Talk, and a scary one from an animal activist group called CLAW advertising their meeting. Odd that there are two talks so close together on the same subject." She shrugged. "The moon must be in Capricorn or something. Anyhow, CLAW's a bit extreme. But their hearts are in the right place so we give them space on the bulletin board."

"Maybe I'll take a look at the Pub Talk flier," I said. Why not? My social calendar was empty for tomorrow night. I glanced over at the café and saw Tris in animated discussion with a bearded young man behind the counter, presumably one of the cooks. Most likely she was interrogating him about the presence of anything healthfully green that might be lurking in the lentil loaf.

I wandered over to the bulletin board, which was covered with fliers and business cards advertising everything from crystal channelers, aura cleansers, rebirthers, and energy balancers to the tax benefits of raising alpacas, the Tellington T-Touch for dogs (unleashing your dog's inner potential, yuk yuk), the ecological benefits of composting toilets, and how to brew a great cup of mushroom coffee. Health food store bulletin boards always induce in me the desire to giggle. Mushroom coffee? I bet it didn't start many hearts.

Alongside the business cards was the Pub Talk flier that Daria had spoken about. It invited anyone interested to come to the pub just off campus at 7 p.m. tomorrow evening, where Dr. Helen Mikita's class would be hosting a discussion on the ethics of testing household products and cosmetics on animals. And sure enough, beside it was the scary flier that Daria had described, the one advertising the CLAW meeting.

THESE RABBITS ARE DYING FOR YOUR NEXT DATE

The headline was printed in bold red letters at the top of the flier. A cartoonish illustration in the middle of the page depicted a row of rabbits in a lab setting, with red rings drawn around their eyes. Really, I thought, CLAW could have done better if their intent was to outrage people.

NO MORE COSMETICS TESTING ON ANIMALS!

I read on. It seemed that an organization calling itself Citizens For The Liberation And Welfare Of Animals, or CLAW (shouldn't their acronym have been CLAWA? CLAW was admittedly catchier, though) was planning an "action meeting," which was to take place Thursday night in the basement of a local church. There was a telephone number at the bottom of the flier for more information.

I thought of my friends Ian Burns and Alison Bell, co-founders of the animal rights group Ninth Life, a group that had been steadily shepherding this issue through local meetings and public awareness talks for years. They were now lobbying in support of the Cruelty-Free Cosmetics Act, Bill S-214, which had passed its third reading in the Senate and was due for a vote in the House of Commons. In fact, they were in Ottawa this very moment.

All at once I became aware that a small redheaded woman with freckles, dressed in a black hoodie and jeans, had come up beside me and was looking intently at the fliers. She had a backpack in her hands, which she clasped to her chest.

"Hard to decide, isn't it?" I said conversationally. "Information or action?"

"God damn CLAW anyhow!" she burst out, ripping the flier from the bulletin board and throwing it to the floor.

"Hey," I said, mystified by her behavior. "I don't know anything about CLAW, but progress is being made. The Cosmetics Bill is in Parliament right now. Why don't you come to the Pub Talk?" I held out my hand. "I'm Kieran Yeats. I'm going to share with the group some encouraging information I have about it. Friends of mine are in Ottawa right now. They're getting close to — "

The young woman turned to me, clearly astonished. "What did you say you name was?"

"Kieran Yeats."

All color fled from her face, leaving her freckles standing out like crumbs on a white tablecloth. She stepped back, staggering a bit, and concerned that she might lose her balance, I reached a hand to steady her. But it was my turn to be astonished.

"You!" she yelled and swung her backpack at me.

I was completely unprepared, and the blow caught me across the side of my head, knocking me backward. I stumbled, dropped my toothpaste, and fell on my butt. When I had picked myself up and dusted off my injured pride, the young woman was gone.

"Kieran?" said a small voice at my elbow.

I turned. Tris was standing there, looking worried.

"Why did that woman hit you?" she asked. "Did you get hurt?"

"Nah, I just fell on my butt," I said. I ruffled Tris's hair and squeezed her shoulder a little, trying to reassure her that all was well. Hey, someone had just whacked her hero in the side of the head and knocked her on her rear end, but all was well. "Don't worry about it, Sprout. I think she had me mixed up with someone else."

A good answer, but privately I wondered. She certainly seemed to know my name. And it had positively upset her. I wondered, too, if she'd show up at the Pub Talk. If she did, I hoped she'd leave her backpack at home.

"Did you figure out our dinner?" I asked Tris.

"Yup," she said. "Lentil loaf and salad."

"Sounds yummy," I said with more enthusiasm than I felt. "Our first meatless meal. Good job."

She beamed up at me. "I hope Aliya will like it."

"I'm sure she will," I said. "In fact, just last week I heard her talking on the phone with Samir, telling him how much she was longing for lentil loaf."

Tris, used to my flights of silliness, giggled. "You're just fooling," she said. "She wasn't!"

"Oh really? We'll ask her," I said. "Let's pay for our dinners, then head on home."

CHAPTER 10

T HE LENTIL LOAF was not a great hit *chez* Yeats. Each of us got a
slice of lentil loaf, a tablespoon of gravy, a glob of mashed
potatoes, and a vole's portion of salad.

"A trifle dry," I commented.

"Kinda icky," Tris said.

"*Sayiya*," Aliya muttered in Arabic. "Listen," she said perkily,
"Tris, you can help me tomorrow when I pick you up from school.
We'll do some shopping at a Middle Eastern grocery store I know.
We'll make falafel and hummus. And serve it with pita. That'll be
easy."

Tris looked doubtful.

"You'll like it," Aliya assured her. "Falafel's like meatballs . . . but
without the meat." She gave me a mischievous look. "And Kieran can
plan something for Thursday night."

I groaned. "Sure. You bet."

Tris cleared away the dinner dishes and put them in the dishwasher. Then we heard her humming in her bathroom, running water.

"How's the toothpaste?" I called to her.

"Weird," she called back. Then, after a moment, "Okay, I guess. There are no bubbles, though."

"Yeah, we're going bubbleless," I told her. "It goes along with meatless. Get your jammies on, Sprout. You can read for half an hour. I'll be in to say good night."

"So you got moved in okay?" I asked Aliya. "Did Samir really help?" I would have been surprised if the feckless Samir had been much help, but I was willing to be surprised.

Aliya shook her head in exasperation. "No. I knew he wouldn't. When the time came to go get my things from home, he arranged to be out taking real estate photos. Lawrence closed the shop and helped me. He's such a fool. Samir. Not Lawrence. I swear he's allergic to physical labor. And if there's a chance for him to show off to a nice-looking woman, then he will. Imagine! He took the drone, just to impress her. Why do you need a drone to take photos in a two-bedroom condo?"

"Hmm," I said, "I hope he had better luck with it than the time he drowned it in a client's fish pond in Uplands. Let's be optimistic. Maybe he didn't lose it off the balcony today."

"Ha," Aliya said. "He's become a real . . . I can't say it. The expression is too rude. Well, at least I won't have to share a bathroom with him anymore. The guy is beyond vain. He has more personal care products than I do."

I chuckled.

"You know, she said pensively, "I wasn't altogether unhappy when our parents sat Samir and me down and explained that one of us would have to move out. I'd been wanting to. Living in a room in my parents' home was getting to be kind of restrictive. And sharing a bathroom with Samir . . . ugh. He never cleaned it. But now I have my own bathroom. And my own apartment. It's beyond amazing!"

I remembered my own first apartment and smiled. "My pleasure," I said. "And I could always set you up with some foamless toothpaste," I teased. "On the house."

We chatted for a bit longer, then I went in to say good night to Tris. She was dead to the world, however, curled up under her Lion King comforter. I felt bad that her sleeping companion, Trey, was at Zee's. Well, if all went well, I could pick him up tomorrow. I turned her bedside lamp off, and saved her place in her latest fantasy novel, "Tailchaser's Song." We were reading chapters to each other at night, and I felt a bit guilty that I hadn't been in to read with her. Well, there was tomorrow. She could catch me up on the adventures of Fritti Tailchaser I'd missed tonight. I made sure her lava lamp was on and pulled her bedroom door mostly closed.

Pouring a glass of wine for Aliya and one for myself, I carried the wine and Shrew's phone into the living room and put them on the coffee table. I took a seat on my old, worn, leather couch, and Aliya joined me. To my surprise, she gave the phone a look of distaste.

"What is it?" I asked her. I'd called Aliya from Zee's and told her to go ahead and see what she could find on the phone. What on earth could she have discovered?

"The phone wasn't locked," Aliya said. "It just needed a charge. The text messages had been wiped, so those aren't available, but her list of contacts seems to be intact. And there's a video. I don't understand it, Kieran. There's a cat, and a man, and . . ."

My stomach sank in premonitory dismay. "Let me see," I said.

She picked up the phone, swiped a few times, then passed it to me. I started the video. There was no sound, only pictures.

Oh yeah. There was a cat and a man all right. A little tabby cat. The cat was being held by the scruff of his neck, struggling and spitting, eyes wide in terror. The man holding him was laughing at his distress. Abruptly the cat swiveled his head and bit the man's hand, hard. Then his flailing back feet gained a purchase in the man's forearm and I could see blood ooze from where his claws had dug in. I cheered the display of feistiness. But it was short-lived. The man's face turned dark with anger and he struck the cat across the head. The cat went limp and the man shook him, stuffing his unprotesting body into a set of restraints on a lab bench. The video stopped. There was a pause, then it began again. The cat now had its eyes clipped open. Two hands appeared close to the cat's head, one holding it steady, and one dripping something yellow from a small squeeze bottle into its eyes. A man's head filled the picture, bending close to the cat, the same man captured in the beginning of the video. He was smiling, saying something to the cat in a parody of endearment. The cat hissed and spat. I put the phone down. I didn't want to see any more.

I put my head in my hands, feeling tears of rage start. "You bastard," I whispered. "You goddam bastard."

"Kieran . . . do you know him?" Aliya asked incredulously.

"Yeah, sort of," I said, wiping my eyes. "And the cat, too." Because the man was the bearded man I had seen driving the Sequoia very early this morning. And the cat was the little tabby now sleeping in a cage in Zee's clinic.

"What's going on?" Aliya asked, eyes wide.

"I don't think I should bring you into this," I told her. "I don't know a lot, but what I do know is pretty damned ugly."

She thought for just a moment. "Well, I helped last year when we thought the stolen Bengals were dying. That was pretty ugly, too. I can handle this, Kieran. Tell me."

"Okay," I said. "Here's what I know."

꿍

Aliya had gone downstairs to bed in her new apartment; Tris was peacefully wrapped in Lion King dreams; and I lay, finally, in my much-longed-for hot bath.

I'd asked Aliya to send the video of the cat and the bearded man to me via email. It was evidence and I wanted to be sure I had it someplace safe. As well, I asked her if she could fool with the video and get me a couple of good stills showing the man's face. I had plans for them. But that was a task for tomorrow. Tonight — what was left of it — I needed to marinate in a hot bath, the place where I did my best thinking. I usually shared my bath time and thinking time with Trey, the big guy nestled in my discarded clothes, always attentive and encouraging of my half-baked theories. Except my theorizing didn't feel so half-baked tonight.

"Okay, Trey," I said, taking a sip of the shot of Method and Madness Irish Whisky I'd brought into the bathroom with me. "I know you're not here but I'm going to pretend you are. I'm calmer now. No more cursing. Let's think. We now know definitively that the bearded guy who drove Julia off the road and the bearded guy who tortured the cat are the same asshole. Here's my guess: the bearded guy caught Julia making the video of him torturing the cat. We don't know why he was doing that, but he was. Julia managed to grab the cat and take off. Somewhere in there she texted me. He fired up his big Sequoia and chased her. She managed to toss the cat and some other things she wanted me to have in the dumpster. She talked to me for a minute, then she took off again. He chased her again and forced her off the road. Sideswiped her car. It jumped the median on Ravine Road and rolled over. She died. Whether intentionally or accidentally, he killed her. I should hand these suspicions over to Mac, and I plan to. The police need to open an investigation into Julia's death. You with me so far?"

I draped the hot, wet washcloth over my face and sank down in the water, the back of my head against the tub.

"Julia bought the little tabby's life with her own, you know. Snatching the cat, fleeing through the night with that asshole chasing her . . . those were awfully brave things to have done. You're being pretty quiet — it may be that you feel as humbled about this as I do."

Silence, of course.

"But talking with you always helps me focus. So . . . let's talk about the job I was paid for. Retrieving the cat and the brown envelope was only half of it. Now I have to find 'the others,' not leave them behind, and accomplish this by Saturday. Easy peasy, right? Wrong. I have no clues as to who they are or where they are or why Saturday is the drop-dead date. I'm hoping like hell the flash drive will give me some answers because if not, I'll be reading tea leaves or casting the runes. But let's leave that problem for a minute, though.

"Now . . . the job I wasn't paid for. Finding the cat torturer. I know, I know, animal torture brings out the dragon in me, and I should probably book myself in for a month of therapy sessions right now. But really, Trey, doesn't the little tabby deserve justice? No one should get away scot free with what that guy did. On a practical note, though, how in hell will I find him? And what will I do with him once I do? Hand him over to the law? Really? You remember how well the Owen Mallory case went. Chasing the torturer won't be good for my mental health, but how can I turn my back on this?"

I sighed. "You're not helping, big guy. I know you would if you were here." I looked down at the empty place on the bath mat where the Animal Crimes Investigator's Trusty Confidant Trey usually snoozed, and sighed. "Maybe we both ought to call it a night: you at Zee's, and me here. I'll see you tomorrow."

I decided I felt too tired to think about anything anymore. In my bedroom, I found a clean T-shirt and a soft, comfy pair of shorts, put them on, lay down on my bed with a groan, and pulled my sheets up over my head. I had another spasm of longing for Trey, but it winked out like a firefly as I fell into the pit of sleep.

WEDNESDAY

CHAPTER 11

SIX-THIRTY FOUND me at the Back Alley Deli, just off Oak Bay Avenue, waiting for Yvonne to open up. I'd turned the coffeemaker on before I left the house and texted Aliya that I was going out foraging for breakfast. She'd see that Tris got up and finished her morning routine: face washing, hair combing, clothes donning, bed making, and backpack packing.

A handsome woman with prematurely white hair cut off stylishly just below her chin, Yvonne had owned the Back Alley Deli for as long as I had lived in Oak Bay. I was one of her first customers. Back in the days when I was a real person with a real job and a paycheck, I used to drop in for a coffee and a muffin on my way to court. Nowadays, I didn't stop by quite as often. I wasn't quite sure why that was. Nevertheless, I was glad to see that the establishment was still thriving. Yvonne pulled on a dark green apron over her white turtleneck, tied it in front, then turned the deli's Closed sign to Open, waving to me as I got out of the car.

"Haven't seen you for a while," she said as the door tinkled closed behind me. "Have you decided to eat healthy?"

"Yeah, the fit comes over me now and then." I smiled. "Usually I resist it, but, you know, I have to think about Tris." The wonderful smell of freshly baked bread made me almost drool, and I vowed to drop in here more often.

"I got your text," she said. "I have your order packed up. Spinach quiche, just out of the oven, a container of freshly squeezed orange juice, a Tofurky sandwich with cranberry sauce and thinly sliced zucchini coins, and a large container of fruit salad." She raised an eyebrow. "Is someone going veggie?"

I grimaced. "Tris. I'm scrambling along behind her."

"Well, Tofurky is a good choice. It tastes like a cross between bologna and turkey." I shuddered, and Yvonne tut-tutted. "Tris will probably like it. Kids do. The cranberry sauce helps."

I paid for the order and was going to say something else to Yvonne — something about bread — but two people came into the deli behind me and I decided to leave her to her customers.

"Enjoy," she called to me on my way out.

❧

Back at home, Aliya was pouring coffee in the kitchen, and Tris was setting the table.

"The mighty hunter returns," I told them. "Quiche, orange juice, and fruit salad were no match for me. And I snagged a sandwich for your lunch, Tris."

She grinned. "Oh boy, quiche! Are we going to have this every day now we're veggies?"

"Probably not," I told her. "But we're sure going to have to think of something for breakfast besides eggs and bacon, or eggs and sausages. Quiche is just a place holder."

"There's always cereal," Tris suggested, making a face.

"Yeah, I know how much you liked those funky, dried-up Os," I said.

"And the scratchy little pillows," she added.

"And the gluey oatmeal," Aliya chimed in.

"Makes you wonder how the Irish thrived as a race," I mused, thinking of my forebears. "All those bowls of oatmeal and plates of potatoes. Maybe there's an unexplored connection between carbs and poetic genius. Sit, my sproutlet," I told Tris. "Chug some orange juice. It's chock full of Vitamin C. Guaranteed to ward off scurvy."

We sat down to a companionable breakfast, helping ourselves to slices of quiche and bowls of fruit salad. I decided in between bites of quiche that I liked it. The companionable part, as well as the quiche. My entire adult life I had leaped out of bed to the banshee shrieking of the alarm clock, turned on the coffee maker, fed the cats, stumbled to the shower, thrown on some clothes, and, barely conscious, dashed out the door. The presence of Tris, and now Aliya, in my life had rendered mornings so much more civilized.

"We could have pancakes or waffles sometimes," Tris said hopefully. "With maple syrup. Or French toast."

"Right after we add a French chef to the household," I said. "We'll have to get you a paper route to afford her. Good ideas, but we need to be thinking of breakfast that half-awake adults can make. It won't always be quiche and fruit salad from Yvonne's. I'll go broke. What's on your agenda at school today?"

"Well, we're working on our big world map of birds," she said between bites of fruit salad. "I chose South America. I have to research all the birds there. There sure are a lot! So I wore my bird shirt."

"Indeed you did," I said. Today Tris wore a dark blue T-shirt shirt with two toucans playing chess on it and the words TOUCAN PLAY THIS GAME beneath the chessboard.

"Where on earth did you two find all those T-shirts?" Aliya asked.

"Online," I said. "Tris and I decided that the selection at the giant superstore didn't quite fit her image. Didn't we, kiddo?"

Tris waggled her eyebrows conspiratorially.

"I'm glad that the college bookstore has as many choices as it does," Aliya said. "I don't have time to shop for clothes." Today she wore another Camosun College hoodie - pale blue with white lettering.

Tris excused herself to go finish getting ready for school, and I poured another cup of coffee for Aliya and myself.

"You're pretty quiet," I observed. "Did you sleep okay? Sometimes the first night in a new place is unsettling."

"I slept okay, thanks," she said with a quick smile. "I just have something on my mind. In fact, I'd like to talk to you about it later if you have time."

"Are you upset by the video on Shrew's phone?" I asked her.

She shook her head. "No. Well, yes, but that's not it."

"Well, you can't want to move out," I said jokingly. "You just moved in. Can I have a hint?"

She nodded. "Yeah. It's my job at Lawrence's shop."

"Is everything okay there?" I asked, a little alarmed.

Aliya sighed. "I think I want to cut back my hours."

"Wow. Is your job interfering with school?"

"No." She paused. "It's, well, something else. And things might be tight financially for me if I do cut back my hours, but that's not what I want to talk to you about. I have savings. I don't want you to reduce the rent or anything like that. It's just that what I have in mind is a little risky. And I don't want to hurt Lawrence's feelings. After all, he gave me my first job here in this country. It's . . . complicated," she said, looking worried.

"Okay, let's talk," I said, mystified. "I'm going up-island to see Miranda Blake in about half an hour. I'm not sure how long I'll be gone, but I should be home at least by dinnertime. As I recall it's Middle Eastern Night, right? Meatless balls and all that. Then I'm planning to go to U Vic for Helen Mikita's Pub Talk. We should be able to find some time in there."

"Okay," she said, pensive.

"Change is sometimes hard. Especially when people you care about are involved. But whatever this is, I think it can be worked out."

"I'll try to believe that." She stood up. "Hey, I'd better go light a fire under Tris. We need to get going. Will you clean up?"

"Sure. See you later."

Before the cleanup, however, I had something to do. I went into my office and found Julia's flash drive where I had stashed it in a desk drawer, then shoved it into one of my computer's USB ports. I was hoping it would hold the answer to this maiden's prayers. Alas, the damned thing proudly proclaimed that it was password protected. It simply wouldn't open.

"For God's sake!" I shouted. "You're making this hard for me, Julia. What's on here? The secret formula for Coca-Cola?" Now I was going to have to consult Aliya, the cyber equivalent of the Delphic Oracle. I quickly scribbled a note for her and left the flash drive on the dining room table. Maybe she would have better luck than I ferreting out its secrets. Time was ticking away, dammit, and I very much wanted to see what was on that flash drive. Julia wouldn't have left it for me if it hadn't been important. I ground my teeth.

I went back out to the kitchen where I cleaned up, my mind only half on my tidying. Overnight, I'd decided I wasn't going to wait for Tris to talk to me about Nigel. I figured the wisest course of action might be to drop into Tris's school sometime today and discuss the Nigel/Dani/Tris situation with Tris's teacher, Marie Linley. Did I think a visit from me would solve things? Maybe. Maybe not. But I didn't want the situation to blow up without having put the school on alert. And it might. Blow up, that was. If, between Tris's threat and what I hoped would be Marie Linley's soft yet stern words whispered in Nigel's ear, the kid still continued to torment Dani and upset Tris, well, then what? I sighed. I understood Tris's frustration. I'd like to cut the tormenting little bastard's nuts off myself. But first, we'd try the civilized approach. When had I become so collegial, I wondered? Hmmf. I put the dishes in the dishwasher and headed for the shower.

CHAPTER 12

I DROVE TOWARD the ocean, indulging myself by taking the long way around to my destination up-island — going south to go north. It was another beautiful day. A faded-denim blue sky characteristic of autumn in the north. Maples blazing red and gold. Tartan sweaters on Corgis. The tang of wood smoke in the air — definitely not good for global warming, but admittedly romantic. At the end of my street, I turned left onto Beach Drive, drove around McNeil Bay, passed the protected marine meadow called Kitty Islet, which as far as I knew had never been visited by a kitty, then followed the coast north into the Royal Victoria Golf Club.

I don't know if this is true, but I read once that the Irish, in a fit of puckish good humor, gave the Scots both the game of golf and the bagpipes. The Scots, dour lot that they were, never twigged to either joke. They never got it that golf spelled backward is flog. And as for the bagpipes, well, the jury is still out on whether the sounds they produce is or isn't music.

Wasn't it the Germans in World War I who called the bagpipes "the ladies from hell"? In my opinion, the bravest souls in that four-year stretch of misery in Northern France were the Scottish and Canadian pipers. Day after miserable day, unarmed, they piped their regiments out of those muddy, smelly holes in the ground, across no-man's-land, into hand-to-hand battle with the foe. The bagpipes put the fear of God into the Germans, if historians can be believed, but alas, not enough fear as the conflict raged on, taking the lives of over 1,000 pipers. Imagine going into battle with nothing between yourself and the enemy but a bag of wind. Frankly, I can't. And as much as I wince musically when I hear bagpipes, I get a little misty-eyed thinking of their history.

A little farther on, I passed the sprawlingly beautiful Oak Bay Beach Hotel — scene of many afternoon meetings with Mac at The Snug — the hotel's quintessentially British pub. Both the hotel and The Snug sit poised on the cliffs right at the ocean's edge and, I may be partisan about this, but I've never seen a more dramatic and gorgeous location for a hostelry. I waste time driving by it every chance I get. Finally, my favorite part of the drive: the Oak Bay Marina. Passing the marina with its thickets of masts always makes me feel nautical, and I whistled a bit from the sea shanty "Bound for Rio" as I drove by.

Friends of mine from Oregon recently decided to chuck all the craziness that was happening on their side of the border, take advantage of one of the couple's Canadian citizenship, apply for permanent resident status for the other one, and emigrate. They rented a berth at the marina, parked their boat — The Catspaw — there, and decided what the heck, why buy an expensive home? For the cost of a modest apartment rental, they'd just live at the marina. Wow. They weren't in residence yet — they were still disentangling themselves from professional obligations on the Oregon coast — but last I heard, they intended to move onto their boat soon. My home and fireplace were always available when the winter winds whipped the seas to twenty feet and froze the lines on sailboats' rigging, I assured them.

I rationalized my time-wasting because I had a disagreeable topic to discuss with my friend Miranda and I needed some balm for my soul first. I'd emailed her the video of the little tabby and the bearded man, and we were going to put our heads together to see if anything bright occurred to us. I knew Miranda had had run-ins with animal torturers over the years, and I was eager to know if the man in the video was anyone she recognized.

Miranda Blake ran an animal sanctuary called, well, The Sanctuary, about fifteen minutes north of Sidney, up the Pat Bay Highway on the way to the ferry docks. A refugee from too many years in the Royal Canadian Mounted Police, she was now in the animal rescue, rehabilitation, and adoption business. She'd traded the red serge and the Musical Ride for cat scratches, fleas, mange, vomit, URI, and dog pee, she joked, and asserted that she was a better woman for it. Six months ago, we'd trailed 26 missing pets to a buncher's holding facility in the woods north of town and sent the animals back safely to their owners. I was hoping she'd want to give me a hand with this.

The parking lot under the firs at The Sanctuary was suspiciously empty of cars. In fact the only vehicles parked in front of the two-story structure were the Sanctuary's dark blue van, Miranda's yellow Jeep, and her assistant, Connie's, black Honda Fit. This was Wednesday — The Sanctuary was open to prospective adopters today — what was going on? I pulled my Karmann Ghia up beside Miranda's Jeep and walked to the front door. A large sign said CLOSED, but a handwritten pink Post-It note beside the large sign said: KIERAN, COME IN. I pushed the door open and walked into the reception area wondering what the heck was up.

"Hi, Kieran," said Connie, looking harried. "It's ringworm, I'm afraid." Today she wore a comfy-looking pink chamois shirt and jeans, her irrepressibly curly gray hair tied back with a hank of purple yarn. Her silver-rimmed glasses had slid halfway down her nose and she adjusted them fussily.

I liked Connie a great deal. Miranda's aunt, she was marooned somewhere in the no-woman's-land between fifty and seventy, and was fearsomely efficient. When I first met her six months ago, I thought her humorless and rather prim, but as I got to know her better, I changed my mind. Once I learned that she often binge-watched reruns of the paralyzingly funny British television series *Fawlty Towers* and could quote whole stanzas from Francesco Marciuliano's laugh-out-loud book of cat poems called *I Could Pee On This*, I realized I'd met a soul mate.

"Things are in a mess here," she said, barely preventing a stack of file folders from heading for the floor. "Administrative chores have had to take a back seat to health issues." She rescued the file folders and tried to make a tidy stack, tut-tutting a little. "I'll never get this lot sorted out, I'm afraid."

"Oh, brother. Ringworm's a bear," I commiserated.

"We've had it before," she said, "but not this badly. Our volunteers are working overtime. They're all parking in the back and using the doors close to the laundry cottage. Miranda doesn't want them traipsing through the reception area. She's right. We need to try to keep the outbreak contained. But they must have done a million loads of laundry. Poor things. And poor kittens, also. A batch of eight-week-olds from a county park brought the ringworm in. Of course, we test everyone for everything, but this is a strain that didn't initially fluoresce under the Woods Light. And they seemed pretty healthy otherwise," she said, plainly puzzled. "They graduated from their isolation period just fine. Then, a volunteer noticed a round hairless patch on one of their necks . . . and it did fluoresce . . . and the rest is, well, a giant pain in the rear end. All the kittens have it. Adoptions have ground to a halt. We're just trying to keep it from spreading to the rest of the cats in the other cottages, and to the dogs."

"Excuse me," she said. "I have to order some more Tyvek coveralls. Miranda insists volunteers wear them to treat the kittens."

"Sounds like you've got things under control," I said reassuringly.

I remembered when Trey was an outdoor cat and contracted ringworm from one of his neighborhood ramblings. He'd had to have several spots shaved on his head and neck, submit to a twice-daily anti-fungal bath, have his shaved spots dabbed with fungicide, and swallow a carefully-measured dose of oral medication daily. He was a very unhappy guy for a few weeks. And I contracted ringworm on one arm from dealing with him — something that freaked me out until Zee assured me that it was nothing to worry about. She got a case of ringworm annually, she said. Fortunately mine cleared up with just daily dabbing with fungicide.

"We're three weeks into this," Connie said with a sigh. "I hope we're turning the corner. We'll know today when the vet comes."

Evidently feeling ignored, Jimmy, the Sanctuary's off-the-beam, doo-wop-singing African Grey Parrot gave me a wolf whistle and screeched for my attention. He was settled on a perch with a window view in the reception area. Once he was certain I noticed him, he danced a bit, then warbled:

"You're my love,
You're an angel,
You're the girl of my dreams."

"Ha," I told him. "That's 'Daddy's Home.' You always think you can stump me. I know more doo-wop ditties than you've ever heard of. A wasted youth, I know. But why haven't you been adopted, cat-bait?"

He stretched a wing, muttered under his breath, and turned away to admire the view out the window.

Connie snorted, peering at me from over the rims of her glasses. "He was pretty close to being adopted twice, but he sabotaged his chances each time. Everyone's enchanted with his doo-wop tunes. It's the cursing they object to. And there's no telling what will set him off. People worry: what will the grandchildren think and all that."

Jimmy whistled, then trilled a new song:

"My boyfriend's back, and you're gonna be in trouble,
Hey-la-day-la.
You see him coming, better cut out on the double."

"Knock it off with the threats," Connie said. "You're going to be a lonely, homeless old bird if you don't mend your ways, mister."

Jimmy leaned over to the window, lifted one claw, pulled the window open, and flew outside, trailing a sound that seemed suspiciously like a raspberry.

I said to Connie, "Is he supposed to be out there?"

"Oh, yes," she assured me. "We built him an aviary. He spends a lot of time in the tree just outside the window. The sun is good for his feathers. And the tree gives him an unobstructed view of the parking lot. He watches for people to drive up, then hustles himself back into the reception area to sit on his perch. Miranda thinks he's checking out potential adopters, but I think he's just nosy. If he suspects someone is interested in him, he erupts into a fit of cursing and head-bobbing. He must think you have no designs on him." She gave me an appraising look. "He just sings to you."

"Yeah, well, I'm a cat person," I said. "He must sense the vibes. Or notice the cat hair on my jeans."

"And what's wrong with a little cat hair on the jeans?" a voice called from the hall leading out of the reception area. "C'mon back, Kieran," my friend Miranda said. A tall, sturdy woman dressed in tan cords, hiking boots, and a navy fisherman-knit sweater, she pulled the hall door closed behind us. Miranda was one of those people with perfectly ordinary faces made incandescently lovely by smiling, which she did now. I couldn't help smiling back, and I am not a smiler.

"The spores from hell have descended upon you, I hear," I said.

"God help us, yes," she agreed. "If it isn't one thing, it's something else. URI last spring, and now ringworm."

"Hey, when I sent you that video, I didn't know," I told her. "You've probably got your hands full."

"Nah," she said. "Our vet developed a protocol for us. And our volunteer coordinator is in charge — she's a former vet tech, and has recruited a brigade of volunteers to help with the actual medicating. I'm trying to stay out of it. The fewer people who come into contact with the spores, the better. Connie's obsessing — we've had to start a file on every sick cat and kitten and record their progress daily. But she's managing."

"It's a little early for drinking," she commented as she showed me into her office, "but I admit the video you sent made me want to pour myself a stiff one."

"It is rather awful, isn't it?"

She took a seat behind her desk, pulled out the bottom drawer, and propped her feet on it. "It's beyond awful," she said. "Where is the cat now?"

"At Zee's," I said. "I should have told you that in my email so you wouldn't worry."

"Thank God," she nodded, tucking a wing of dark hair behind one ear. She turned to look out the window and when she turned back, her pale blue fighter-pilot eyes blazed with anger. "I don't even know the circumstances behind the video, but I can tell you that I'm pretty angry. Fill me in?"

"Sure. Here's what I know," I said, giving her the details of everything that had happened yesterday.

"Have you told Mac about what you suspect?" she asked. "That Julia was deliberately driven off the road by the driver of the white Sequoia?"

"Uh-huh. I sent him an e-mail just before I left to come here. Her death — that's a matter for the law to investigate. I'm sorry as hell it happened, but I have other fish to fry, so to speak."

"Such as finding the guy in the video with the cat?" Miranda guessed.

"How well you know me," I said. "Yeah, that, among other things. Including discovering who and where these mysterious others are. The second part of my job for Julia."

She was silent for a moment, then added, "It's a damned sad fact of our legal system that animals get such short shrift. Except in egregious circumstances. Sorry," she apologized. "I don't mean to rake up the past for you. I was thinking out loud."

"No problem," I said. "I'm over that. The Owen Mallory thing."

Miranda raised an eyebrow. "Fibber."

I sighed. She was pretty perceptive. During the course of our becoming friends, I'd told her about the case that had scuttled my law career for me, swore on many occasions that I'd put it behind me, yet still found myself weeping into my beer with her from time to time.

"Yeah," I agreed. "My nose just grew an inch. Someday I'll get over it, though."

"There's no rush," she said. "It'll take as long as it takes. Okay, tell me what your plans are."

"Ha," I said. My unplans, you mean. I thought I'd just ask questions and turn over rocks until something crawls out. Someone, somewhere, knows who the cat torturer is. And where he is. So I've already started asking. I sent email to an attorney friend of mine this morning. Caroline Edwards. We were close when I worked in the Crown Counsel's office. I asked her to make some inquiries for me. Find out who's been prosecuted for animal cruelty since I left. She'll get back to me," I said. Glumly, I added, "I only prosecuted one animal-torturing bastard. Owen Mallory. And he looks nothing like the bearded guy."

Miranda took some file folders out of a desk drawer. I was appalled to see that the stack wasn't exactly thin. "Here are some more bastards for you," she said.

"Jesus," I said. "Quite a few."

"Yeah," she agreed. "Quite a few."

We sat in silence for a moment as I flipped through the folders, then she said, "I have another idea. You know, we've got a Facebook page with a few thousand followers. And a Twitter account with a few thousand more. Connie's the Sanctuary's Queen of Social Media. She prides herself on her expertise in that area. God knows I'm useless. I'm too busy speaking to Chambers of Commerce or going to lunch with wealthy prospective donors." She smiled. "I was thinking Connie might be willing to help. It would take her mind off the ringworm cats. She's fretting."

I frowned. "Yeah, but that would mean she'd have to look at that awful video, Miranda."

"It would," Miranda said, "but I wouldn't worry about Aunt Connie. She's no shrinking violet. She's an animal activist from way back. In fact, she's writing a book about her years in animal activism. Some people in animal rescue are, well, fragile, but Connie isn't one of them. I think when she sees the video she'll be as incensed as I am. Let's ask her."

"Okay," I said, and Miranda picked up the phone.

Connie came down the hall and leaned against the door frame. Miranda motioned for her to come around her desk. "I have a video I want you to look at here on my laptop," she said. "Kieran sent it to me. It's pretty ugly. But someone knows who this man is. Maybe even someone on our social networks. We're thinking you could ask them. Put the photos out there."

Connie bent a bit to get the angle on Miranda's laptop just right, then uttered an exclamation of disgust. She gave me one eloquent look, and I was afraid that the video had been too much, that she was about to tell me to go to hell. Instead, smoothing an imaginary wrinkle from her already wrinkle-free jeans, she tightened her lips, narrowed her eyes, and nodded. Drawing her shoulders back, she stood a little taller. Suddenly, I got it. Connie had just received her marching orders. She was preparing to go into battle.

"Of course I'll help," she said. "Miranda, send me the photos? I'll start now."

Did I hear the echo of bagpipes?

CHAPTER 13

As I HEADED to my car, I noted that the weather had turned iffy and I found my mood deteriorating with it. A nasty cold breeze had sprung up from somewhere, and I zipped my windbreaker a little higher. A flotilla of eggplant-colored clouds had drifted in from the south, and they now sat on the horizon like a dark-sailed armada. Rain was clearly in the offing.

Putting Miranda's folders on the floor in front of the passenger seat, I headed out onto the Pat Bay Highway. I wasn't up for thinking about what lurked inside them, or inside the file that Caroline Edwards had just emailed me — animal cruelty cases the Crown Counsel's Office had prosecuted over the last few years. Actually, to be honest, my incipient grumpiness was due to the fact that I didn't want to pour over files of animal torturers right now. I simply wanted to — I don't know — grab a sub sandwich, visit Kitty Islet, and look at the sea.

I turned my mp3 player on, and Bachman Turner Overdrive's paean to economic independence blasted out of my speakers:

"If you ever get annoyed, you can be self-employed
And love working at nothing all day."

Ain't that the truth, I thought. Some days I positively longed for the annoying CC's office and a few straightforward prosecutions: theft, blackmail, breaking and entering, assault. Days like today, for instance. After my midnight ride with the tabby cat, and the video Aliya had found on Julia's phone, I felt smothered by ugliness.

In fact, more days than I liked to admit, I keenly regretted my choice of *métier*. And what the hell was it anyhow? Interdicting. Thwarting. Depriving predators of their prey. Intervening before harm was done, small lives snuffed out, hearts broken, charges filed, cases argued. Keeping the living alive.

A few raindrops spattered on my windshield. Perfect, I thought. Just perfect. I turned the car's wipers on and headed for Oak Bay.

❧

At the Oak Grove School, I sat in my car for a couple of minutes, wondering how badly I was about to betray Tris. I just hadn't gotten around to telling her I'd overheard her talking to Jen about removing Nigel's testicles. For that matter, Tris hadn't followed Jen's advice and talked to *me* about Nigel, either. Ah, well. We'd have to see how all that played out. The main thing was, I figured, that someone (alas, that someone was me) would have to tell Marie Linley about what was happening. I didn't want Dani to have a nervous breakdown, or Tris to pick the lock on our gun safe so she could extract her air pistol and go gunning for Nigel.

I'd called Marie Linley from my car, and fortunately I caught her at lunch. She'd told me to come right in, and I made my way to the office, where she said we could talk.

We sat on either side of a small, round table, and Marie came right to the point. "Bullying, you say?" Her otherwise pleasant green-eyed gaze became stern. The motherly-looking redhead was absent. In her place was a no-nonsense Athena, goddess of wisdom. "We have a zero-tolerance policy for bullying."

I cleared my throat. "Well, yes, bullying."

"Tell me about it," she said.

So I did, filling her in on everything except Tris's threat to neuter Nigel. I translated Tris's graphic warning into a promise by my daughter to visit some unspecified bodily harm on the kid if he didn't stop tormenting Dani.

Marie nodded. "This isn't unexpected."

"It isn't? Then you know what a little jerk he is?"

"We know. Dani isn't the first child Nigel has bullied. He tends to pick on those he considers helpless." She frowned. "Last year it was a little Haitian girl. This year it's Dani."

"Well, at least he's an equal opportunity bully," I said. "Although he does seem to be stuck on refugees."

"You could say he's on probation," Marie said. "We hoped that would give him a wake-up call. Curb his bullying."

I sighed. "Ah, yes, probation. Forgive my cynicism, but I bet you had a parent-teacher-student crisis meeting with him also. Where he got a lot of attention and was the star of the show for about an hour. I'm certain he was enjoined to try and feel how the poor picked-on little girl felt. Be empathetic." I snorted. "I'm sure he even cried a bit. Said he would try. Said he was sorry."

Marie had the good grace to blush. "Something like that."

"In my experience, Marie, bullies don't change. Sensitivity sessions don't confer empathy upon them. Nothing does. If they haven't learned it by Nigel's age . . ." I shook my head. "Kid bullies just grow up to be adult bullies. Tormenting little kids at school turns into . . . something else."

I had the feeling Nigel's fate was about to be decided here. Did I feel sorry for him? Not a bit. True, we were just kicking the can down the road, but I didn't really give a rip. At least this particular can would be on someone else's road. Who knew? Maybe the parents would get the kid some meaningful therapy. Although I thought age nine was way too late for a turnaround.

"What's Plan B?" I asked.

"Plan B?"

"Yeah. You said he was on probation. What comes after probation?"

She sighed. "Expulsion. He knows that."

I shook my head. "Nah. He doesn't know it. He's counting on the fact that nothing will happen to him. After all, has anything bad ever happened to him? I bet his parents have tacitly enabled his bullying for years — never administered any meaningful punishment. Now he has the bit between his teeth. He likes what he's doing to Dani, Marie. Oh, he could get some therapy, but . . ." I trailed off, not wanting to engage in any more fantasies.

Marie looked miserable. "You may be right. And I'm afraid this is partly my fault."

"Your fault? How?"

"Despite our zero-tolerance policy, I agreed to give him another chance. I bowed to . . . pressure," she said, clearly ashamed.

"Pressure?"

"From his father. I let myself be persuaded. Everyone deserves a second chance, he asserted. Strongly. Part of me wanted to believe that we owe people, especially young people, a chance to change. That no one is irretrievable. That we shouldn't give up on the . . . misguided."

"Sorry if I sound cynical, but I don't believe that," I said. "Oh, I might have, once, but not now. I believe some kids *are* irretrievable." We took each other's measure, her gaze meeting mine.

"What if you're right?" she asked. "In that case, what are we to do with them? The irretrievable children."

I looked over her shoulder out the window where rain now beat down steadily on the school's eponymous oaks. *Sub Quercu Felicitas* proclaimed the school's motto on a sign buffeted by the wind-driven rain. Happiness Under the Oaks. A nice sentiment. Had Nigel found happiness here as he selected his victims and watched them suffer? A sad, sick, and nearly incomprehensible idea: to cause pain to another and take pleasure in it.

And did the grown-up Nigels, emboldened by their success as children, continue to act in similarly horrible ways, sending the horrible errors of childhood, as poet William Stafford said, storming out to play through the broken dike.

Troubling concepts. But I had long ago put my philosophy books away. This was a problem in the here and now, and I found that I didn't give a rat's ass. I was more concerned that Dani and Tris find happiness here. As for Nigel, well, he could take his shtick elsewhere.

"I haven't a clue about the irretrieveables," I told Marie. "But fortunately that's not my business. I'll let the psychologists and social workers and priests sort that out."

Marie nodded, looking sad. "I'll contact Nigel's parents. I don't think this will be an unexpected phone call for them." She walked me to the office door. "I'll write up my report of our meeting. And thank you for bringing this to my attention, Miss Yeats."

I smiled sadly. "Kieran, please. And you're welcome."

❧

My phone rang as I was starting the car, saving me from the guilt I was feeling at being the one who ended Nigel's academic career here at The Oak Grove School. Although really, this was a self-inflicted wound. He'd done it himself. For crap's sake, I told myself, if it wasn't you, Yeats, it would have been someone else. It was just a matter of time. I sighed. If I carried on, I could dredge up half a dozen homilies intended to make myself feel better. So far, though, none of them was working. If I'd done the right thing, why did I feel like a worm? And what would I tell Tris when she came home tomorrow or the next day, bursting with the happy news that Nigel was MIA? If she even shared it with me, that was. After all, it was Jen who had been her confidante, not me.

I saw that my phone call was from Zee, and my stomach clenched a little. Please, no more ugliness right now.

"Yeats," I said, hoping I didn't sound as crabby as I felt.

"Good news," Zee replied, as if anticipating my rotten mood.

"Yeah? Tell me. I crave good news as the desert craves rain."

"Oh-oh," Zee said. "With you, ennui always results in bad similes and metaphors. Must be your ancestry: all those brooding Irish

87

scribblers. Well, my news is a little complicated and quite unexpected. But uplifting. You'll have to see it to believe it. Can you drop by?"

"To be uplifted? Absolutely," I said. "I'm about to founder in a fen of guilt."

"Tsk, another bad metaphor," Zee said. "Tea will help. I'll put the kettle on."

"You might as well be British," I said testily. "Oh, don't mind me. I can be there in a fifteen minutes."

❧

Brandishing a large, black umbrella, Jen was waiting for me in the little covered entryway outside Zee's front door. As I drove up, she hurried to the car to greet me.

"Charlie and I just got in from school," she explained. "We got soaked. So I thought you'd appreciate staying dry."

"You're a thoughtful kid to think of an old lady," I said, joining her under the umbrella as the rain pattered down around us. "I do appreciate it." Then, "Charlie?" I asked.

We hurried to the front door where a girl of about Jen's age waited, a tall girl with a sandy ponytail and an enchanting, gap-toothed smile. "This is Charlie," Jen said. "Well, Charlotte really." She and Jen gave each other goofy smiles and I thought, *oho.*

"Pleased to meet you, Charlie," I said, holding out my hand.

Charlie took it solemnly. "Are you really a private investigator?" she asked. "Jen's been telling me about you."

"Indeed I am," I said. "Do you have something that needs investigating?"

"No," Charlie said, giggling.

"Well, keep me in mind," I told her. "Any friend of Jen's . . ."

"Kieran," Jen said, brown eyes flashing with excitement, "I wanted to talk to you out here. I wanted to be the first to tell you about Jeoffry."

"Jeoffry?"

"The tabby cat. Mom's assistant Ginny named him. Oh, Kieran, you won't believe it! It's a miracle. But you have to pretend that I

88

never spilled the beans. I know Mom wants to be the one to tell you the good news."

"You're making me crazy," I said, laughing. "What beans? And of course I'll be amazed at whatever your mom tells me."

"He can see! The tabby cat can see! Well, a little, anyhow. He won't be blind!"

"You're kidding!" I exclaimed in surprise. "Jen, that's terrific."

Jen opened the front door, shook off the umbrella, and propped it up on the tile floor. Charlie followed Jen inside and I followed them, closing the door behind us.

"And — " Jen started, but broke off abruptly as Zee appeared in the hall leading to the clinic. "Remember," she whispered, "shhh."

"Mum's the word," I whispered back. "No puns intended."

"What deviltry are you three cooking up?" Zee asked.

"No deviltry," I assured her as Jen and Charlie fled laughing, arm in arm, down the hall to her bedroom. "Jen was telling me about, um, a new weather app she's downloaded for her phone."

Zee, who was, along with me, a member of the tech-challenged club, raised an eyebrow. "Oh? You need a weather app to tell you it's raining outside?"

"It's complicated," I said. "But I'm here ready to be uplifted."

"Come on back to the clinic," she said, unable to conceal the satisfaction in her voice. "It's the tabby."

Uh-huh, I thought to myself. Tabby, shmabby. He already has a name. A bad sign. Someone's halfway to pet ownership, I bet.

"Look," she said, opening the exam room door and showing me in.

All thoughts of the cat's name left my mind. Because in one large cage together were Trey and the tabby, arms around each other, heads snuggled in each other's fur. Hearing us come in, Trey raised his head, squinted at me, gave the tabby's head a couple of tender licks, then sighed and put his head down again.

"Yikes," I said. "When are the nuptials? Talk about the loved object! How on earth did this happen?"

"It was Ginny's idea," Zee said. "She was in here cleaning. Trey had persuaded Ginny to let him walk on the counter while she changed his litter. The tabby must have heard him, or seen him, and began to call out. Trey hustled over to his cage and began to groom him through the bars. When the tabby began to purr, Ginny decided to make them roommates."

"Wow. I would never have guessed Trey for a nurturer."

"Sometimes neutered male cats are very sweet," Zee said. "And, here's more good news . . . Jeoffry is not blind, as I feared."

I feigned amazement. "Zee! That's wonderful! How much can he see?"

"I can't be certain," she said. "I'll have a feline ophthalmologist look at him in a few days, but he can definitely perceive objects. He can eat from his food bowl and drink water without bumping anything. So I'm hopeful."

"And his name? Jeoffry?"

"Ginny suggested it," Zee explained. "Apparently it's from an eighteenth- century poem called 'My Cat Jeoffry' written by a madman named Christopher Smart. Ginny studied it in school, she said."

"Yeah, I know it," I said. "It's a great, if under-appreciated poem."

I looked it up online," she admitted. "Smart said his cat was a combination of gravity and waggery. We'll have to see if this Jeoffry comes to emulate his predecessor. You're not the only one with a famous forebear," she told me.

"Indeed not," I said, trying not to smile. "I assume Ginny has dibs on Jeoffry?"

"Heavens, no," Zee said quickly. "She lives in the dorm at U Vic. No pets allowed. No, we'll have to find him an owner when the time comes."

Uh-huh, I told myself.

"And Trey?"

"He's eating normally, using the litterpan, grooming himself, and seems altogether more interested in life."

Oh, brother, I thought. Jeoffry and Trey: a bonded pair. Should I pack Trey's sponge balls and catnip mice? Well, one thing at a time.

"I hear the kettle," Zee said, smiling. "Jen put it on for us. Let's have some tea. It's been a good day."

☙❧

I drove slowly through the puddles in Zee's hazelnut orchard in the watery sunshine of late afternoon. The rain had slackened off, but the remains of the day had turned me maudlin again. The hazelnut leaves lay like heaps of gold coins — pirates' plunder discarded between rows of trees whose wet, dark branches reached entreatingly heavenward. I found this infinitely depressing. Of course next year there would be froths of white blossoms and explosions of pistachio-colored leaves, but at the moment, the barren orchard chilled my soul. Perhaps I had fallen under the spell of another of those maudlin Irish scribblers Zee alluded to, Gerard Manley Hopkins, who, in his downbeat poem "Spring and Fall" asked a child named Margaret if she was grieving over Goldengrove unleaving. Damned straight she was. As was I. At the end of the poem Hopkins rather cruelly pointed out to Margaret that death was *'the blight man was born for,'* and suggested that it might be she herself, Margaret, and not the leaves that she mourned for. Nothing like the dirty rotten truth for a kid, Hopkins, right?

I turned out of Zee's little road back onto the highway. Sometimes I thought my head was stuffed with too much poetry, too many unanswerable philosophical conundrums. And I had those blasted files to look at yet. Well, maybe Aliya had been able to unlock the flash drive. Who knew what delights lay there? Or perhaps Aliya's meatlesss balls would cheer me up. Followed by a discussion of torturing animals in order to make our shampoos safer. It promised to be a fun evening.

But Jeoffry could see. I'd take my miracles, however small, where I found them. I managed a tiny smile as I headed for home.

CHAPTER 14

B ACK AT HOME, the house felt empty, chilly, gloomy. No Trey to hustle to the front door, chirping a greeting, butting my leg with his head; no Tris to call a happy hello from where she worked on homework at the kitchen table. I put the file folders down as I made coffee, then took them into my office once the coffee was finished brewing. Fie on it, anyhow. I'd just have to read Miranda's and Caroline's accounts of animal cruelty. In Miranda's case, the files were from her DNA stash — Do Not Adopt — based on past mistreatment and cruelty to repossessed Sanctuary pets. Caroline's files were somewhat grimmer: accounts of men who had been prosecuted for animal neglect and cruelty. Some of these jerks were incarcerated, some not. I sat down heavily. My goal was to compile a list of likely culprits and call my online investigator. Photos. I needed photos. I wanted to see who these animal torturers were. If I was lucky, one of them would be the bearded man. A long shot, I knew, but still a shot worth taking.

Two cups of coffee and a fair amount of anger and disgust later, I had my list. Nine names. Now I hoped Edgar Poe, my go-to guy for hacking, could help me. To my surprise he answered Poe Enterprises' phone himself. Once a thoroughly disreputable database snoop, Edgar had morphed into a regular nine-to-fiver, cobbling together a band of former hackers like himself. Now they wore white hats and called themselves Poe Enterprises. Now they had a suite of offices overlooking the Inner Harbor, a view of the Parliament Buildings, a ruffled raven perched atop a computer for a logo, and a business motto of "Nevermore." Cute. According to Edgar, they performed cybersecurity for some of Victoria's top tech companies. Quite a metamorphosis. I was touched that Edgar took my phone calls himself. And that he still agreed to hack databases for me. I think he enjoyed the challenge. After all, how exciting can repelling ransomware attacks be?

"I recognized your number, sweetie," he said. "I knew you'd have something to spice up my day. I'm bored to death constructing firewalls and removing malware. Entertain me."

"How well you know me," I bantered back. There was always a fair amount of back and forth BS necessary between Edgar and me before we got to the point: what I wanted and what it would cost me.

"How does burgling the ICBC database sound? Spicy enough for you?" I asked. ICBC was the Insurance Corporation of British Columbia, and in its database, I hoped, my bearded man's driver's license and photo were lurking.

"Ooooo, sweetie, that'll be a tough nut to crack," he demurred.

"Tough, I'm sure, but not impossible for someone of your skills," I said unctuously.

"True," he admitted, "but it will cost you a little more than my usual fee. They've recently beefed up their security. Thanks to us," he added.

Uh-huh, I told myself. "I'm sure you still have my Visa card on file. Just go ahead and charge me. I have a list of nine names and addresses. What I want are drivers' license photos. Can you do that?"

"Can I do that?" he asked indignantly. "Of course I can do that. Photos, you say? Now that's an interesting request. But, as I said — "

"I know, I know," I groused. "It'll cost me a bit more. I'm going to email you the list in a jiffy. When do you think you can send me the photos?"

"Let me consult my schedule," he sighed. "If nothing else pressing intervenes — "

"Like a hospital going dark or Air BC's computers failing?"

"Mock all you like, Kieran, my dear," he said testily, "but we have prevented disasters very like those. Do you know that last year Canadian businesses spent over fourteen billion dollars on cyber-security? One in five companies was hit with cyberattacks. And it wasn't personal information the thieves were after. No. They wanted money. These were ransomware attacks."

"I'm not mocking, Edgar. Really. I'm not. I'm full of admiration for your skills. It's just that —"

"You're under the gun, to coin a phrase," he said. "You always are."

"Yeah," I said. "Something like that. I need those nine photos asap."

"I'll do my best, sweetie," he cooed.

"I'm sending you the list right now," I told him, sending the email while I had him on the phone.

"Got it," he said.

"And you'll get right on it?"

"For you, sweetie, and old time's sake, I will."

"Even if a hospital is about to go dark?"

"Even if," he said.

I ended the call wondering what on earth had happened to Edgar. Was he mellowing? In times past I would have had to engage in at least five additional minutes of blather before we concluded our business. Or maybe Poe Enterprises really was busy. Shaking my head, I put my phone down on the desk. Things were in the hands of the gods, or at least Edgar, now.

I tidied up the file folders and was just locking them away in my bottom desk drawer when my phone rang. Miranda.

"Don't tell me Connie's social media requests have paid off already?" I asked.

"Not quite yet," Miranda said. "But she learned something interesting from one of her animal rights groups. Well, a couple of things."

"Oh?"

"Apparently there's to be a Pub Talk on cosmetics testing on animals tonight at seven at U Vic."

"Yeah, my upstairs tenant, Helen Mikita, is in charge. I saw a flier at the health food store. I don't think you've met Helen. She's a part-time lecturer at U Vic. Her class is presenting the talk."

"Connie showed me the flier," Miranda said. "She's hot to go. You might not know this about my aunt, but in her animal activist past life, she knew Henry Spira. She was a small part of his Revlon campaign."

"Wait!" I was stunned. "What? Henry Spira? The activist? Really? The guy who brought Revlon to its knees?"

"Yup."

"Miranda . . . I'm . . . flabbergasted. How did I not know this about Connie?"

"Oh, she's pretty modest," Miranda said. "Although she's mad as hell that we're still fighting the battle about cosmetics testing all these years later. So she's very interested."

"I can see why," I said.

"I thought I'd go, too," Miranda said. "Do you want to come along?"

"Sure I do. I need to talk to Aliya and have dinner first. Then I'm free."

"Why don't we pick you up about six-thirty?" Miranda asked.

"Sounds good. See you then."

After I ended the call with Miranda I realized I'd forgotten to tell her the good news about the tabby. Not only could he see — well, some — but he had a name. Jeoffry. She'd be pleased. So would Connie. Lord, but it would be wonderful to share good news.

I sat in my office, feet up on my desk, after Miranda's phone call. Things were moving, albeit glacially. Cases were sometimes like this. I regularly despaired, thinking I would never get to the bottom of whatever it was I had been paid to get to the bottom of. Closing my eyes, I thought I might nap for a moment. But I couldn't shut my mind off. Maybe I could just sit here quietly; maybe that would be as good as a nap. Seventeenth-century French mathematician Blaise Pascal said that the sole cause of human unhappiness is our inability to remain quietly at home in our rooms. An odd philosophical observation for a non-humanist. Well, here I was, at home in my room, quiet, but admittedly unhappy. So maybe Pascal was wrong. He may have had a computer language named after him, but how much did he really know about the human heart, anyhow? Hmmf.

I heard Aliya's car pull up in the driveway and the happy sounds of Tris's and Aliya's laughter as they made their way up the front steps and into the house. Time to make some fresh coffee and abandon philosophical musings, I thought. I wondered what Aliya wanted to talk to me about. Well, I was sure I would soon find out.

☙

We left Tris at the kitchen table with oatmeal cookies and milk, working on her report about birds of South America, and took our coffee into the living room. Aliya sat at one end of my comfy old leather sofa. I sat at the other.

"First, the flash drive," Aliya said. "I had some trouble with it. My friend Natalie is helping me out. She should have it unlocked pretty soon. She'll email the files to me."

"Sure," I said. "I appreciate the help."

"What I wanted to talk to you about, well, it's really not such a big deal," she said. "It's just that I've been thinking about it for so long that it's gotten big in my mind."

"You mentioned that you want to cut back your hours at Lawrence's shop," I said, "and you're worried that things will be a little tight financially? Is that right?"

"Yes. No. Oh, Kieran, I feel awful about this. I can work the money out. It won't be regular, but it will be enough. Maybe more than enough. It's leaving Lawrence that I feel bad about."

"Tell me about it."

"Okay. Well, I have another job."

"Ah." I nodded. Somehow I wasn't surprised. Designing T-shirts and note cards for Lawrence's auxilliary business, and writing the photo shop's blog, had gotten to be less than fulfilling, I was willing to bet.

"I feel so guilty. It was designing those T-shirts and note cards that, well, started all this. You see, we — the shop, really — had to buy the Adobe program called InDesign. It makes graphic design so much easier. Then I took a little course on graphics at Camosun and found that there was so much more that could be done with the program. Our assignment was to design a couple of book covers."

"Book covers? Like . . . book covers for authors?"

"Yes," she said. "I discovered that I love it. And I'm good at it. And," she said, shaking her head in evident amazement, "people want to pay me to do it for them!"

"That's great," I said. "But how much? Is there real money in book covers?"

She nodded. "My clients are paying me a couple hundred dollars a cover."

"Wow, Aliya! I imagine that beats your salary at Lawrence's shop."

"It does. And I don't know how to tell him that I want to quit. I have four orders, and I need time to myself to design them."

"Did you get hired by a design company?"

"No," she said. "This is the part where you need to tell me if I'm crazy or not." She took a deep breath. "I'm going to work for myself."

I laughed. "No, you're not crazy. This is pretty exciting. So you'll be working . . ."

"Downstairs. On my laptop first of all. I need a better computer setup — a bigger monitor. For graphics. That can come later. And I need my own version of InDesign. I've been using Camosun's."

"And you've got four orders waiting for your design skills."

I was happy for her. "Wow, Aliya. You're on your way."

She smiled for the first time since we'd started talking. "Did you know that over a million new self-published books were added to Amazon's database last year alone?" she asked excitedly.

"No. And let me guess — every one of them needed a book cover."

"Exactly. So you think this is not too crazy an idea?" she asked, chewing her bottom lip a little.

"Not at all. You seem to have thought this through pretty well. Now all that remains is — "

"To tell Lawrence," she said sadly.

"Aliya, it'll be all right," I told her. "I've known Lawrence for a long time. He'll be happy for you."

"You think?"

"I think."

"I have a possible replacement employee for him," she said in a small voice. "If he doesn't want to advertise my job, that is. She's a classmate. She's good with computers and very reliable. And she'd love to have a part-time job. Should I mention her to him?"

"Sure," I said. "He was thrilled when you and Samir walked in. He told me that putting his HELP WANTED sign in the shop window was all the advertising he wanted to do."

"I can train her on the T-shirt equipment. It's a snap."

"Why don't you talk to him tomorrow?" I suggested. "Then you can get working on those book covers and bill your clients. A very important part of working for yourself . . . billing."

She gave me a dazzling smile. "Thanks, Kieran."

"My pleasure," I said. "And before I forget, I wanted to tell you that I visited the tabby cat at Zee's today."

"Oh, Kieran, how is he?"

"Well, you may not believe this, but he's regained some of his sight."

She teared up. "I'm so happy for him. Those photos — what that guy did to him was awful."

"And he has a name. Zee's assistant named him. Jeoffry. After a cat in an old poem."

Aliya sniffled and blew her nose on a tissue she fished out of the front pocket of her hoodie. "I was thinking," she said. "When my friend Natalie sends me the contents of the flash drive, I could look at it while you're away this evening. I wonder what's on it. Something pretty important, I bet, if Julia tossed it in the dumpster along with the cat and her phone."

"Probably so," I said. "If you can look at it, great. I do need to know what's on it. I guess I'll be back around nine or so. But right now, why don't we get started on those meatless balls? I'm a lousy cook, but a dynamite chopper. Just tell me what to do."

CHAPTER 15

W E WERE LATE — rain and evening traffic held us up — so the Pub Talk had already begun when we walked in. Helen had evidently just finished speaking and I was a little irked — I had wanted to hear what she had to say.

Dark paneling, dim lighting, a long mahogany bar, small tables here and there, a few couches in conversation groupings, the smell of stale beer — the pub seemed like every university watering hole I'd ever been in. I could have been back in the pub at University of Toronto where I did my undergraduate work, or Queen's University where I studied education before I fortunately came to my senses and realized I would make a lousy teacher. The only table left was one in a back corner, but we took it. Wow. Who would've guessed that maybe sixty people wanted to come out on a rainy night mid-week to talk about cosmetics testing on animals? The perennially guttering flames of my faith in humanity burned a little brighter.

My upstairs tenant Helen Mikita had taken a table with two of her students at the front of the pub. A part-time lecturer in the psychology department, Helen's field of inquiry was anthrozoology — the emerging field of animal-human relations. Tall and slender, with curly prematurely silver hair and bright blue eyes, Helen was a hit with her students. Her classes were always over-enrolled: apparently dozens of students wanted to consider why we don't eat kitten casseroles and if mice feel empathy. The department periodically offered her an assistant professorship, but Helen repeatedly turned it down. That seemed a little idiosyncratic to me, but Helen said that although she liked teaching, she liked writing more, and as proof of this, was at work on her fifth book. On one side of her was a young man with sandy brown curls, rimless glasses, and an earnest expression. Swallowing nervously, he introduced himself tentatively as Howard. In contrast to Howard's diffidence, a young woman with straight, shiny brown hair and a lively smile introduced herself forthrightly as Shannon. No nervous swallowing for her. But only two students? Hmm. I guessed they were the spokes-students.

The questions began right away. From a table beside us, a young woman called out, "Really, how can we know that what's in our soap or shampoo or whatever is safe unless we test it? I read somewhere that before nineteen thirty-eight, before the Cosmetics Act was passed in the States, all sorts of horrible stuff was on the market."

A female voice from across the room chimed in. "I looked into this — the cosmetics crap that was for sale back in the thirties. Anyone can find this information using Google. It was like the Wild West back then." Heads turned to look at her, and she continued. "I'm a pharmacy student. This stuff is grotesquely fascinating. There was a face cream that contained mercury and made people's skin turn black and their teeth fall out. And something called Lush Lash that blinded people. And then there was Koremlu, advertised as a permanent hair-removal cream, that poisoned people! Do we want things like those on the market?"

"Stuff like that isn't on the market anymore," a young man scoffed. "Those were the bad old days. Oh, I get it. You say you're a pharmacy student. So of course you'd be on the side of testing this stuff on animals."

"Actually, I'm not," she said. "But even if I were, don't cosmetics manufacturers have a responsibility to keep us safe? We don't need any more Lush Lashes. Looking at the photos of what happened to people who trusted those cosmetics makes you want to throw up."

I looked at Helen, worried that this might devolve into a donneybrook. She saw me looking and winked. Ah. The kids who had just spoken were students taking her class. I got it. Clever. She had probably seeded the audience with students primed to ask difficult questions in case the audience members didn't.

"Keeping us safe is one thing," an older guy in a baseball cap said, "but damn, that was eighty years ago. Haven't we tested enough? Why do we have to keep on doing the same tests? Don't we really know by now what's harmful and what's not?"

"In fact we do," said a man with a bushy brown beard. He stood up, introducing himself. "I'm Jonathan Myers. My wife, Sara, and my daughters and I own Foggy Meadows Soap Company. We sell our soap here and there on the island. On the mainland, too. We've been in business for years. Twenty of them, as a matter of fact." Murmurs of recognition. "Our soap has only eight ingredients. We use substances that were declared safe decades ago: butters, oils, fragrances. Heck, there's a list of over five thousand ingredients that soap makers or personal products manufacturers can choose from. I'm sad that these ingredients were once tested on animals, but if cosmetics makers stuck to the KISS principle —" laughter erupted here, "— no more rabbits would have to be blinded. Of course we're small fries," Johnathan said, "but there's still no reason the big guys can't do what we're doing."

"Some of the big guys do," a voice called. "And they're right here on our doorstep. Island Naturals. They're pretty big. They sell their products here and on the mainland, same as Foggy Meadows. They're even on Amazon. And they've been cruelty-free since they started. They believed in something and stuck to their guns. They've never tested on animals. The whole island's proud of them."

"Let's get back to the big guys," someone said. "Why *do* big companies keep on testing anyhow? Why don't they all go cruelty-free? Like Foggy Meadows and Island Naturals? They figured it out."

Shannon spoke up. "The only circumstances under which testing needs to happen is if, for example, a company wants to produce a new formulation of an old product. Say they wanted to make, oh, mango shampoo, and the ingredients weren't on the list of five thousand."

"Then they'd have to test the ingredients on rabbits, right?" another voice called.

"Absolutely not," Howard said vehemently. "There are plenty of alternatives to animal testing. It's not rocket science. These alternatives, called *in vitro* tests, have been around for decades, and more keep being investigated and refined all the time. You can Google them if you like. There's an institute at the University of Windsor, the Canadian Centre for Alternatives to Animal Methods, that's in the forefront of this movement. They have a website describing affordable, reliable alternatives to animal testing. There's really no excuse for continuing to blind rabbits."

"Yet companies keep doing it, don't they?" someone called out heatedly. "There are way more companies that test on animals than there are cruelty-free companies. Just take a look at the shelves of body wash and shampoo in any store. Only a minority say they're cruelty-free. Why in hell do the others keep on doing it? Don't they realize they have a choice?"

Howard chimed in. "Partly because that's the way things have always been done. If a company thinks it needs that mango shampoo, well, they know they'll get approval for it a lot quicker if they have animal data to show the regulators. Animal tests are familiar, even if they're flawed. And researchers admit they're flawed," he said bitterly. "Animals' eyes are not our eyes, after all. Regulators whose jobs it is to approve new products are very conservative and can delay approving a new product if the manufacturer provides safety data that is unfamiliar to them."

Shannon added, "Also, there's a huge subsidiary industry supported by testing — specialty animal breeding and all the associated costs such as cages, instruments, restraints. There's a lot of money at stake there."

"These alternatives to animal testing," someone asked, "are they more expensive than testing on rabbits? I don't know a thing about this, but maybe cosmetics manufacturers are thinking about their bottom lines?"

"Yeah, what *does* all this testing cost, anyhow?" another person wanted to know.

Shannon said, "In fact it's more expensive to do animal testing than to use any of the alternatives."

"What?"

"Are you sure?" voices from the audience called.

"I'm sure," Shannon told them. "The cost for a traditional Draize test on a rabbit — the so-called gold standard for eye irritation — is eighteen hundred dollars."

"What in hell is a Draize test?" someone asked.

"It's a toxicity test devised in nineteen-forty-four by United States Food and Drug Administration toxicologist John Draize," Shannon explained. "Do any of you recognize the name Henry Spira?"

Silence. Then someone said, "Wasn't he an American animal activist? Didn't he force Revlon to stop testing cosmetics on rabbits? In the eighties?"

"Exactly," Shannon said, referring to notes on the table in front of her. "He described the Draize test like this. These are his exact words:

'You start with six albino rabbits and clip their eyes open, checking that the eyes are in good condition. Then, holding the animal firmly, you pull the lower lid away from one eyeball so that it forms a small cup. Into this cup you drop 100 milligrams of whatever it is you want to test. You hold the rabbit's eyes closed for one second. A day later you come back and see if the lids are swollen, the iris inflamed, the cornea ulcerated, the rabbit blinded in that eye.'

The room was silent.

"They look like this," Shannon said, clicking a remote, which projected a photo on a screen behind her. It was a side view, a close-up shot of an albino rabbit held in a restraint on a lab bench. The eye we could see was blood red, the eyelids swollen. On the fur around its eye was the residue of some yellow substance. Its sides had been shaved in a pattern and the bald patches blossomed crimson, goopy yellow gunk around the red sores.

Several members of the audience gasped.

Suddenly, realization hit me with the force of a blow. "Jeoffry," I whispered to Miranda and Connie, dipping my head so only they would hear me curse. "For God's sake, it's Jeoffry! What was done to that rabbit . . . that's what was done to Jeoffry!"

"Oh, my God," Connie exclaimed. "You're right, of course. Why in hell didn't I see this when I was looking at the video?"

Thoughts tumbled through my mind, but I found I couldn't concentrate. For one thing, the audience had erupted in shouting.

"Turn that thing off!" a voice called. Others agreed.

"It's obscene."

"It's awful!"

"Get that picture off the screen!"

"Omigod, we get it!"

"Sorry," Shannon said, clicking the photo off. "Sometime a picture speaks more eloquently than even Henry Spira's words."

There was silence for a bit in the pub as if the audience paused in a moment of respectful mourning for the rabbit in the photo, who had, in all likelihood, died for someone's next date.

My thoughts circled back to Jeoffry. What the hell? Had someone used him in a Draize test? But why? Everyone knew about rabbits being used in cosmetics testing, but cats? They would have been impossible subjects: they bit, they scratched, they screamed. Just as Jeoffry had done in the video. No way was the Draize test that been performed on Jeoffry anything legitimate. So . . .? So had it been torture, masquerading as research? Or just plain torture? Jesus. And where the hell had it been done? Maybe I should go home, I thought, and lock myself in my office in the dark with my bottle of Method and Madness and think. Or drink.

"The Draize test . . . labs . . . I just had an idea," Connie whispered to Miranda and me. "Let's listen to a bit more of this then go."

Abruptly, at the table immediately in front of us, a middle-aged woman expensively dressed in a black turtleneck and dark pants, blond hair drawn back in a fashionable knot behind her head, rose quickly to her feet, jostling the little table, spilling her coffee. She looked a lot like the actress Catherine Deneuve in her younger days. She made a grab for her purse and a black coat, then, weaving between tables, fled. As she passed our table, the coat slipped out of her hands. I picked it up off the floor, intending to call to her, but she was already gone. What the hell? I folded the coat carefully and placed it on my lap, intending to give it to the bartender after the talk was over.

"I want to get back to animal testing," someone said. "Eighteen hundred dollars? Per rabbit? For God's sake!"

"Yeah," another voice added. "How many rabbits are, well . . ."

"Sacrificed?" Shannon asked. "They call it sacrificed. At the end of the test the rabbits are, of course, killed. But researchers call it sacrificing the animals."

Exclamations of disgust bubbled around us.

"They seem to have trouble using the word 'kill,'" she said. "So they've appropriated 'sacrifice' from religion. Like they're offering this animal to God, sanctifying its suffering when what they're really doing is killing it. After a predetermined number of days of unspeakable suffering, of course. I'm sure God is beaming down favorably on this practice. It's doubly disgusting that they further distance themselves from the word kill by shortening sacrificed to sac'd. As in 'I sac'd two dozen mice this afternoon.' Or worse yet, in a paper I read about testing, the researcher said he said he 'sac'd the heterozygotes.'"

"What the hell does that mean?" a young woman asked.

"It means he killed the mice," Shannon said.

"For God's sake, he should be ashamed of himself," the young woman continued heatedly. "Okay, they may be just mice, but they deserve to be thought of as more than hetero . . . whatever you said. I mean, they're *alive*. They're not *things*."

Murmurs of agreement arose.

After a moment, Howard adjusted his glasses and cleared his throat.

"To answer someone's earlier question," he said, "it's six. Six rabbits for the Draize test. And the really economically stupid part of this is that the alternative test would cost considerably less than eighteen hundred dollars."

"And no rabbits would have to be sacrificed," someone said. "Or sac'd, if you're a moral wuss and can't cope with the guilt of calling a spade a spade."

"Right," Howard said. "And no rabbits would have to be sacrificed."

"What's the number . . ." someone began.

"What's the number of rabbits sacrificed every year so cosmetics companies can have the equivalent of a mango shampoo? Or a household products company can market a new lemon-scented oven cleaner?" Howard asked.

"Yeah. How many?"

"Last year, maybe one hundred and fifty thousand," he said. "But here's another way of thinking about it. For each new ingredient being tested — for that mango shampoo — at least fourteen hundred animals will die. It's not just the Draize eye test. It's the skin corrosion test, the phototoxicity test, the embryotoxicity test . . . shall I go on?"

"No," voices called. "No, don't."

"This is a dirty rotten business," someone called out. "It needs to be opposed. Thank God we have a bill in Parliament that might put an end to this."

Silence fell in the pub. For the time being, it seemed, there were no more questions.

Miranda reached across the table and touched my hand. Bending toward me, she whispered, "The woman who ran out a minute ago . . . she's Portia Curran. She and her brother Philip own Island Naturals. She's one of The Sanctuary's big donors. I had lunch with her not so long ago at the Empress. Island Naturals really came through for us when we needed to fund a vetting room for new arrivals."

I raised my eyebrows. What in hell was Portia Curran doing here at U Vic at a talk about animal testing? Island Naturals was one of the good guys. Had she intended to speak up as Jonathan Myers had? To lend her voice to the arguments against testing? If so, why hadn't she?

And what had upset her? I realized that I'd missed some discussion, so I tuned in again.

" . . . a philosophy student," a young dark-haired woman was saying. "I'm writing a paper on ethics — that's why I came. I just wondered, no one here has brought up the issue that what's being done to rabbits, blinding them for the sake of mango shampoo or whatever, is just plain wrong."

Heads turned to look at her.

She cleared her throat and continued.

"I mean, it's not as though philosophers haven't been debating for ages how to think about animals. They have. I don't want to bore people, just leave them with one thought. An eighteenth-century philosopher named Jeremy Bentham believed that actions are right if they increase the happiness, pleasure, and good of the greatest number of people. He called this utilitarianism. But he's remembered in animal rights and animal welfare circles for stating this about animals: 'The question is not can they reason? Nor, can they talk? But can they suffer?' The issue is really pretty simple, I think. It's morally indefensible to cause another being's suffering. Bentham had a great influence on Peter Singer, the famous philosopher who wrote "Animal Liberation." And Singer had an influence on Henry Spira. All three of them would agree that this all boils down to right and wrong. And suffering is the litmus test, so to speak."

There was silence again in the pub. Then someone said, "I agree. You just have to look at those awful photos of rabbits in labs to see that they're suffering. And I don't see how any of the researchers involved in making mango shampoo, or whatever they think needs to be tested on rabbits, can get up in the morning and look at themselves in the mirror. This is just plain . . . evil."

"Let's all hope the cosmetics bill passes," someone else said. "I read a story last summer in the newspaper about the bill. It's not perfect, but it's something. If it passes, then Canada can hold its head up. We can join the EU and the thirty-seven other countries that have banned animal testing. What's the bill's status? Anyone know? Is there anything we can do to help the bill along?"

"Yeah, and what's the situation in the States? I heard they have a bill that was dropped in twenty-fourteen because no one wanted to sponsor it," someone commented, and the discussion began to veer away into what could be done in this country to help the bill's passage, and what the situation south of the border was.

Connie leaned over the table again. "Miranda, Kieran, let's go have coffee and talk about Jeoffry and the man who tortured him. We might not know who the guy is but we might be able to find out where he is. And that should lead us to who he is. C'mon. These people will probably debate this bill and its chances for passing until the cows come home."

"Sure. Let's go to my place," I said. "There's plenty of free coffee there. Probably some banana bread, if I remember correctly. Aliya's a great baker. And I can make a fire."

As we passed the bar, I paused, intending to give Portia Curran's coat to the bartender, but he was away somewhere, washing glassware or unloading beer kegs or whatever bartenders did when they weren't tending bar. Fooey. Now I'd have to hang onto it. And then what? Ship it off to Island Naturals, I guessed. With more than a little annoyance, I tucked the coat under my arm and hurried to join Miranda and Connie.

∽

Aliya was in the living room looking at her iPad when the three of us got back to my house. As if she had intuited my plans for a fire, one crackled in the hearth. It was undeniably cheery on a miserable night like tonight, but I had already decided that this was the last year for fires. In an effort to do my bit for the planet, I had my eye on the Pleasant Hearth Twenty-Inch Electric Fireplace Plus Grate for ninety-nine dollars at Amazon. Faux fire. No more guilt about burning wood. Apparently the electric fireplace put out ersatz firelight as well as real heat, which was good. Necessary even. My forbears and I — poets, soothsayers, bards — we know all about the darkling wood, the bleak midwinter, the frosty winds moaning, the dying of the light. Pale, delicate things that we are, in eons past we huddled around our guttering fires, chanting, praying for the return of the sun. Longing for a fire in wintertime was in my genes. But this winter . . . well, it would be my woodpile's swan song. Next winter, it was the Pleasant Hearth for me.

"What's up?" I asked Aliya, hanging up Connie's and Miranda's jackets, then depositing Portia Curran's black wool coat on the dining room table. I'd deal with that later. "I thought you'd be downstairs lost in the world of book covers." A troubling thought crossed my mind. "Everything okay with Tris?"

"Sure," she said, but her brows were drawn together in a frown. Hmm.

Miranda glanced at Aliya and, picking up on her disquiet, said, "C'mon, Connie. Let's go into the kitchen and make coffee. Okay, Kieran?"

"Thanks, yeah," I said. "You know your way around."

Aliya looked at me.

"What is it?" I asked her, standing with my back to the fire, warming my hindquarters.

"Well, I checked out the contents of the flash drive," she said. "Natalie emailed the files to me."

"And?"

"There's lots on it," she said. "Lots and lots. I just took a stab at what I thought might be most important. There's one folder that stands out because it's so big. It's board meeting minutes. Anyhow, I printed the whole thing."

"Okay."

"It's there." She gestured to a stack of paper about three inches thick on the coffee table.

"Wow, okay," I repeated.

"Kieran, the place where Julia downloaded this stuff onto the flash drive — I guess she worked there — well, was that the same place where Jeoffry was tortured?"

"Yeah, I guess so," I said.

She shook her head. "Then I don't get it," she said. "Because the folder of board meeting minutes and some of the other files — email, shipping and receiving, personnel — they belong to a local business. A cosmetics company."

"A cosmetics company," I said, comprehension dawning. "Someplace where they'd have the facilities to do the Draize test."

"The what?" Aliya asked.

"Nothing," I said. "Go on. Did you find out the name of the company?"

"Yeah, I did," she said. "It's Island Naturals."

"What?"

"Island Naturals."

I sat down on the couch in disbelief. "Island Naturals? But they don't do that damned test — they're cruelty-free. God, we just heard a roomful of people singing their praises. Are you sure?"

"Yeah, I'm sure." She gestured to the heap of documents. "It's all here."

Connie had come into the room beside me. "Well, crap," she said. "So much for my idea. I thought we could send email to the local cosmetics companies. Ask them who's doing the Draize test. Tell them some fairy tale and send them the bearded man's photo. But now we won't have to."

"Because?" I asked, my brain short-circuited by too much information all at once.

"Because I bet I know where he works."

"You do?" I asked.

"I do," Connie said. "It's not a big leap of logic. Island Naturals."

"Jeoffry's torturer works at Island Naturals?" I said in disbelief. "But the Draize test . . ." I sputtered. "No one there does that."

Connie raised an eyebrow and inclined her head to the printout on the coffee table.

"Don't they? Let's find out."

CHAPTER 16

"**I**S THIS a party?" a sleepy voice called from the living room doorway.

Oh, crap. It was Tris, standing there in her giraffe print pyjamas, knuckling sleep out of her eyes. Maybe she'd been awakened by the doorbell announcing the arrival of pizza. The three of us, and Aliya until she'd gotten too tired, had been reading for five hours. It was now after one. We were bleary, weary, and starving.

"No, Sprout," I told her. "It's work. Connie and Miranda are helping me. We have a bunch of stuff to read. Aliya went to bed."

"Okay," Tris said, eyeing the pizza hopefully. "That looks good."

I was tempted to let her have a piece, but good sense took over. "I don't think you should have any, Sprout. It would just sit in your stomach like a lump of lead and stop you from getting back to sleep. We'll save you some for tomorrow, though. Are you hungry?"

"Not really," she said in a small voice.

Uh-oh. Something was wrong. "Let's go into the kitchen," I said. "We'll make cocoa."

"Okay," Tris said.

"I'm going to return that call from the shelter I got a while ago," Miranda said, stretching. "Sheryl said she'd be there all night. I expect it's about Beatrice."

Connie nodded. "Probably so. I can return it if you want to keep on reading."

"Hmm, okay," Miranda said. "If you don't mind. Will you tell Sheryl that if she thinks she needs to call the vet, she can? Or you can do it. Twelve puppies won't be fun to deliver. Poor Beatrice. I'll keep on here. We still have a fat stack of board meeting minutes to read."

"Connie, you can go on into my office to make the call if you like," I offered. "It's around the corner by the kitchen. The light's just inside the doorway on the left."

"Thanks," she said, pulling out her phone. "I'm not sure how long I'll be. I'll try to keep it short, although I might have to talk to the vet too. I probably should."

"What's up?" I asked Tris as water heated in the microwave for cocoa. We sat across from each other at the kitchen table, and I remembered how I had sat here in this very spot last year with another troubled kid. Jen. And how Trey had hopped up on the table to comfort her. I wished he were here for Tris now.

I put her mug of cocoa in front of her and she took a sip. In a few moments she came to what was bothering her.

"Kieran, um . . . well, I had a bad dream."

"Oh, I'm sorry, sweetie. Was it the ooms?"

The ooms were our catch-all code for things that bothered her enough to wake her up. I, too, had suffered from bad dreams when I was a kid, and I called the huge, dark, shapeless, terrifying blobs that haunted my dreams ooms. I wasn't sure if these were the same entities that visited Tris nocturnally, but when I told her about my ooms, she adopted the term. Sometimes I felt as though I was letting her down — not inquiring more deeply into the substance of her bad dreams. But I trusted that she would let me know if she was plagued by more than ooms. On the other hand, that was probably a lot to expect from a kid.

"Yeah," she said. "When I have a bad dream I hug Trey. He keeps the ooms away."

Oh. Trey. Was that what this was about?

"Trey will be coming back pretty soon." I told her. "Zee thinks he's okay . . . not sick or anything."

"But he was really sad, wasn't he? Did Zee fix him?"

I thought about Trey and Jeoffry. "You know what Zee found out? She found out that Trey needs someone to hug."

Tris looked at me in concern. "He does?"

"Yeah. Apparently he missed Vlad a lot, although they never hugged. But he's found a buddy at Zee's clinic. Why, they're probably hugging right now."

"Can he come to our place? Trey's new buddy?" Tris wanted to know.

I thought about Jeoffry and the rehabilitation he would undoubtedly need. Zee wasn't sure how much the cat would ever see. He'd need a special kind of family when he was ready to be adopted. "Probably not," I said. "But we could still get Trey a buddy. Miranda's shelter is probably full of potential buddies. Let's talk to her about that. We could go up there tomorrow."

"Okay," Tris said, sounding a little more hopeful.

"So that's settled then." I reached over and tugged one of her curls. "While we're up there we could drop in and see Tiffany for a haircut. My mane could use some trimming, too. How about it? I could pick you up after school."

Tris nodded, yawning.

"Okay, then. It's a date," I said. "C'mon. Let's go back to bed."

I tucked her in, made sure her lava lamp was turned on, and sat on the bed beside her. "Want to hear some sleep music?" I asked her. I'd made her a playlist of soothing songs to promote sleep — at least I hoped they were soothing. They certainly promoted sleep for me when I was having a bad night. Tris seemed to like them.

"Uh-huh. Play the one about the moon keeping watch?"

I thought for a moment. Oh yeah. *"All Through The Night,"* a traditional old Welsh lullaby, translated into English in the nineteenth century by a Brit named Harold Boulton. I found the song on the CD I'd made for Tris, and started it playing, listening with her, waiting for the part Tris liked:

"While the moon her watch is keeping
All through the night.
While the weary world is sleeping
All through the night.
O'er thy spirit gently stealing
Visions of delight revealing
Comes a pure and holy feeling
All through the night."

I looked down at Tris. Just the top of her curly blond head was visible on her pillow, face turned away. She might have been asleep, feeling safe with the moon keeping watch. I hoped so.

I pulled her door partly closed and left her to her music and, I hoped, sleep. Poor kid. She probably did miss Trey a lot. Well, maybe he could come home tomorrow. But what about his beloved, Jeoffry? Hell.

Miranda was busy in the kitchen, making more coffee.

"Good idea," I commented brightly. "This is like my study group in law school. We consumed vats of coffee. I'd kind of forgotten what that was like."

"You won't believe what we found in the board minutes," Miranda said, flipping the switch on the coffeemaker.

A pleasant burbling sound ensued, followed by the smell of coffee brewing — one of life's great olfactory pleasures. Orange blossoms, freshly-sanded cedarwood, the smell of baking bread: all great, but distant seconds and thirds to coffee.

I sniffled a little, and she looked at me in concern.

"Everything okay? How's Tris?"

"She's all right. Just a little upset that Trey's not here."

"Hmm," she said shrewdly. "How about you?"

"I'll be okay." I laughed a little. "I think I'm pulling Fs in the mother department. But tell me what you found."

"The minutes I'm reading now are several months old, but at that meeting the board, well, voted Portia off."

"Voted Portia . . . what? Why? Wasn't she one of the founder's children? I thought she and her brother were running the place."

"Yes and yes," Miranda said. "But for several months the board had been debating a motion introduced by Philip and adamantly opposed by Portia."

"Oh yeah? What sort of motion?"

"You won't believe this," she said. "I didn't believe it. But it's true."

"You're making me crazy. What?"

She shook her head. "Island Naturals is going to start testing on animals."

"On . . . "

"On animals, Kieran. Rabbits. The Draize test."

I sat down heavily at the kitchen table. "Screw the coffee," I said. "I need a drink."

CHAPTER 17

I BROUGHT THE bottle of Method and Madness and three glasses into the living room, pouring two fingers of amber whiskey into each glass. Connie had rejoined us, taking a seat in an armchair by the fire. Miranda and I sat at either end of the sofa, and we all sipped whiskey in silence. With only one lamp lit, and the fire giving off a subdued orange glow, the room seemed cavernous, unfamiliar, mysterious.

"How did this happen?" I asked. "A company that built its reputation on being cruelty-free, a company that's an institution on the island, that produced *television commercials* touting its ethical purity, for cripe's sake, is now going to test future products on *animals*? I'm beyond disgust."

Miranda tossed the last batch of board meeting minutes she had been reading onto the coffee table. "So am I. And hundreds and hundreds of island purchasers of their shampoo and soap and body wash will be also. The company will lose its Leaping Bunny certification. And thousands of customers. Portia was so proud of it. It will be a PR nightmare."

"But a financial success," Connie said quietly, in counterpoint to Miranda's outrage.

"How do you figure that?" Miranda asked.

"Philip Curran will have finally prevailed," Connie said. "I know a little bit about the company and its inner workings. I have a friend on the board. When Curran senior, Porter Curran, died two years ago and the company came to Philip and Portia, Philip started lobbying like hell to take the company down a different path. To make it more profitable. It just wasn't making enough money, he felt. And that different path led, he believed, away from being cruelty-free."

I asked, "So how did he get the board on board - no pun intended - with his plan? Presumably the board once believed in Island Natural's original way of doing business. In Porter Curran's ethos. They wouldn't have been serving on the board unless they believed. So what siren song did Philip sing to them? How did this happen?"

"More easily than you'd think," Connie said. "Island Naturals is not a publicy held company. There are no shareholders to be concerned with. Philip sweet-talked the board into his point of view — well, a majority of them, anyhow. There were a few who disagreed. And at that meeting, Portia was voted out. I guess he lobbied like hell and finally staged the coup he had been planning for two years. It's all here in the minutes. Island Naturals abandoned the company's original mission for, well, the lure of dollars. It's all about money. Sadly, most things are."

"But public sentiment is with Portia," I said in exasperation. "Most people are opposed to cosmetics testing on animals. There was a big story about this last summer in *The Globe and Mail*. Bill S-214. Our local television station even ran a segment on it. Interviewed Victorians on the street. Something like seventy-nine percent of the people they talked to think animal testing is cruel and unnecessary. You heard the people at the Pub Talk."

"Yeah, if the bill passes," Connie said. "It's not a done deal. And what about the companies that are already testing? They'll probably be grandfathered in."

"This is beyond depressing," I said. "So I guess Island Naturals really isn't too worried about the bill's passing."

Connie nodded. "I'd say they're not. After all, there are more companies that do test on animals than don't. Just look at the bottles on drugstore shelves." She shrugged. "They'll just join the majority. And they'll survive the PR nightmare."

"Wow," I said. "The payoff is that big?"

"The payoff is huge," Connie replied.

"How huge?" Miranda asked. "Even with its exports, Island Naturals is a tiny fish in a big pond. So they, what, maybe double their business. Or will they? Will the customer base they lose be made up for by the base they gain? There'll be a scandal, sales will fall off, then they'll have to grow their other market — people who don't care about killing rabbits. They'll lose Europe because the EU doesn't test on animals. So I guess they'll cater to the U.S. market? Different TV commercials. Different print ads. It'll take time."

"Forget the U.S. They have another market in mind, all right," Connie said.

"What do you mean?" I asked. "What other market?"

Connie finished her whiskey and put her glass on the coffee table. "A market of over one billion potential customers. It's been there for some time. And all Island Naturals has to do to reach it is abandon its ethical roots."

"C'mon, what market is that big?" Miranda scoffed.

"China," Connie said. "China. Where the government is very friendly to imports from foreign personal products companies, but those companies have to agree to one thing."

"Oh, my God. They have to agree to test their products on animals," Miranda whispered.

"Bingo," Connie said. "Maybe someday China will see the light and test *in vitro* instead of *in vivo*, but they've not seen it yet. One day they're convinced that animal testing is the way to go, and the next day they're investigating alternatives. Add to that the fact that the whole process of securing a contract with China is rife with bribery and, well . . ."

"Well, shit," Miranda commented. "What a mess."

"So Philip and his followers on the board hardly care about what happens in this country," I said. "I get it. If they have to agree to testing on animals in China, they'll lose their Leaping Bunny certification here, but what's that to them? They're rubbing their hands together, counting all that *yuan* they'll make for the company. So they might as well go all in. Go backward. Go cruelty, as opposed to cruelty-free. Abandon ethics. They'll win here and they'll win in China." I looked at Miranda. "No wonder your friend Portia ran out of the Pub Talk. She must be so damned ashamed."

"Actually, I wonder why she was there at all," Miranda said. "Maybe she was going to confess. Give people a heads-up." She shrugged. "Not likely. But still . . ."

A thought crossed my mind. "Do we have the latest board meeting minutes? Has anyone read them?"

"I read them," Connie said.

"When is this . . . transformation going to take place? You can't just start testing without a lab, personnel, equipment."

"And animals," Miranda added.

"They've been working toward those things for about six months," Connie said. "They've retrofitted an old storage facility at the back of Island Naturals' main building. Built offices, storage space, a testing lab. Equipment has been ordered. Ditto animals. Lab personnel have been hired. They're ready to go. Backward."

"And Julia got the goods on them." Then, after a minute, after I thought a bit, I said, "But so what?"

"What do you mean?" Miranda asked.

"If Julia planned on letting the cat out of the bag, let's say to a newspaper or TV reporter, *before* Island Naturals was ready to announce its change in business model, well, so what? It would be a juicy story for, what, a week? The story the board meeting minutes tells - 'Island Company Sells Its Soul To China' — that would be a juicy, nasty, embarrassing PR debacle, but it would die down. Then

Island Naturals would put its recovery plan into effect, as Connie said. It would recover. Life would just . . . go on."

"Yeah, probably," Miranda said. "So what's your point?"

"My point is, why kill Julia for a premature release — by her or by someone she would hand the flash drive off to — of information Island Naturals would release anyhow? It doesn't make sense."

"Yeah, I see," Miranda said. "Okay, here's something else. How did the guy in the white SUV know Julia had the flash drive? With all that juicy information on it?"

"Huh," I said. "Good question. I don't see how he could have known."

"Okay, assuming he didn't know," Connie said, "he still chased her for something, right? What does that leave?"

"Jeoffry," I said. "And her phone. He knew she had the cat, and he must have caught her recording what he was doing."

We were all quiet for a couple of minutes, then Miranda ran her hands through her hair. "This is making me crazy. So he wanted Jeoffry. And Julia's phone. But *why?*"

"The Draize test?" I suggested.

"Oh, crap," she said. "Not that it wasn't awful, I'm not saying that. It was rotten and horrifying, but even if the asshole was charged with felony animal abuse, well, what are the chances he'd do jail time? Kieran? What do you think?"

"It's a weak case," I said. "I wouldn't like to argue it. It was done in the lab at Island Naturals, so he could always say he was pioneering a new eye irritancy test or some such BS. Fall back on his professional credentials."

"So why chase Julia then?" Connie asked. "Like you said, Kieran, it would be a hard case to argue. It's hardly worth running someone off the road and killing them just to avoid an iffy prosecution."

"So where are we?" Miranda asked.

"Stranded up that creek where no one wants to be," I said. "I'm stumped."

I drank a little more whiskey. Who knew, maybe it would lubricate the rusty cogs of my brain.

"Here's another way of thinking about this," Connie said. "Maybe Julia was working with or for someone else and he found out about it. Someone who made him desperate. Desperate enough to kill."

"Who or what could have unhinged him that badly?" I said.

"Maybe an animal rights group," Connie suggested. "No one wants to run afoul of one of the big alphabet groups. Maybe Julia was going to hand the information or the cat, or both, over to them and let them take it from there. They might be able to administer a PR tar-and-feathering that Island Naturals could never recover from. Something that would devastate future business as well as their image."

"Yeah, maybe," I said doubtfully. "But it's not Ninth Life." They were the biggest group on the island, as I knew, but they were in Ottawa, lobbying for Bill S-214.

"Connie?" I asked. "Do you have any ideas? You know the local groups."

"Most of them are pretty responsible," she said. "What you mean is do I know a group of nutcakes that would do something like put Julia undercover to get the dirt at Island Naturals, and plan something off-the-wall? Well, there are the Sisters of Outrage," she said, tightening her lips in disapproval.

"Connie!" Miranda scolded. "She means CLAW," Miranda said to me. "They think the way to win hearts and minds is to demonstrate. Horrify people."

"That approach worked in the last century," Connie said. "But people are tired of being horrified. We have outrage exhaustion. CLAW doesn't realize that, though. They're young, they're mad as hell at society's mistreatment of animals, but they have no sense of history."

"Aren't they the group that threw red paint on the fur coats at The Bay a few years ago?" I asked. "It was supposed to simulate blood, as I recall."

"Yup," Connie said.

"Hmm, you know, I had my own run-in with them yesterday," I continued. "Well, with one of them, anyhow." I recounted my meeting with one of the CLAWs at the health food store, described the flier she ripped off the bulletin board, and ruefully included the fact that she sucker-punched me with her backpack.

"You mean she *knows* you?" Miranda said.

"Well, my name anyhow. For the life of me, I can't think how. I've never met anyone from CLAW."

"You say they're meeting tomorrow night?" Miranda asked with interest.

"Uh-huh. Some church downtown."

"I think we should go," Connie said. "Somehow this is all tied together — Julia, Island Naturals, the bearded man, the cat, maybe CLAW. How can it not be?"

"I can send you the meeting details," I said. "From looking at their flier, I can tell you that they're incensed about cosmetics testing on animals. I'm kind of surprised that they didn't show up at the Pub Talk. Disrupt things."

"That would have been too tame for them," she said. "They're probably planning something showy. What about it? Want to go? Miranda?"

"Why not?" Miranda said. "In for a penny and all that. Cosmetics Testing two-point-oh. Tomorrow night. And gee, I was going to wash my hair." She grinned at me and I grinned back. For Miranda, I guessed outraged animal activists were a distraction from ringworm and the other vicissitudes of running an animal shelter. The fate of all those rescued animals in your hands — I knew I couldn't do it.

We sat in silence for a few minutes, then Miranda yawned hugely.

"I confess I have a whopper of a headache," she said. "Hard liquor and disillusionment always do that to me. Maybe we should drink the coffee that's been cooking in the kitchen and call it a night."

"Better make it coffee to go," Connie said. "It's pretty late. We should get on the road. Who knows what's happening with Beatrice."

"Thanks a lot, you two," I said. "I almost fainted when I saw the stack of paper Aliya had put on the coffee table for me. I'd still be reading next week if you hadn't pitched in."

"Our pleasure," Connie said. "Text us the details of the CLAW meeting?"

"Will do."

I ushered Miranda and Connie out the front door, locked it, turned off the outside light, and was thinking fondly of my bed, when my phone buzzed. What? At two-fifteen in the morning? I almost let it go to voicemail, but a peek at the screen showed me it was Edgar. Ah. The photos, I hoped.

"Miz Yeats," he said, clearly surprised. "I thought I'd have to leave a message."

"I'm just about to pass out from fatigue," I told him, "so we'll have to make this short, Edgar. Although I do appreciate your thinking of me so late, or early, in the day."

In fact, I wondered why he was still up. Hadn't he become respectable? In earlier years, when Edgar was a devil-may-care hacker, it seemed I always spoke to him in the wee hours. Fancifully, I imagined him a species of bat, flitting into his closet at the first blush of dawn, hanging there by his toenails until the sun extinguished itself somewhere below the horizon, then emerging in the gloaming to haunt the information highway. But now that he had become a nine-to-fiver, I wasn't sure. After all, I *had* spoken to him on the phone in the daylight.

"Check your email, sweetie," he said. "I sent you a large file. Mug shots. Faces to go with those names you provided. Although, I must say, a less attractive bunch of faces I've seldom seen."

"Thanks, Edgar," I said. "I'll look at them tomorrow. Right now, I'm fried. I have to go to bed."

I ended the call, torn between checking my email, staggering off to my bedroom, and having yet another glass of Method and Madness. I'd already had two, so this would make three. But was three really too many to have at the end of a difficult day? After all, it wasn't as if I planned to sit in front of the dying fire polishing off the bottle as I had after my abrupt departure from the Crown Counsel's office years ago, brooding, listening to minor-key music.

Quiet, I told my inner nag. Quiet. I was over that. But . . . surely it wouldn't hurt to have just one more. I sighed. Yes, it would. Had I forgotten the headaches the size of Newfoundland? Or the unpleasant fuzz I discovered on my teeth in the mornings? Sighing, I picked up the bottle of whiskey, put it in the kitchen cupboard, and deposited the three used glasses in the dishwasher.

One cup of coffee the hue of molasses remained in my Krups, and instead of pouring it down the sink, I poured it into a mug and took it back into the living room with me. To hell with tired. Did I really think I could go to bed without looking at my email?

∽

Nine photos. Nine animal abusers who'd shot, fractured, burned, microwaved, starved, dismembered, frozen, abandoned, hanged, drowned, or otherwise tortured their pets. And, along the way had molested children, abused wives, parents, and girlfriends, and beaten kids. Jesus. The seldom-appreciated link between domestic violence and animal abuse. I was truly glad I had left it all behind me at the Crown Counsel's office. Finally, I shut off my phone and lay back on the couch, despairing. Because he wasn't there. The bearded man, the saturnine face, the dark hair, the sharp profile . . . he wasn't there. The fire's dying embers seemed demons' eyes taunting me.

Wasn't it Sting, that sly poet of rock, who neatly nailed evil in his song "Wrapped Around Your Finger"?

> Mephistopheles is not your name,
> But I know what you're up to just the same.

∽

I may not know who you are or why you did what you did, I said to my mental image of the bearded man, but I do know *what* you are, and dammit, now I know where you are. Island Naturals. Sighing, I made my way to my bedroom, flipping off the kitchen light as I went. I kicked off my sneakers, shed a few clothes, and slid under my comforter, intending to wrap myself up like a burrito.

But I must have dozed off and wandered into a dream, because when I opened my eyes, I was no longer in my bedroom, and the eyes I looked out of were not my own. I had awakened in a large, dimly lit room, and the colors my human eyes should have seen were shades of gray. I knew, without knowing how I knew, that it was dark outside. I looked around, puzzled. I was in a steel box with a barred front, my feet scrabbling on a smooth, cold metal floor. Something panicked me and I opened my nostrils to the smell of those trapped here with me — smells of urine and feces, sweat and vomit, and an acrid smell that I could not identify. Smells of terror and despair. A few of us moaned in uneasy sleep, but I could sense that most were awake. Awake and terrified of something in the room with us. The thing we feared most, more than we feared the man who hurt us. I squealed, as did several of the others — a feeble show of defiance — as in the shadows, I saw the monster begin to grow. I heard its voice, smelled its hot breath, felt —

I awakened abruptly, feverish and panicked. Too much comforter, I thought groggily, kicking it aside and wondering whose mind I had inhabited for those few dream moments. And the hot, huge presence in the room where I had been imprisoned — what the hell had that been? My last thoughts were, strangely, not of Julia, or Jeoffry, or the bearded man, but of the others, whoever and wherever they were, and the days trickling steadily away to Saturday. But then my consciousness winked out like a snuffed candle and everything mercifully stopped.

THURSDAY

CHAPTER 18

D EAD TO THE world, I slept through my alarm, missing Buzz and
Mandy's patter, an hour of the oldies program (although I
remembered something about a bustle in my hedgerow), and breakfast
with Tris and Aliya. I rejoined the land of the living around nine, a
hungry, testy, decaffeinated zombie. Yawning, I opened my bedroom
door to find two notes affixed to it: one from Aliya telling me that
there was fresh coffee in the Krups and a fried egg sandwich in the
microwave, and one from Tris telling me that she'd see me after school
for our haircut and kitten-shopping. Oops. I'd forgotten about the
ringworm at Miranda's sanctuary, so kitten-shopping would have to
wait for another day. I hoped Tris would understand.

The sky outside the kitchen window looked gray and fretful. I
sympathized with it — I didn't feel too sparkly myself. Oh well, it was
late October on the island. The best days of the year were behind us.

What did we have to look forward to anyhow but a miserable time change and a swift descent into Stygian gloom.

As I ate the sandwich Aliya had left for me and drank coffee, I sat at the kitchen table thinking about the discussion Miranda, Connie, and I had had last night. Overnight, I had changed my opinion a bit. I just didn't believe that a mystery alphabet animal rights group had anything to do with Julia's death. We were probably wasting our time going to the CLAW meeting, although I'd go along for the sake of being agreeable. And who knew, I might be wrong.

In my mind, we were looking down the wrong rabbit hole. Forget the information on the flash drive. Forget the mystery animal group with sufficient cachet to terrify the bearded man. Nope. Julia's death was all about Jeoffry. And if I believed that, I'd have to venture a trip to Island Naturals, the likely site of his torture, the place where, if I was right, the bearded man worked. I had no idea what questions I might ask there, or whom I might ask them of, but I felt I had to go. Taking a last look at the pewter-colored sky, I put my breakfast dishes in the diswasher and tried to coax the vestiges of a plan from my sluggish brain.

❦

"So we'll have to dissemble and mislead?" my friend Lawrence asked, clasping his hands behind his head, leaning back in his office chair, studying the ceiling.

"Well, yes," I said, dismay niggling me. Since when had Mr. Fox become so morally fastidious? He'd helped me with my cases for years.

"Good," Lawrence said, grinning, sitting up straight in his chair. "My life has been too quiet lately. Tell me about your case."

I picked up an elastic band from his desk blotter and zinged it at him. "You had me worried there for five seconds, junior," I groused, filling him in on everything that had happened from my midnight rendezvous with Julia on Monday to last night's marathon reading session with Connie and Miranda.

Tall, slender, sandy-haired, Lawrence was another old friend. A journalism student at U Vic years ago, he'd been fortunate enough to land a part-time job at Henderson's Photos in Oak Bay. He and the now-departed owner had hit it off so swimmingly that when the old guy shuffled off his mortal coil, he left the business to Lawrence, who had never changed its name. Recently, after hiring two Lebanese immigrant college students to help in the shop — Aliya and her twin brother, Samir — he'd found himself with a little spare time and was in the process of rediscovering what had led him into journalism in the first place: his love of photography. On the wall behind him were a series of framed prints — beautiful shots of Canada geese, cattails, and mist. I noticed that one of his cameras and a camera bag sat on a filing cabinet behind him, and a navy waterproof jacket hung on the back of his chair.

"Oh, were you about to leave on a photography adventure?" I asked.

"Well, yeah. But if we can make one stop at the cattail pond I've been photographing, I'll be all yours."

"Sure," I said. "I love cattails."

"Lame, Kieran," he chuckled, peering at me over the tops of his gold-rimmed glasses. "It'll be mucky there. If you want to do anything other than sit in the car, you can use the spare pair of boots I keep in the Range Rover. We'd better take it and leave your car here."

"Drat," I said. "And I had our disguises carefully stowed away in the Karmann Ghia. Ah, well. I'll transfer them, then tell you my plan as we're driving. Oh, can we bring the flying robot?" The flying robot was Tris's name for Lawrence's photography drone, and the kid's name for it had stuck.

"Sure, but you know who Henderson's best flying robot driver is, don't you?"

"I do?"

"Yeah, you do. Aliya. Remember our last case?" he said.

"Uh-huh. Wilderness exploration. The search for the stolen Bengals." The flying robot did great, as I recalled, until Tris in her persona as that pesky kid Trouble shot it down. Of course, we didn't have to worry about that this time, but I took his point. "Isn't Aliya in class right now, though?"

He looked at this watch. "Yeah, she is, but I'll text her. We could pick her up at Camosun when she's done. But we can't leave until Max gets back — and Samir makes an appearance." He pulled a long face. "I have to do boss duties before we go. Samir is in the doghouse. Too many latenesses. I'm getting a tad tired of opening the shop. After all, one of the perks of being the owner ought to be that I can sleep late and wander in with Max at ten."

"Speaking of Max, where is the ferocious beast?" I teased.

Max, Lawrence's Belgian Malinois — a small German Shepherd with a black face — was one of the mellowest dogs I'd ever met. A calm, gracious, serious sort of dog, not at all given to licking and writhing, Max was a rehabbed RCMP sniffer dog. He and his human partner, Duncan, had gotten snootfuls of fentanyl on an investigation and, tragically, Duncan hadn't survived the overdose. Max, stricken with grief, developed canine PTSD, had been retired from the force, and spent a long, difficult time recovering at Miranda's sanctuary, mostly under her desk.

Lawrence and I had been consulting with Miranda as part of our last case, and Max had been, as usual, on a blanket under her feet until he heard Lawrence's voice. He came out from his cubbyhole, sized Lawrence up, sniffed his sneakers, laid a paw on his knee . . . and it was all over but the adoption application. The two bonded in that instant, and as far as I knew, they had never been separated for more than a few hours since. Lawrence blushingly told me that he had had Max's name embroidered on his brand-new doggie bed, his collar, and his saddlebags. As well, he had had Max microchipped, and affixed a top-quality Pet Tracker GPS tag to his collar, with the matching app on his phone. The words *stray* or *lost* were never going to be in Max's future.

Max, however, was a working dog, and had to be kept busy or he fretted. His morning duty was to go to the corner coffee shop for coffee and bagels or whatever treat Lawrence had ordered by text in advance. Max had been outfitted with a spiffy red pair of doggie saddlebags, and the staff at Serious Coffee just loaded him up whenever he appeared. Max was so smart that he knew how to open and close the door to Lawrence's shop as well as the door to the coffee shop. He was famous in Victoria and had had his photo and story in the paper twice, but he remained unfazed by fame.

The front door of the shop tinkled and Max appeared at Lawrence's office door, a dog biscuit — a treat from the Serious Coffee staff — held daintily between his teeth. Max never ate anything unless Lawrence told him it was safe to do so, and when Lawrence had examined it and said, "*Gut*," Max took it delicately from his fingers, tossed it in the air, snatched it, and chomped it down. The staff at Serious Coffee were goofy about Max and would have spoiled him silly with innumerable biscuits, but they had learned that just one was an acceptable treat, and that Max would carry it back to the photo shop where Lawrence would vet it. Max had had a long, danger-filled career as a criminal investigator, and Lawrence was keenly aware that he shouldn't have lived through his fentanyl misadventure. Accordingly, he vowed he wasn't going to lose him because he wasn't vigilant about what the dog sniffed, ate, or drank. I thought Lawrence was a little overly protective of Max, but who was I to carp? After Trey had gotten lost in my own neighborhood, he never set a foot outside the house again.

Lawrence hugged Max, unloaded three to-go cups of coffee from one saddlebag and a paper bag of goodies from the other, unhooked the dog's saddlebags, and said, "*Platz*, Max." Most of the commands Max was familiar with were German, and this one meant "Down," or "Sit." In this case, it meant "You can go lie in your comfy doggie bed now," and he did, settling with a sigh into his orthopedic-foam padded red fleece dog bed with his name sewn in ornate white script on the front. He gave a Kong toy in his bed a perfunctory chomp, wagged his tail a few times, then put his head on his paws and looked at Lawrence. He might as well have said, "What's next, boss?"

"Help yourself," Lawrence said to me, indicating the coffee and bag of goodies on his desk. "When you told me you would be dropping in, I took a stab at what you might like." The shop's front door tinkled again. "Samir," he said with a frown. "Be back in a jiffy. This won't take long." He took one to-go cup, folded a bagel from the bag into a paper napkin, then closed his office door on the way out. Max and I regarded each other.

"He's in trouble," I told Max.

Max did the doggie equivalent of raising his eyebrows.

"It's either sex, drugs, a heavy school schedule, or another job," I told him. "I doubt it's his school schedule. From comments his sister's made to me, Samir isn't a scholar. And I doubt if he has another job. Apparently he's not exactly enterprising. He fancies himself a ladies' man, so it could be Number One. You may not remember it, but sex is a great distraction for males. And I sure hope it's not Number Two. Addiction is a life-wrecker. You know, Max, the kid doesn't appreciate what a great deal he's got here. Decent pay, benefits." I opened one of the to-go cups and sniffed. Hazelnut cappuccino. Nope. In the other was plain black coffee. Thank heavens. Coffee should not be frou-frou. In the goodie bag, two onion bagels remained. I took one out. "And how many bosses provide coffee and bagels as a perk?"

Max thumped his tail.

"I bet Aliya always opened up on time."

At the mention of Aliya's name, Max raised his eyes to mine, looking hopeful.

"No, she's not coming until later," I said. "She doesn't open up any longer. Job reassignment. Schedule change. I think she'll be here this afternoon to clear out her things, though."

Max wilted a little.

"You're a good man, Charlie Brown," I told him. "I'm not a dog person, but I've made an exception for you. You make Lawrence very happy."

"Okay," Lawrence said, opening his office door and gathering up his camera, camera bag, jacket, coffee, and bagel. "Chastisement dispensed." He looked down at Max in his doggie bed in the corner. "Max, *bleib*."

Max sighed and closed his eyes.

"I'm telling him that I'll be gone but not for too long," Lawrence said. "Samir will take him to the park about noon. So . . . let's take off. We'll pick up Aliya and you can fill us in on your plan as I drive."

೧

As it turned out, rain dampened Lawrence's plans for the cattail pond photography session. We picked up Aliya in front of Camosun College, then headed north, out of town toward the ferry docks.

"It's not much of a plan," I admitted. "As a matter of fact, it has more holes in it than one of Tris's socks. But it's the best I could come up with on short notice. I need to get inside Island Naturals. And not just on the PR tour either. I mean, I need to get *inside*. Into that renovated storage facility at the back of the building. Apparently that's where the new testing lab is located."

Aliya, who was sitting in front with Lawrence while I cuddled up to the flying robot in back, turned around, frowning. "But Kieran, if these are the people who ran Shrew off the road, and tortured Jeoffry, won't it be a little risky to just, well, waltz in and start asking questions? Will they even let you in?"

"Well, we'll be discreet." I told her. "Lawrence and I are going to make a delivery. Everyone's glad to see delivery persons. They bring stuff. Aren't you happy to see the UPS delivery person or the FedEx driver?"

"Well, yes . . ." she said uncertainly. "That makes sense. So what do you need me to do?"

"Ah, I need you for a little bit later. I'll explain when Lawrence and I are done."

"So we're going to be delivery persons?" Lawrence asked. "What will we be delivering?"

"You'll see in a minute," I told him. "Turn in here."

"Here?" he asked as he pulled the Range Rover off the highway into the little parking lot for a farm supply store. "This is Buckfield's Feed Store."

"Yeah, it is," I said. "And it has just what we need. I called ahead. It'll be waiting for us — a couple of bags of generic critter chow. Let's put our disguises on first. Better here than in the parking lot of Island Naturals."

Fortunately the rain had stopped. We stood in Buckfield's parking lot and climbed into the navy coveralls I had brought from home — another two of my extremely useful disguises. The left breast of each set of coveralls had a white patch with AZ ENTERPRISES on it blue.

"AZ ENTERPRISES?" Lawrence wondered aloud. "In case anyone asks, just what . . ."

"No idea," I told him. "Animal Zone? Alien Zoos? Acoustic Zoetropes? I bought a bunch of them at a secondhand store. Different colors, different logos. Thought they'd come in handy."

He adjusted his glasses, frowning a little.

I patted him on one shoulder. "Don't fret, junior. It'll be okay. You told me you were yearning to dissemble, right? And you look fetching in blue. It's always been your color."

 space

Island Naturals was just a few miles down the highway from Buckfield's. At a sign bearing the company's name and logo — three green pine trees, a field of yellow flowers, a blue ocean — we turned down a wooded lane that skirted the front of a long, low, cedar-shingled building. There was a small parking lot in front, but I directed Lawrence around back.

"I used Google Earth," I told him. "The old storage facility that now contains the testing lab is off the back parking lot."

As we drove around the side of the building to the back lot, we came to a white-painted guard hut. Nothing but a large shed with windows. A young guy in khaki pants, a dark green logo jacket, an Island Naturals baseball cap, and a clipboard in one hand, came out to greet us.

"Now what?" Lawrence asked.

"Just roll down the window," I told him. "Project calm. Remember, we're delivering. I'm sure they get deliveries here every day. Especially deliveries for their brand new animal testing enterprise. You're on, junior."

"Hi," Lawrence said to the guard. "Delivery for the lab."

The young guy smiled and nodded. "Sure. Straight on," he said. "The employees' lot will be on the left, shipping and receiving for the lab will be on the right. You'll see the loading dock. You can park there. Go on inside up the little staircase beside it." Disconcertingly, though, he wrote down our license plate on his clipboard and, as we drove on slowly, he pulled a cell phone out of a pocket in his jacket. Hmm.

"See?" I said to Lawrence with a lot more confidence than I felt. "The kid is just there to direct people. He's not guarding anything. No sweat."

"Here's the deal," I told Lawrence and Aliya as we drove up to the loading dock. "Right now I need to discover three things: if the bearded guy really works here, as I think he does; as much information as I can find out about him; and if the test animals are here. I have no idea what they might be — rabbits, mice, guinea pigs." I sighed. "Aliya, I have the photoshopped picture you produced for me, the one isolating the bearded guy from Jeoffry, so I have a pretty good three-quarters face."

"And you're just going to wave that around?" Lawrence asked skeptically.

"Nope. No waving. In fact, I won't even pull it out unless I have to. My plan is to just stick to questions."

"Okay," he said, shrugging. "Your plans usually work out. Just tell me what to do."

"Follow me, carry the heavy stuff, and act dumb," I told him. "You're the brawn today. Think you can handle the food bags and grunt now and then while I carry a clipboard with the invoice?"

He gave me a crooked smile. "Any day."

"Once we get in and look around, I'll tell you more. I confess my plan contains a lot of winging it."

"Where will you be?"

"Looking for a guy with a beard, a shredded arm, and one helluva nasty cat bite."

For a moment, I almost believed in my own bravado.

CHAPTER 19

LAWRENCE PARKED JUST to the left of the loading dock, in front of a series of four concrete steps that led to a white door marked DELIVERIES. The loading dock itself was a wide, elevated concrete extension of the building, intended for trucks to drive up and disgorge their bags and boxes easily. The loading bay door — a wide green metal overhead door resembling an oversized garage door — stood open. A black van, its back doors ajar, was parked in front of the loading bay, the driver busy heaving cardboard boxes onto the dock while a couple of employees of Island Naturals, dressed in dark green pants and shirts with the company's logo on the back, carried them on into the dark recesses of the facility. No one even looked our way.

"See?" I murmured to Lawrence as I loaded him up with the bags of critter food, fetching my clipboard from the back seat. "We're invisible. Let's take the stairs. Sit tight, Aliya," I said. "We'll be back in a bit."

Lawrence preceded me, and we were halfway up the stairs when, with a deafening rattle and clatter, the loading bay door crashed down, frightening me witless, squashing several of the cardboard boxes the van driver had heaved onto the dock.

"Shit!" one of the Island Naturals employees yelled, the one on the outside of the door helping the van driver. "I thought they fixed this bloody thing. It's gonna cut someone in half. Leroy, give that chain a heave! Get the door up then put a screwdriver in that damned chain."

The Island Naturals guy on the inside yelled back, the van driver started shouting about his squashed boxes, and under cover of this verbal tempest, Lawrence and I slipped inside the door marked DELIVERIES. In the interior dimness, a guy with a large screwdriver met us. Presumably Leroy.

"Piece of garbage door," he muttered. "Doesn't work worth a damn. Never did. Not even when we just used this place for storage. Throws the breaker half the time. Crappy wiring, I guess. Now I have to heave the damn door up with the chain," he complained. "It's murder on my back. Well, they need to get this fixed — we have a shitload of deliveries tonight and tomorrow night. And will they pay us overtime? They better."

"Renovation," I commiserated. "Always a challenge."

Leroy gave us no more than a cursory glance. "Go see Darlene," he said, struggling with the chain so he could lift the overhead door manually.

"Sure thing," I said agreeably.

"Down the hall to the right," he told me. "There's a T-junction. Stop at the office marked RECEIVING. Darlene'll check your stuff in. Looks like it's meant for the lab. That's farther along on the left."

"Yup," I agreed, trying not to grin at this serendipitous flurry of information. "C'mon, AJ," I told Lawrence.

"AJ?" he whispered as we left Leroy struggling with the door.

"Don't ask," I muttered. "Someone burly and silent from my past. Let's find Darlene."

❧

The office with RECEIVING on the door was just where Leroy said it would be — at the T junction. The door was ajar and I knocked, pushing it open. Under fluorescent lights was a twenty-square-foot space, two desks, two computers, two gray three-drawer filing cabinets, a stand with a laser printer/scanner, a drooping ficus tree in one corner, another stand with a coffeemaker and paper cups, a water cooler, but no Darlene. I edged into the office.

"Should I take the food to the lab?" Lawrence asked. "Leroy said it was on down the hall."

I was about to answer him when something on the desk nearest the door caught my eye. A photo, taped to the side of the computer monitor. A photo of a smiling woman and a small tabby cat. I bent closer. Jesus. It was a photo of Julia and Jeoffry, taken outside in a little alcove near the loading dock. I recognized the spot from when we drove along the back of the building.

"Holy crap," I said, going around the desk and sitting down in what I presumed was Darlene's desk chair, bending closer. Julia was kneeling, one hand on the cat's head, smiling at the photographer. Jeoffry had a full kibble dish beside him, ditto a water dish, and was looking up at the photographer with big, golden eyes. *So that's what color they are,* I said to myself. What the hell was a photo of Julia and Jeoffry doing here?

"Kieran?" Lawrence asked.

"I think I'll just stay here and get our invoice signed," I announced loudly, then whispered, "Yeah, go on down to the lab. See if you can get in using Julia's key card. You know what we're looking for."

He nodded, settled the bags of food more comfortably on his shoulder, and trotted off down the hall.

As I sat at Darlene's desk, listening to music playing on her computer, I thought I heard noises coming from behind a door at the rear of the office. Maybe an office supplies closet? That seemed odd. I turned Darlene's music down. Uh-huh. Voices. Two voices. One male, one female. Arguing voices. I frowned. What kind of disagreement would require the privacy of the supplies closet? An in-office lovers' quarrel? And what business was it of mine, anyhow? I took another look at the photo of Julia and Jeoffry and decided, yup, it was my business. Sighing, I crossed the office just as one of the voices, the male's, got louder.

"I want that cat, dammit!" he yelled. "You must know where it is. You and that other woman . . . you two were always cooing over the filthy thing. Where is it? Did she hand it over to you Monday night?"

"I keep telling you I don't have it," said the female voice, sounding desperate and frightened. "And I didn't see her Monday night. I don't know what you're talking about!"

A woman's cry of pain made up my mind for me. Enough was enough. I knocked on the door. "Darlene, I've got paperwork for you to sign," I called.

"Go away!" the man's voice shouted.

"Can't do that," I said, opening the door.

A small sandy-haired woman in jeans, a paisley vest, and a blue turtleneck was backed up to a bank of shelving which held reams of paper, boxes of envelopes, and an assortment of other office supplies, one hand raised to her cheek. She was crying. Half-turned from her was a dark-haired man in a lab coat. A bearded dark-haired man. The same bearded dark-haired man whose photo I had folded up in my coveralls' pocket. He gave me a furious look.

"Who the hell are you?" he said. "Get out or I'll call someone."

Someone? Boy, was I intimidated. Still, I thought it better to play-act. "Didn't mean to interrupt," I told him with feigned meekness. "I was looking for Darlene. Hey, there you are! AJ and I are on a tight schedule today."

I took a step forward, removed a page from my clipboard, and handed it to her. She looked at it, blinked a few times, looked back at me, then squeezed past the bearded man and fled out the door behind me to the outer office.

The man turned slowly to look at me and as he did, my brain froze. But why? Really, he was nothing unusual — a man of medium height and medium build, dark hair and beard, thin face, very dark brown eyes, black pants, blue Oxford-cloth shirt, a white lab coat worn unbuttoned over his clothes. But there was something in those eyes . . . something dreadful that seemed to raise its head and look at me from where it crouched in a dark, diseased place.

Mephistopheles *is* his name, I realized, shivering. In fact, he has had many names over the centuries, most of which we don't want to believe in any longer. Something gleeful, cruel, and completely inhuman looked out of the man's eyes, and I had to mentally shake myself to not start gibbering in fear. I thought, this must be what a deer feels like brought to bay by hounds, or a rabbit the minute before the bobcat pounces, or the mouse under the cobra's gaze.

In an immense effort of will, I forced my eyes away from his. I forced myself back into my Kieranness — a brave, capable, resourceful woman. I was not a deer, a rabbit, a mouse. Or a tabby cat. I was not prey. Then, as often happens to me when I've been scared half to death, I got mad. I entertained a fantasy of kicking the shit out of the cat-torturing, murdering bastard. But I didn't. I didn't even voice an objection to his assault on Darlene.

"Sorry, man," I said, forcing myself to cringe a little. "I didn't know Darlene had something . . . going on here."

The bearded guy smiled, fussily pushing the sleeves of his lab coat up above his elbows and I was surprised and immensely gratified to see twin lines of deep cat scratches on the inside of one forearm. Moreover, like the cherry on top of the sundae, he had what looked like a festering bite on his right hand. *Way to go, Jeoffry,* I cheered silently.

"Yes, well," he said. "We just needed some privacy. You know how it is."

"Sure," I said. "No problem. I know how it is." I avoided looking at him directly, because I didn't want him to see the disgust in my eyes.

"Hmmf," he said. "All right then. Collect your paperwork and get going."

In the outer office, Darlene and I stood looking at each other until the bearded guy disappeared down the hall. Then she sat down heavily at her computer, put her head in her hands, and broke into tears.

"Who are you?" she asked through her fit of weeping. "The paperwork you gave me is the paid invoice for work done on someone's Karmann Ghia."

"I'm a friend of Julia Stevens's," I said. "And the tabby cat, too."

"Oh, Tom!" she cried. Tom . . . I guessed that was her name for Jeoffry.

Lawrence appeared at Darlene's office door and I motioned for him to come inside and close the door. He took a seat at the desk across the room and raised his eyebrows. I held a finger up to my lips.

"Talk to me," I urged Darlene. "Who was that guy in the supply closet?"

"Dr. Maleck!" she said hysterically. "The lab director. But I don't know why he thinks I have Tom."

"Hmm," I said. "Tell me about Dr. Maleck. And the cat. And Julia."

More weeping. I handed her a tissue from a box on her desk. "Dr. Maleck's only been here for a couple of weeks," she said. "He's a very disagreeable man. He's managed to alienate almost everyone. And he hated Tom." She wiped her nose, then continued. "The poor little guy was abandoned here on the grounds when he was only a kitten. Someone had just thrown him away. He was starving until some of us started to feed him. Lots of us chipped in. We took up a collection to get him neutered, too. We named him Tom — short for tomcat. He lived in the warehouse at night and visited people in their offices during the day. He never did any harm. Everyone loved him."

"Except Dr. Maleck," I commented.

Darlene nodded. "Him!" she said bitterly. "He'd started trying to kick him whenever he saw him. Called him filthy. He wasn't. He was pretty and clean and smelled good." More tears.

Hmm — did I detect an undertone of guilt in all that crying? Maybe. So many times these abandoned cat stories ended up badly. I always wondered why the well-intentioned cat enthusiasts didn't take the cats who aroused their care and kindness to a shelter or, better yet, home with them. But people always have excuses. Boyfriends with allegies. New husbands' dogs. The landlord.

"So you and Julia were both looking out for Tom?" I gestured to the picture on her computer monitor.

"Yes," she said. "I called CLAW about Tom. They're an animal welfare group. I hoped they'd come and get Tom, take him away, find him a home. Instead they sent Julia. They got her a job here as a temp.

That was last month. With the expansion, we were hiring a lot of people. She got a job in Receiving, right here." She gestured to the desk where Lawrence was sitting. "We needed another clerk. We became friends, well, because of Tom. We were trying to keep him away from Dr. Maleck." She laughed bitterly. "As it turned out, though, Julia — oh, it sounds stupid — was undercover. CLAW put her here to get proof that Island Naturals was going to be testing a new product on animals. On animals! She said that they'd stopped being cruelty-free!" She looked at me in disbelief.

I looked back at her in an equal measure of disbelief.

"But you're here in Receiving. You must have, what, *received* plenty of stuff for your new lab. Cages, counters . . . what on earth did you think would be going on in the new lab."

"I thought . . . I didn't really know what animal testing was all about. I didn't realize they'd hurt the animals."

Oh, my God. Was Darlene one of those people who thought that testing shampoo on rabbits meant that you washed their fur to see if it needed conditioner? And had she not been aware of the fact that the Cosmetics Testing Bill was making its way through Parliament, that Canada was maybe on the cusp of joining the other sane nations of the world in a stand against animal cruelty? How deeply was Darlene's head in the sand?

"But Julia set me straight about all that," she said sadly. "About testing, About what might be going to happen in the lab."

Might be? This woman was still in denial. Jesus.

"Julia became very worried about Tom," she said. "More worried than me, even. We tried to keep him in here but it wasn't working. He wanted to do what he always did — visit the other offices, go outside. I guess he went down the hall to the lab one too many times and Dr. Maleck got mad. Scooped him up and put him in one of the lab's cages. His lab assistant liked Tom. He came to tell Julia and she got very upset. She said she was going to take him away herself."

"When was that?"

"Let me see . . . that was Monday. I think she was planning to come back after work and get him."

That fit. She came back, found Maleck at work on Jeoffry in the lab, shot a video, grabbed the cat, texted me . . . yeah, it all fit. It was her tender-heartedness that saved Tom/Jeoffry's life. And cost her her own.

Darlene carried on. "But if Julia came to get Tom, and took him home or to CLAW or wherever, why didn't she come in to work the next day?" She dabbed at her eyes. "And why is Dr. Maleck so angry? He should be happy — Tom's gone. I should have taken him home myself. I wanted to. But my boyfriend said no," she said shamefacedly. Uh-huh. "He loved it here — he had the grounds to roam, and the warehouse, and his favorite people. I guess I told myself a story, that this could be Tom's home."

I felt sorry for her. "It could have been," I said, thinking of Miranda's Rodent Ranger program. "Plenty of cats live in warehouses. But everyone has to want them."

"Until Dr. Maleck came along, everyone did want Tom," Darlene said.

I had a quick fantasy of my own — making Maleck disappear, returning Jeoffry to Island Naturals, where people loved him . . . where busy people could learn to take care of a half-blind cat? Ha. He'd get squished by a forklift on Day Two. Nope, Jeoffry was Zee's project. She'd find a home for him.

"What's going on? Who are you really?" Darlene asked, suddenly realizing that she'd been babbling away to a stranger in blue coveralls with a bogus invoice. There was no paperwork to be signed. "And him?" she said, gesturing at Lawrence.

I decided to offer half the truth — the half that she seemed most concerned about. I hoped she wouldn't ask about the other half. "We're not from CLAW, but we work for animals, too," I said.

"Is Tom . . ." she started, eyes filling with tears again, wanting to ask the question, wanting to hope.

"Is Tom all right?" I finished the question for her.

She nodded.

"Tom's all right," I said.

"And Julia?"

I sighed. Of course she would ask about Julia. Even if they'd been just work friends, they'd still been friends. Had Julia's death made the papers? The news? I hadn't been paying attention, and presumably, neither had Darlene.

"The last I saw of her was when she gave me Tom," I said. "Monday night, late. Well, Tuesday morning actually." There. That was, strictly speaking, the truth. And that was all I intended to say about Julia.

Fortunately Darlene didn't ask me more. Maybe she imagined that Julia, amateur undercover investigator, had been folded back into the arms of CLAW. I decided to let her believe that.

"And Dr. Maleck? What do I tell him when he comes around again wanting information about Tom and Julia?" she asked, fear plain on her face. "He only went away because you came into the supplies cupboard."

I thought about this. Maleck's obsession with repossessing the cat was way over the top. He'd already killed Julia. If my arrival hadn't stopped him, what might he have done to Darlene?

"Do you have vacation time?" I asked her. "Or sick leave?"

She nodded. "Both."

"Take some sick leave. Maybe just a few days. I have a feeling this is all going to blow over soon." I took a notebook and a pen from her desk, scribbled my name and phone number on one of the pages, ripped it out, and handed it to her. "Call me if you need to," I said. "But, Darlene?"

"Yes?"

"Maybe leave as soon as you can."

"Oh," she said. "You're serious, aren't you?" She raised her hand to the place on her cheek where Maleck had slapped her.

"I am," I said. "Call your supervisor. Say you have the flu. It came on suddenly."

She shut off her computer, clearly alarmed. "All right," she said. Then, "Miz Yeats? Will I ever . . . that is, can I see Tom again?"

I thought about this for a moment, how a visit could be arranged, where it might take place . . . weighed the logistical problems against Darlene's obvious love for the little warehouse cat named Tom.

"Of course," I said finally. "Of course you can."

Her smile was incandescent.

CHAPTER 20

"I FOUND THEM," Lawrence told me in a low, excited voice as we closed the door to Darlene's office and hurried back down the hall to the loading bay. "In the lab. Right there . . . in a bank of stainless steel cages. Six black and white rabbits. Here, I got a photo when the lab guy was putting the food away." He held out his phone and I took it.

"Crap!" I said, looking at the photo on his phone. Sure enough. Six big white rabbits with black noses, ears, and paws. The others. And a sign on one of the cages read 10/31. Saturday. Now I knew what the last part of Julia's instructions meant. "Crap," I said again.

"So that procedure you described to me, the Draize test thing, well you're not going to let that happen, are you?" Lawrence asked, worry plain on his face. "You can't."

"No, I can't," I told him.

"But how . . . how will you stop it? Short of stealing them?"

I said nothing, and when he looked at me, he must have seen the answer on my face.

"Oh my God, that's what you're going to do, right? Steal them. But, Kieran, even if you go in after hours, you heard Leroy — they're getting after-hours deliveries. This place will be crawling with people."

"Yeah," I said gloomily. "I heard him."

We passed the ladies' room door on our left, and suddenly an idea bubbled up into my brain. Not a great idea, and not a fully formed one, but an idea nonetheless.

"Did the magnetic card I gave you, Julia's card, open the testing lab door?" I asked him.

He nodded. "Yeah. Although the lab assistant saw me and came to intercept me and take the food. The card did work, though." He patted a pocket of his coveralls. "I have it right here."

"Okay. Just loiter here for a minute." I handed him the clipboard. When he opened his mouth to object I said, "Lawrence, Yeats's Second Rule of Investigation is this: wear a uniform and carry a clipboard, and you can go anywhere. That includes loitering."

"I won't even ask what the first rule is," he said.

"Won't be a minute," I told him.

Inside the bathroom, I checked under each of the three stalls for feet. Nope, none. I was alone. Praying for privacy, I hopped up onto the counter, standing between two smallish sinks. The window over the sinks was maybe three feet by two feet, hinged at the top, and opened inward easily once I turned the latch. I looked closely at the window, but there was nary a sensor — it was, as I had hoped, not on the alarm system. Small windows usually aren't. A security oversight, but ah well. I fished a roll of duct tape from a coveralls' pocket, ripped off a small piece, taped the window latch open, smoothed the tape down carefully, and closed the window. There. Now it would open easily from the outside — all I would have to do was push.

"C'mon, let's go see Aliya," I said as I rejoined Lawrence in the hall. "Time for the flying robot."

Lawrence parked the Range Rover in a little clearing just outside the back fence that separated Island Naturals' employees' parking lot from the forest. A narrow, rutted road ran along the fence, but the two shallow tracks made by vehicles bore several flourishing varieties of weeds. Nothing had driven down this road lately. A screen of huckleberry bushes separated us from the fence, which I thought just as well. We needed the camouflage. The rain that had been off and on all day was currently off and the sky was uniformly gray, the light flat. Good, I thought. Aliya would need decent visibility to find what I wanted her to look for.

"I hope to hell we're not still on their property," I said. "I don't think so. It would be pretty awkward if someone from Island Naturals drove up and rapped on our windows."

"It certainly would," Lawrence agreed. "Does Yeats's First Rule of Investigation apply to that?"

"To window rapping? Nah. We'll just have to improvise."

Aliya rolled her eyes at us and got out, setting the drone down on the ground in front of the Range Rover. "Here we go," she said, hopping back into the passenger seat. She used the controller to fly the drone smoothly up and over the fence where it hovered over the rows of parked cars. "This is a new drone, isn't it?" she asked Lawrence, who sighed. "Oops, is that a sore subject?"

"Oh, not any longer," Lawrence said in resignation. "I was pretty hot the day Samir gave the old drone burial at sea at the Oak Bay Marina. We were photographing a million-dollar yacht. But I've gotten over that. Thank God for insurance. And a patient yacht owner."

I sat in back looking between the seats as the video screen on the controller let us see what the drone was seeing. Our own private eye in the sky.

"I'm sending this to your phone, Kieran," Aliya told me. "You can watch the video later if you like. But right now . . . tell me what you're looking for?"

"A big white SUV. A Sequoia, I think. With damage to the driver's side and, if we're really lucky, scrapes of red paint on it. Maybe a dent or two. Unless I'm totally wrong, it's the car that drove Julia off the road and it's in this lot. I'm guessing it's Dr. Maleck's car."

"Okay," she said. "Let's do a quick flyover and pick out likely vehicles. When we find the Sequoia, I'll drop the drone lower and we can examine the car."

The drone cruised over the roofs of parked cars: black, blue, red, silver; Civics, Focuses, Hondas, Subarus; vans, sedans and SUVS. I was getting antsier by the minute. No Sequoia.

Then, when I was about to admit that maybe the trail of crumbs I was following was, well, invented, Aliya exclaimed, "Bingo. There." Sure enough, a Sequoia. A white one. "I'll take the drone down lower," she said. Then, "Wow, look. Scrapes and scratches on the driver's side. A huge dent. And red paint. Just like you wanted to find, Kieran. I'll take the drone around it one more time."

When the drone passed behind the car, I said, "Can you hover this thing? Make it stop for a minute? I need to see something up close."

"Sure," Aliya said. "What do you need to see?"

"The license plate." The drone hovered, and I said, "Well, for crap's sake." "What's wrong?" Lawrence asked.

"Look close, junior. At the top, there's a logo of a *fleur-de-lis*. And the word Quebec. And under the numbers and letters, there's a line of type."

"I see it," Lawrence said. "Barely, though. Can you read it?"

"Yeah, it says *Je me souviens*. Literally, I will remember. It means that the people of Quebec will never forget their ancient lineage, traditions, and memories of the past. It's the province's motto. Brother, I sure missed all that Monday night. Good work, Aliya."

I wrote the license number on the bottom of my car repair invoice, mentally high-fiving myself. *I've got you now, Maleck, you murderous, cat-torturing, secretary-slapping sonofabitch.*

"Are we done, Kieran?" Aliya asked.

"Yup, done. Thanks a million you guys," I said. "Say, why don't we get a sub sandwich on the way back to town? My treat. I'll drop you two back at your shop, Lawrence. After all, you have to do *some* work today. As for me, I have a car and a kid to pick up."

I arrived at the Oak Grove School with about fifteen minutes to spare. Having shed my coveralls back at Lawrence's shop, I now looked presentable. Parent-like, even. I settled back with a sigh, noting that among the drab and leafless oaks in a little garden by the parking lot was a lone maple still bearing a crop of crimson leaves like a defiant shout. *Good for you*, I thought. *Do not go gentle into that good night.*

I figured I had just time enough to make a phone call and *mirabile dictu*, Edgar answered the office phone himself. Again.

"Edgar," I said, "this is getting to be a habit, your answering my calls in person. A nice habit."

"Well, your inquiries are usually a lot more interesting than our present data security jobs," he said. "So I reconfigured our phone system a little. Now your calls come directly to me."

"I'm flattered," I said, not sure if I should be.

"Oh, don't let it go to your head, sweetie," he said. "It's just that constructing firewalls does get a tad tiresome."

"Happy to rescue you from the slough of tekkie despond," I said. Imagine that. Edgar was bored. "Here's a request reminiscent of the work you used to do: I need dirt."

"Ooooo, do I still do that?" he asked. "Dig up dirt?"

"I sure hope so," I told him.

"Who's the subject?"

"A guy named Maleck. Don't know his first name, but he works at a company called Island Naturals. I'm pretty sure this is his car's license plate." I rattled off the string of letters and numbers I'd copied. "It's a Quebec plate."

"Oh, good thing you told me," he said. "I might have wasted my time prowling in the BCIC database. Although what you want will be an extra fee. I'm not, ah, familiar with Quebec's vehicle database."

"Meaning you've never burgled it," I groused. "So of course it will cost me more. You know, it occurs to me that I'm actually subsidizing your continuing education."

"Tut-tut," Edgar chided,clearly enjoying our back and forth. "What is it you need on Mr. Maleck?"

"Dr. Maleck, supposedly. I need anything and everything you can find. The dirtier the better. Taxes, medical records, work history, criminal history, marital history . . . everything. Did he run out on child support? Dodge a speeding ticket? Assault his wife? I'm interested in those misdeeds, Edgar, but what I'm really looking for is something worse. Putrid peccadilloes, sordid sins, woeful wrongdoings. I don't know yet what I'll do with the dirt you might find. Something will occur to me, though."

"Ooooo, sweetie," Edgar cooed. "You've become a veritable virago. I'm shivering. What's our boy done to upset you?"

"You don't want to know," I said. "But I want to see that he pays for it. If there's anything I can use from his past, I want it."

"I can hardly wait to get started," Edgar said. "I have a couple of marvelous ideas already. Of course I will have to, ah, visit several databases . . ."

"Yeah, yeah, yeah," I sighed. "Just do it. And Edgar?"

"Sweetie?"

"Do your visiting sooner rather than later, all right?"

"Will do," he said cheerfully.

I ended the call, feeling drained. Negotiating with Edgar always felt like rolling a boulder uphill. Still, the aggravating little twerp invariably came through. I might be getting a trifle too old for witty repartee, though, I thought. That was the downside of dealing with Edgar — phone conversations as performance art. But it wasn't as though one could go, say, to Amazon and order up dirt — amend that to "deep background" on people. Oh, you could extract a certain amount of information from online public records, but that wasn't what I wanted. No, I wanted a misdeed so awful that it would not stand the scrutiny of sunlight.

Edgar was a ferret, a digger. He loved the challenge, loved the chase. If the dirt I wanted existed somewhere online, he'd find it. After all, Maleck might never even stand trial for running Julia off the road. Or for torturing Jeoffry. In that case, if I could find something in his past that could be used against him, something so egregious he would want it to stay hidden — ideally something I could send on to Mac — perhaps justice would be served.

It had started to rain a little, and as I turned on my wipers, Tris came bounding out of the front doors of the school, wearing an odd combination of grey cargo pants, a yellow anorak and a knitted blue cap with red snowflakes and dangling earflaps. She seemed dressed for rain, snow, or anything in between. I chuckled.

"You're a sight," I told her as she tossed her backpack in the back of the Karmann Ghia. "I haven't seen you for, oh, over twelve hours. How the heck are you?"

She took off her cap and frowned a little. "I'm fine. But Dani wasn't in school today. She never misses. And she wasn't sick yesterday."

Immediately I thought of Nigel. No time like the present. "Tris, maybe Dani was a little afraid to come to school today."

Tris gave me a questioning look but said nothing.

"Maybe she was afraid of Nigel," I suggested.

"Did Jen —"

"No, Jen didn't tell me anything. I was outside the barn the other day and heard you talking to her. About Nigel and Dani. About, ah, threatening to remove certain of Nigel's body parts."

Tris looked down at her sneakers "You're mad at me, I guess."

"Actually, Sprout, no, I'm not."

"You're not?"

"Nah. You didn't do it, did you? And you wouldn't have, either. It was just talk," I said, not at all sure of this. Tris was a tough, resourceful little kid.

"No, I guess I wouldn't have," she agreed. "I was just trying to scare him. But y'know, Nigel wasn't in school today either."

Ah, I thought. Thank you, Marie Linley.

"I have something to confess, kiddo," I said.

Tris looked at me, eyes huge.

"Sometimes people need help. And it's okay to ask for it when you have a tough case. I'm working on a tough case right now."

Tris nodded, clearly connecting the dots. Then she said what I hoped she would say. "So you had to ask for help. Last night. You asked Miranda and Connie to help you. Aliya, too. You said they were helping you read stuff."

"Uh-huh," I said. "That's what you have to do when you're in a little over your head. Ask for help. Like you did with Jen. That was smart."

Tris nodded. "Yeah. She told me to maybe ask you." She looked down at her sneakers again. "But I didn't."

"Well, as it turned out, that was all right," I told her, hoping like hell I was going to say the right thing.

Tris looked at me intently.

"Tris, what you told Jen about Nigel, about how he was so mean to Dani, well, being mean like that is really, really wrong. Kids just can't treat each other that way and expect to get away with it. In school it's called bullying. Do you talk about bullying in school? With your teachers?"

Tris nodded. "A little."

"What do your teachers say to do if you see or hear bullying?"

"Tell someone."

Oh Tris, why didn't you just go to Marie Linley? "Okay, so you did that," I said, trying to put the best face on this situation. "You told Jen. That was good."

"Well, yeah, but I should have talked to you. Or Miss Linley. Right?" Tris said miserably. "Even though Dani asked me not to tell anyone. She was afraid. She said she didn't want her parents to get in trouble. So I didn't say anything."

I decided to cut to the chase. "Well, Sprout, the long and short of it is that as soon as I heard about this, I realized we all needed help — you, Dani, and me. So I talked to Miss Linley myself."

"You?" Tris said, panicked. "Is Dani in trouble? Are her parents in trouble? Is that why she wasn't in school?"

"No, Dani's definitely not in trouble. Neither are her parents. You know who's in trouble?"

Comprehension dawned on Tris's face and she grinned hugely. "Nigel! Nigel's in trouble! Kieran!"

"Nigel is in a whole lot of trouble — a boatload of trouble, a whole ocean liner of trouble. He won't bother Dani ever again," I said. "Bullying is serious stuff, Sprout. Your school doesn't stand for it. Nigel was expelled. He's gone."

Tris stared at me. "Gone? Gone where?"

I shrugged. "Who knows? His parents will find another school for him."

"Can I phone Dani?" Tris asked. "I know her parents' number."

I thought this over. Tris had a flip phone that hardly had a brain in its electronic head, a not-smart phone that I had given her for emergencies, programmed with my phone number, as well as Aliya's, Jen's, Zee's, Lawrence's, and Miranda's.

"Sure," I said. "I think this qualifies as an emergency. A good emergency. Give Dani a call. Tell her it's safe to go back in the water."

"Go back in the water?" Tris asked.

"A line from an old movie, kiddo. We'll watch it together sometime. Go ahead and make your call."

Tris chattered enthusiastically to Dani for a few minutes, then ended the call, bouncing a little in her seat.

"Kieran, can we sing?" she asked me.

I'd introduced Tris to the joys of old-fashioned rock and roll, and often when we rode in my car together, we'd sing along with the golden oldies.

"I thought you'd never ask," I teased her. "Any requests?"

"The song about the candle and the handle and the broom and perfume. The one we sing in two parts."

"Oh, you mean 'The Way You Do the Things You Do.' That old chestnut ."

"Uh-huh."

"Sure." I advanced the songs on my mp3 player to the one Tris wanted, possibly the silliest song in rock and roll, and we sang along with The Temptations. In two parts. Call and response.

I looked over at Tris bobbing her head, singing along to that silly song, the rain pattering a little on the windshield, the car's heater chugging valiantly, and a sudden, unlooked-for certainty came over me. *Damn. This is happiness.*

CHAPTER 21

TRIS AND I, freshly shorn, headed out from Supercuts, she eating a granola bar I found in the glove compartment, and I finishing up a phone call to Miranda. The ringworm epidemic at The Sanctuary had slipped my mind, I explained to Tris, so we couldn't kitten-shop today, but I still needed to visit The Sanctuary. Tris was a little down in the mouth about the kitten-shopping but rallied at the prospect of revisiting Jimmy the doo-wop-singing parrot. I had my own reasons for visiting The Sanctuary. I needed information, and I needed someone to bounce ideas off. Miranda had volunteered for both roles.

We parked under the dripping pines, dashed through the rain, and arrived inside The Sanctuary's lobby to be met by two cagefuls of very small kittens, perhaps six weeks old: tabbies, torties, some Siamese crosses, and a couple of tuxedos. A kaleidoscope of kittens.

"Oh, kittens!" Tris exclaimed. "Oh, wow!" She looked at Connie, who was down on her hands and knees putting a large bowl of wet cat food in one of the cages. "Do they have the worms too?"

Connie laughed. "No, honey, they don't have the worms. They're out here so they don't get the worms."

"They're just babies," Tris said wistfully. "I guess they can't go home with anyone until they're bigger."

"I'm afraid not," Connie said. "And they haven't been vetted, either. They'll have to stay here for a while." She stood up and brushed a speck of dried cat food off her cream-colored turtleneck, dusted off the knees of her brown corduroy pants, and looked at me in disgust. "When we opened up this morning, they were here on our doorstep. In the rain. Two big U-Haul cardboard boxes of kittens, thoughtfully taped up. I guess they weren't important enough to make the move. No air holes, though. Sometimes I hate people."

"Na na na na, na na na na, hey hey hey, goodbye." Jimmy trilled from his perch atop one of the kitten cages.

"He's jealous," Connie explained. "He's been in a funk all morning."

Jimmy trilled on, fluffing his feathers and bobbing his head.

❧

"He's telling them to go away, isn't he?" Tris said. "He's mad. But I can help with the kittens. And then I could play with Jimmy and make him feel better."

"You're on, sweetie," Connie told her. "Hang your jacket over there on those hooks by the door. We need to log the kittens in. I've got them ID'd. Now we need to make sure the right collar goes on the right kitten. We can do that together." She winked at me. "It's always good to have an experienced pair of hands around here."

"Oh, fuck you!" Jimmy shrieked, flapping his wings. "Goodbye! Goodbye!"

"Beast," I told Jimmy. "You think you've stumped me? That's 'Na Na Hey Hey, (Kiss Him Goodbye)' by Steam. And watch your beak. Kids are present."

Tris wrinkled her nose and laughed, having heard plenty of cursing from Jimmy before.

"Miranda?" I asked Connie.

"In her office in a terminally grumpy mood," she replied. "Maybe you can extract her from *her* funk."

I walked through the lobby and made my way down the hall to Miranda's office. "So I hear you're in a funk," I said.

She looked up from her computer, face set in a scowl. "Grant proposal," she said, raking her hair with one hand. "My least favorite job. Come on in. If you want coffee, I moved the coffeemaker in here. It's on the bookcase by the window. Help yourself. Hordes of kittens have commandeered the lobby. We literally have no more room in the inn."

"Do you want coffee?" I asked her.

"Ha! I'd rather break out the Scotch. It's a bit early for that, though. Even though the sun is over the yardarm somewhere. Sure, I'll have coffee. Let me just record a few more bits of visionary prose, then I'll be right with you."

"You are in a mood, aren't you?" I said as she closed up her laptop and sat back in her office chair.

She rolled her eyes. "I am. I've been sitting here in one place for too long. I feel ossified. If it weren't raining I'd suggest we go for a bracing trot around The Sanctuary grounds. We could look over the two cottages I'm having renovated."

I recalled that Miranda and Connie each lived in a cottage behind The Sanctuary's main building. Apparently four cottages had come with the property and Miranda had had two renovated. I wondered what plans she had for the other two. Rentals? Maybe. She certainly had a cadre of volunteers — perhaps one of them needed a place to live.

She took a sweatshirt that she'd draped over the back of her chair and pulled it on over her head. The sweatshirt, a faded blue, had the letters RCMP and GRC on the front, separated by an iconic Mountie in ceremonial red serge, lance in hand, atop a horse in mid-gallop. I guessed the well-washed sweatshirt was a hard-to-abandon souvenir from Miranda's time in the RCMP. Interesting that she still wore it,

I thought. She rubbed her arms and shivered a bit. "I'm chilly and crabby. Are you warm enough? I could turn on the heater."

"I'm okay, thanks." I handed her a cup of coffee, took mine, and sat across the desk from her in the only other chair in her crowded little office.

"I'm not good at this kind of fundraising," she said. "I'm better at lunchtime meetings at which I describe big visionary programs that capture donors' imagination. And require large checks. I should hire a grant writer. For sure I'll do that right after I deal with the other twenty-seven things that are vying for position at the top of my list. So you mentioned that you were . . . what did you say on the phone?"

"On the horns of a dilemma," I said.

She threw back her head and laughed. "You just made my day. That must be very damned uncomfortable."

"Somewhat," I agreed. "Mostly it's frustrating."

"Tell me about it," she said, pulling out her bottom desk drawer and propping her feet on it, a favorite position. She tucked a wing of dark hair back behind one ear — a gesture she made when she was preparing to attend carefully to something. Gamblers would call this a tell. It was. It meant she was giving something or someone her full attention.

"Okay, first a story," I said. "It has four chapters. Then the dilemma. Here's what I learned this morning." I took a deep breath. "One, CLAW placed Julia Stevens at Island Naturals."

Miranda's eyes widened.

"Yeah," I continued. "I had a chat with a secretary named Darlene in Island Naturals' Receiving department. CLAW must have learned something, somehow, about Island Naturals' plans to begin testing on animals. I'm guessing they wanted Julia to get proof, so they arranged a job for her."

"That's how she came to have all that information on the flash drive," Miranda said. "Okay, what's two?"

"Two is that I met the cat torturer." Now Miranda's eyes opened *very* wide. "A guy named Maleck. The lab director. I interrupted him in mid-assault on Darlene. He accused her of having the cat.

Apparently it was well-known around the warehouse that Julia and Darlene had a soft spot for the little tabby named Tom."

"Tom?" Miranda asked.

"Jeoffry," I clarified.

"Ah, gotcha," she replied. "And three?"

"Three, Lawrence paid a visit to the testing lab as I was rescuing Darlene from Maleck. The animals are there — Julia's 'others.' Six rabbits. Waiting for their Saturday date with the Draize test."

Miranda winced. "God. Four?"

"Aliya came with us and used Lawrence's drone to get the license plate of the car I believe drove Julia off the road. My, ah, internet researcher, Edgar Poe, is finding out what he can for me about the car's owner."

"Quite a morning," Miranda said. "And you think the car's owner is this guy Maleck, the lab director. Hmm."

"Maleck is a piece of work," I said. "He's a spooky guy, Miranda. And he's over-the-top batshit crazy about getting that cat back. And I'm just curious enough to want to know why. Anyhow, I'm hoping that once Edgar gets back to me, I'll know more about Mr. Maleck . . . or as he's called at Island Naturals, Dr. Maleck."

Miranda snorted. "Dr. Moreau might be more apropos. He seems like a character out of that horrid Jules Verne novel."

I finished my coffee and tossed the paper cup in the trash. "In the meantime, I need to know about CLAW. If Julia was working for CLAW . . . "

"Then CLAW may be your employer," Miranda said. "Ugh. No wonder you're on the horns of that dilemma."

"Yeah, and from what I've seen of them — the flier on the bulletin board, their behavior at The Bay years back — I'm not impressed. So tell me about the Sisters of Outrage."

Miranda laughed. "Well, Connie knows a lot more about them than I do. They're not high on her hit parade. She should know — she's looked into the history of just about every animal group on the island for her book. Let's ask her. Last I saw she was getting our new kittens squared away in their cages. Comfy beds, bowls of food. She may be finished. Did you leave Tris with her?"

I nodded. "Poor kid. She probably wants to adopt all of them. She about drooled when we walked in and saw the kittens. Trey is very much missed *chez* Yeats. Tris badly needs a cat fix."

"Well, I'm sure Connie is letting her cuddle every one of them," she said. "I'll go out front and see what's going on there." In a minute she came back with Connie. "Tris is settled down on the floor between the cages reading to the kittens," she reported. "Today's newspaper. I think she's deep into the real estate section. Describing to the kittens the amenities of those four-million-dollar estates in Uplands."

I chuckled.

Connie leaned against Miranda's office door frame, arms crossed. "So you want to know about CLAW," she said to me, shaking her head. "They're the kind of animal group that gives the others a bad name. They've been activists since their inception five or six years ago. Not that marching and demonstrating and making a fuss is necessarily bad — it isn't — but in my opinion, you need to choose your battles. CLAW seems to have no focus. One year it's fur coats, another year it's goosedown parkas. They like to dress up in animal costumes and demonstrate, terminated by 'die-ins.' Very dramatic. They usually get arrested for trespassing and property damage. That often results in media exposure, which they adore. It appears, however, that notoriety doesn't increase their membership, or win people to their causes. This year they've taken on the cause of cosmetics testing. Great cause but wrong approach. Dress up as rabbits, ring your eyes in red paint, lie down and 'die' outside stores selling lots of products tested on animals. Oh, and hand out fliers and brochures with those awful photos of Draize-tested animals."

"Connie calls their literature 'animal porn,'" Miranda said.

"They sound . . . provocative," I said diplomatically.

"They piss people off is what they do," Connie said. "Deliberately. They're of the mistaken belief that if you make a godawful fuss and rub people's noses in the dirty rotten truth, that will change hearts and minds. Demonstrations helped advance the cosmetics testing bill years ago, but we're way past that, thank God."

"Yeah, we are," I said, thinking of Ninth Life's patient lobbying efforts. "The bill is a little stalled in Parliament right now, but a demonstration won't goose it along. Calls to our MPs will. Who's in charge of this merry band?" I asked.

"Two women. Giselle Hadley and Liz McLaren," Connie said. "They came from Ninth Life. The Lifers were too tame for them. Patient persuasion is not CLAW's long suit. They've gathered a bunch of agitators around them — I expect we'll meet them all tonight. After all, this is the night of their 'action meeting,' right?"

"Hmmf," I said. "I want to know if CLAW is my employer. If they are, well, hell, I ought to hand over the flash drive. After all, I took their money. But dammit, I don't want to. There — that's my dilemma."

"Then don't do it," Connie said.

"I'm inclined not to," I said. "Giving CLAW the flash drive will accomplish nothing. And it may well ruin Island Naturals. Do I want to be responsible for handing over to a group of agitators information for a story that might put the company out of business here on the island? It might still be viable here even after it abandons its cruelty-free ethos. It seems to me that's for its customers to decide. I mean, the truth will come out sooner or later, but do I want to have a hand in hastening it along?"

"You heard people at the Pub Talk," I said. "They're proud of both Island Naturals and that soap company whose name I've already forgotten. Foggy Whatsit." I looked from Connie to Miranda. "Okay, poke holes in my reasoning."

Miranda shrugged. "I don't have a problem with it. In your place, I probably wouldn't give them the flash drive either. And here's another thing. Apart from the nasty story about Island Naturals' plans to get in bed with China, the flash drive has personnel information, financial information, and for all we know, the super-secret formula for ginseng body wash. And it's all stolen information."

"Indeed," I said.

"Which doesn't help you off the horns of that thing you're stuck on," Miranda said. "If I follow the trail of your ethical misgivings, it seems that you're perseverating about the fact that you took someone's money to do something. You did part of that something, but you don't really know whose money you took and what it really obligates you to do."

"Perseverating?" I bristled.

"Yeah," Miranda teased. "You ex-law types perseverate. You think things to death. We ex-law *enforcement* types are more, um, action-oriented."

"Oh, really? You mean you would've just grabbed the cat, the phone, and the flash drive, banked the money and called it a night?"

Miranda grinned. "Okay, maybe not. You could be right. Some perseveration might be in order. Maybe thirty seconds' worth."

"Yeah, touché," I said. "I suppose I'll just go to the CLAW meeting tonight and see what's what," I said.

"And if you don't like it, you can always leave," Miranda said. "Decline them as your employer. Oh, be sure to take your checkbook with you."

"To do what?" I asked.

"To refund their money," Miranda said.

"You know," Connie said. "About CLAW. I joined them. Paid my membership dues and everything. No laughing," she warned us. "Strictly for research purposes. I didn't want to omit any animal group, no matter how wacky they might be. And this group is wacky. Some of their members objected to the sensational tactics they used, and went off to form their own group." She shrugged. "These things happen. Animal welfare groups are sometimes as bad as rock bands in terms of re-creating themselves. It's sociologically fascinating. But Giselle and Liz — the original Sisters of Outrage — are firmly in charge of the remaining members. You'll not get sweet reason out of them."

"I guess when we go tonight, I'll just listen, and see what's what," I said. "I'm certainly not handing Jeoffry over to anyone, and as for the flash drive, well, I've pretty much decided I'm not inclined to hand that over either."

"So are you still on those horns?" Miranda asked.

"No so much," I said. We were all quiet for a moment, listening to the rain patter against the window of Miranda's office. I sighed.

"So, will we meet up at the church?" I asked. "The shindig is at seven-thirty. I have to get Tris home and buy dinner along the way."

"Seven-thirty at the church," Miranda said. "See you there."

CHAPTER 22

TRIS WAS UNCHARACTERISTICALLY quiet on the drive to the Chinese restaurant where I'd ordered ahead for food.

"What's up, Sprout?" I asked. "Cat got your tongue?"

She managed a dutiful smile. "It's Trey."

"Yeah," I said. "I miss him, too. But what did you think of the kittens at the Sanctuary? Do you think one of them might make a good buddy for Trey? They're too young to be adopted, but you could ask Miranda to put a hold on one for you."

Tris sighed. "It's not that they aren't nice, it's just that . . ."

I was mystified. "What, sweetie?"

"Well, maybe Trey should pick out his own kitten. When he comes home. I asked Connie about that and she said people sometimes bring their own pets in when they want a new pet. To be sure they get along. We could take Trey in."

"Huh. That's a good idea." I was seriously impressed. Which kitten might the big guy like, she must have asked herself. A little Siamese? A tabby? A tuxedo? "You're in mortal danger of being hugged," I told her. "Lucky for you I'm driving."

Tris squirmed, laughing. Being hugged was clearly a new experience for her, and I knew she was still a little ambivalent about it. Heck, I was, too. By nature, I'm pretty reserved. But Tris just brought out the hugger in me.

"Are we getting Chinese food?" Tris asked.

"We certainly are," I told her. "Moo goo gai pan. Hold the chicken and pile on the tofu, please." At that moment, my phone buzzed. I handed it to Tris. "Tell me who it is, sweetie? If it's worthwhile answering, I'll pull over."

Tris took the phone. "It's Edgar," she informed me. "Is it worthwhile answering?"

"It is," I told her. "I want to talk to him. Will you answer for me? Tell him I'll be right with him."

"Kieran says she'll be right with you," Tris said self-importantly. Whatever Edgar said to her by way of reply sent her into fits of laughter. I hoped it was age-appropriate. You never knew with Edgar. I pulled off the highway at a branch of ScotiaBank, parking the Karmann Ghia between a dark blue Prius and a greenish-gray Subaru Forester.

"Edgar," I said, taking the phone from Tris. "I'm in the car. I'll have to call you when I get home. But tell me you have something that will make me happy."

"Sweetie, I have so many things," he said. "A cornucopia of things. And I guarantee they'll make you swoon with delight. I must say even I was thrilled. I've emailed you quite the file. Your person Maleck has been such a naughty boy. Call me?"

"You betcha," I told him.

∽

Down the road at the Lucky Dragon, Tris and I were informed we'd have to wait a few minutes.

"I guess they're harvesting the tofu," I said. We took seats along the wall beside a middle-aged woman with golden gelled hair that resembled a cockatoo's crest, too much eye makeup, and a phone in one hand. Beside her was a girl about Tris's age with long brown hair and freckles, dressed in sparkly pink sneakers, lavender tights, a purple dress, and a puffy pink jacket.

Tris was sitting beside the little girl, giving the pink sneakers sidelong glances, when the kid turned to her and said, "Hi!"

"Hi!" Tris said in return, a friendly smile on her face.

The little girl looked curiously at Tris, who had just taken off her knitted cap with the earflaps and shaken out her short blond curls. Inspecting Tris thoroughly, she asked, "Are you a girl or a boy?"

"Sophie!" the woman with gelled hair exclaimed. "We don't ask questions like that!" She looked over at me in apology.

"No problem," I said.

"I'm a girl, silly," Tris said, giving Sophie a mischievous grin.

Holy crap. Was this going to be one of *those* conversations? Tris and I hadn't had to weather one yet, although I'd imagined it was coming. I decided to let Tris talk for as long as she seemed comfortable.

It was a little toasty in the restaurant, and Tris unzipped her yellow rain jacket, revealing one of her animal-themed T-shirts. This one was long-sleeved and indigo — a starry night sky with two gray cats on a fence, one looking away, the other looking back over its shoulder. ALWAYS WISH UPON A STAR, the shirt read. Sophie studied it, frowning. Then her gaze traveled to Tris's grey cargo pants and down to her skateboarder's black sneakers with white laces.

She screwed up her face and asked, "If you're a girl, why are you wearing boys' pants?"

Tris shrugged, not at all put off. "They have lots of pockets," she said. "They close with Velcro so stuff is safe in them. I have lots of stuff."

Sophie thought this over. "Like what?"

"Oh, my ID wallet, my keys, my phone, a notebook, and a pen," Tris said. "I write down things I want to look up on Google."

"You have a *phone*?" Sophie asked, giving her mother a meaningful look. Her mother, who was absorbed in her own phone, said nothing.

"Uh-huh," Tris said nonchalantly.

"Can I see it?" Sopie asked.

Tris shook her head. "Nah. It's just a flip phone to make emergency calls on. Not a smart phone. I'll have one of those when I'm older. Probably a 5G phone."

"What's your name?" Sophie asked, clearly impressed by Tris, or her pants with pockets, or her phone.

"Tris. It's short for Tristan."

"But isn't that a boy's name?" Sophie asked.

"My tutor and I looked it up," Tris said breezily. "It was the name of one of King Arthur's knights. But now it's a gender-neutral name."

A gender neutral name? Now *I* was impressed.

At the mention of gender-neutral, Sophie's mother looked over at Tris and frowned. "Is she, well, you know?" she asked me.

Well, you know. What the hell did that mean, I wondered, although I had an inkling. I decided I'd have some fun.

"We think she's two-spirited," I told her confidentially. "Such a lucky thing to be, don't you think?"

The woman gave me a spooked-horse look and returned to her phone.

In the meantime, Tris and Sophie had other things to talk about.

"Do you like cats?" Sophie asked Tris, looking at her T-shirt.

"Oh, yeah," Tris said enthusiastically. "We have a big gray cat. He's at the vet's right now, though. Do you have a cat?"

"No," Sophie said sadly. "My dad's allergic."

"Oh," Tris said. "Too bad. You know, maybe he could take allergy pills or something. Or there's a spray you can use on the cat. People don't sneeze after you use it. My friend who runs an animal sanctuary told me about it."

Sophie looked hopefully at her mother. "Mom?"

Mom was texting now and shook her head. "We'll see, dear."

Allergies, fooey, I thought. Mom would get Sophie a cat when pigs flew.

"What school do you go to?" Sophie asked Tris. "Do they let you dress like that at your school? Like boys? It's cool."

"Oak Grove School," Tris said. "And kids dress any way they want."

Fortunately our food arrived at just that moment.

"Moo goo gai pan with tofu. A double order." A handsome young Asian guy held out two paper bags of food.

"That's for us," Tris announced. "We're vegans," she told Sophie, who looked at her with eyes wide with wonder. Clearly it was too much: a vegan girl with a gender-neutral name, a tutor, her own phone, boys' pants, and a cat.

I paid, Tris took the bags of food, and we prepared to go.

"I hope you get a cat," Tris said to Sophie. "I think that allergy spray stuff is called something like Allercat. You could Google it. Bye now."

After we climbed into the car and buckled up, Tris turned to me. "What's two-spirited?"

"It's a First People's concept," I told her. "They believe that some people have two spirits — male and female — inside them."

Tris looked thoughtful. "So kids could be boys sometimes and girls other times? Grown-ups, too?"

Oh, lordy, I hoped I had this right. "Uh-huh," I said. "Depending on which spirit was speaking to them that particular day."

"Cool," Tris said.

"We could look it up on Google together," I offered. "Then we could talk about it if you like."

"Yeah, okay." Tris shrugged, her interest clearly fading. "You know what? I saw a tall white bird with a long neck standing in a pond on the way here. I want to look it up on Google. I think it might be an egret. So maybe spirits can wait 'cause I only get half an hour of Google time every day," she said, reminding me of one of our house rules.

"Whatever you like, sweetie," I told her, privately relieved.

Two-spirited? Whatever was I thinking? Did I really think Tris fit somewhere on the LGBTQA2 spectrum? Or, as common parlance would have it, that she was genderqueer? I really had no idea. Right now all I knew was that Tris was an avid birdwatcher, was contemplating veganism, didn't like pink, preferred pants with lots of pockets, liked animal-themed T-shirts, and seemed to like herself. She hadn't seemed at all put off by Sophie's question about her gender. Hmmf. Sufficient unto the day were the spirits thereof, I told myself as we turned inland onto Oak Bay Avenue and headed for home.

❧

With the Chinese food keeping warm in the oven, and Aliya and Tris at work on homework at the dining room table, I closed my office door and called Edgar.

"At last," he said, sounding a bit testy. "I was thinking you'd lost interest in the delinquent Mr. Maleck."

"Not a chance," I assured him. "I've just gotten in. I have your email right in front of me, but can you give me the Cole's Notes' version? I'm kind of pressed for time."

"Well, I suppose so," he said, reluctance in his voice. "I was rather hoping we could pore over his peccadilloes together, but if you insist."

I smiled. Edgar, Edgar. The guy wanted to preen, to have me high-five his cleverness, but I really was pressed for time. Still, I could be a little admiring. He was in fact a most ingenious database burglar.

"Thanks, Edgar," I said. "I realize what you found must have taken serious digging."

"To say the least," he replied. "All right, here we go. Full name Evan Louis Blalock, born in Gatineau, Quebec — "

"Wait . . . what?" I asked. "I thought you were researching a guy named Maleck?"

"Tsk, tsk," Edgar said, "all will be revealed. As you'll discover, Maleck is an invention. So bear with me. Evan Blalock created an aka — Yvon Denis Maleck — same birth date and birthplace — to keep two steps ahead of the law. Confusion to his enemies and all that."

"Ha!" I said. "So Maleck really does have something to hide. I was hoping for that. Any idea why Blalock needed an a.k.a? Why he became Maleck?"

Edgar giggled. "Sweetie, he's in trouble no one ever wants."

"Edgar, don't tease me. What trouble?"

"All right, all right. Revenue Canada trouble. It seems that Mr. Blalock is just a smidge in arrears on his taxes."

"And how long is a smidge?"

"Three years," Edgar said. "And there is a certain Angus McLachlan in the Ottawa office of investigations for Revenue Canada who has been working on the Evan Blalock case, and would love, I'm sure, to know about Evan's a.k.a. and his whereabouts." Edgar cleared his throat. "I do have that, I might add. His whereabouts. Or rather Mr. Maleck's whereabouts. A north Victoria address, a landline number, and a cell phone number. Also," he chortled, "an email address and his Twitter account."

"I'm seriously impressed, Edgar," I said. "But do I sense there's more?"

"Oh, yes. It seems that Blalock has a mountain of credit card debt that he's been ignoring. But that hardly seems to matter because in his new incarnation as Maleck, he now has several freshly-minted cards, which he's been using to finance his flight across Canada and the establishment of his new life here. Needless to say, several credit card companies are pursuing him."

I gave a soft whistle, impressed by Maleck's chutzpah.

"And there's even more," he said. "I saved the best for last. It's ugly, though, sweetie. It seems that in Quebec, Evan Blalock worked in several labs, testing household products and cosmetics on animals. At the last one, in Montreal, he was the lab director. That was the position that proved to be his undoing."

"Really?" I asked, my pulse accelerating.

"Really," Edgar said. "Sadly, he mistreated a lab animal. Deliberately, it seems, from the court proceedings. It had to be euthanized. One of his assistants turned him in. He was arrested, charged with felony animal cruelty, stood trial, and went to prison. It's complicated sweetie, but I have the trial transcript. I was able to get it from CanLaw database. You'll want to read it. The long and short of it was, though, that the judgment prohibited him from working with, owning, or having any future contact with animals. Any animals. It effectively brought Mr. Blalock's career to an end."

"But it didn't, did it?" I said in exasperation. "End his career. He was released from prison, reneged on all his obligations, reinvented himself as Yvon Maleck, and fled the east for a job in British Columbia."

"It seems so, sweetie."

"Shit," I said, appalled. "How in hell did Yvon Maleck end up at Island Naturals as director of *their* new lab? Didn't their HR department do a background check? It should have turned up his felony. I don't freaking believe it!"

"How?" Edgar said. "Easy. Forged documents. A doctored resume. A lazy HR department. A lab too eager to hire someone with Blalock's, oops, Maleck's credentials. It seems that some wool-pulling went on. However, there's a bright spot in all this, if you want to call it that."

"Surprise me," I said, disgusted.

"He served two and a half years of his four-year sentence, but was released thanks to some legal shenanigans. I don't quite understand them, but you will. Anyhow, the conditions of his parole were quite clear: any contact with animals, and he would go back to Quebec and finish serving out his term. You should read the judgment — it's a doozie."

"Thank God," I said. "I could kiss you Edgar. Your worth is far above rubies, as the saying goes."

"Sweetie, *puh-leese*," he said. "I'm blushing. I think that saying is from Proverbs and pertains to worthy women. But I'm flattered nonetheless. I'll hold that thought and your Visa card number equally close to my heart. And do call me if you need anything else."

I ended the call and sat back, thinking. So I had what I wanted. The explanation for why Maleck was so desperate to get his hands on Jeoffry and the video. He couldn't take a chance on anyone finding out what he'd done in the testing lab that night. If they did, he'd go back to Quebec and prison. That meant he had to make both Jeoffry and the video disappear.

And as for Julia? What was he thinking that night? That he could chase her, run her off the road, snatch the cat and the video, and then what? Intimidate her into saying nothing? Maybe. After all, once he had the cat and the video, Julia would have no proof. But could he take a chance that she would say nothing? Any accusations she made would be sure to stir up his past, his previous peccadilloes, as Edgar called them, and they would inevitably rise to the top of the septic tank. No, Julia had to be silenced. And once she was, and he discovered that the cat was not in her car, Jeoffry had to be found. What a mess. But it was a mess of Maleck's own making. All caused by the fact that he couldn't keep his hands off Jeoffry.

I put my feet up on my desk and sat back, closing my eyes. Mac would have a field day with all this. I should have felt exhilarated. Instead, I felt depressed. This was déjà vu. This had too many echoes of the case that had driven me from the law several years ago, the Owen Mallory case. And here was Yvon Maleck/Evan Blalock — another grinning animal-torturer who managed to evade full punishment for his crime but couldn't resist re-offending.

Frustrated, I ran my hands through my hair. What in hell good was the new maximum penalty for felony animal cruelty — five years — if the law allowed the guilty to slip through the bars after serving a fraction of their sentence? I was glad I was out of the whole flawed system.

But what about me? Would I never be free of animal torturers? Maybe not. Maybe in my line of work I'd keep tripping over them. So maybe I needed to understand them better. Forewarned is forearmed, as the wags say. But who to consult? A moral philosopher, a priest, a psychologist, a cop, a neuroscientist? I snorted.

Sometimes I thought that animal torturers shared with drug addicts the dopamine hit they both craved. Heroin, opiate, or fentanyl addicts got it from their street drug; animal torturers from the rush cruelty gave them. It was something to consider, I thought, when I had the leisure to contemplate such things.

In any event, the law might be wiser than I appreciated, as in several cases I recalled, the judgments against animal torturers involved keeping the felons, upon their release, away from anything that would remind them of their craving. No puppies or kittens, no dogs or cats, no "owning, having custody of, or residing on the same premises as an animal or bird." I wondered how that was working out for other released felons — clearly it hadn't worked out for Maleck. He was drawn to animals like a magnet draws iron filings.

And what about Maleck anyhow? What had come over him with Jeoffry? The cat wasn't one of his products-testing subjects. He was simply a small creature Maleck had taken a dislike to. Was the urge to torture so overwhelming that he'd risk someone discovering him at his malign obsession, as Julia had? Was he held in thrall by his compulsion to . . . do what? I didn't have a verb for it. I truly didn't get it.

Abruptly I made a decision. I was getting the rabbits the hell out of Island Naturals ASAP. Julia had bought the rabbits' lives, as well as Jeoffry's, with her own. I owed this to her.

Maleck/Blalock was a murderer. That was clear enough to me. The murder of Julia Stevens and the torture of Jeoffry seemed to trump his Quebec parole violation, but those were jurisdictional problems, and they were certainly not mine. What the law did or didn't do to him was not my business. I'd subtracted myself from that process some time ago. So I needed to take everything I knew to Mac, show him Julia's video, share Edgar's email with him, tell him how I believed this all fit together . . . and let him take matters from there. Let the law deal with Maleck/Blalock. My job? To remove the rabbits from Island Naturals. That was what I'd been paid to do. But by whom? CLAW? I certainly hoped not. But perhaps I was about to find out.

CHAPTER 23

MIRANDA, CONNIE, AND I heard the shouting as we walked down the hallway leading to the church's basement community meeting room.

"We don't know what happened to your girlfriend!" a voice from inside the meeting room yelled. The double doors just ahead of us burst open and out stormed a tall, skinny woman with bushy dark brown hair, dressed in a baggy denim shirt and jeans. Ahead of her she was pushing small, red-haired woman in a black hoodie, moving her on when she resisted. With a start, I realized the readhead was the same young woman who had whacked me with her backpack in the health food store. Well, this was interesting.

"Go the hell away!" the denim-clad woman shouted, scowling fiercely, giving the redhead a few more shoves. She noticed us and, clearly frustrated, said, "Will someone take this brat home and put her to bed? We have a meeting to run."

"Giselle," Connie said in a friendly tone. "What's going on?"

I was surprised that Connie knew the redhead's assailant, but I recalled her saying that she'd joined CLAW. This must be Giselle Hadley, one of CLAW's co-founders. How encouraging. I could hardly restrain myself from writing a check for membership.

"Oh," Giselle replied, recognizing Connie, "c'mon in, Connie. We're just about to start the meeting."

The redhead turned around to say something to Giselle, and Giselle pushed her again, toward us. "Not you, Ro. Just go the hell away. I'm sorry your girlfriend had a traffic accident, but we don't know anything about that."

"You must know!" the redhead said. "She was working for you! At Island Naturals. In some office there. Trying to get stuff from the computer that *you* wanted. And dammit, what about the cat she called me about? I don't believe she didn't call you — she was frantic on Monday night! "

Giselle made an exasperated sound and shook her head. "You're crazy. We don't know anything about a cat!"

"Dammit, why won't you *talk to me?*" The red-haired kid yelled, raising hands balled into fists.

"Oh, brother." Miranda took two steps forward, putting her arms around the kid, immobilizing her and lifting her off the ground.

"Put me down!" she shrieked.

"Shhh," Miranda said. "This is a church, after all."

Connie stepped past us, skirting Miranda and the struggling kid. "Catch you later," she said quietly. Miranda nodded as Connie and Giselle went into the meeting room, closing the door behind them.

"Let's go into the ladies' room," Miranda said to the kid. "If I put you down will you stop being a butthead?"

The kid yelled something incoherent, then collapsed, all fight seemingly drained from her. We walked back down the hall toward the stairs, and I held the ladies' room door open as Miranda stepped through it, the red-haired kid dangling limply in her arms, sobbing.

"Okay, okay," Miranda said, sitting her down on the counter between two sinks. She released her and stepped away. I wetted a bunch of paper towels and gave them to the kid. "Wash your face," Miranda said kindly. "It'll make you feel better. It always makes me feel better when I've been crying."

The kid wiped her face, sniffling, and I handed her a wad of toilet paper. "Blow," I suggested. She did. Then she really looked at me and I could see rage spark in her green eyes.

"You," she said ominously. "From the health food store. Kieran Yeats. The investigator. CLAW talked about you at the meeting last month. About hiring you to get the information they needed on Island Naturals. People seemed to know you."

"They might have known *about me*," I said. "But no one from CLAW has ever contacted me to do anything."

"Yeah, they didn't have to," she said bitterly. "Julia just bloody volunteered. But what did — "

"Shhh," Miranda said again. "We'll get this all sorted out. Is that your name? Ro?" she asked. "I'm Miranda."

The kid nodded. "Yeah. Rowan. Rowan Finnerman."

Ro looked down at the floor, miserable. She was calmer, although she probably wanted to punch me, too. Well, maybe she was worn out. Rage does that to you. Ditto weeping.

"Ro, I have an idea," I said. "Let's go down the street to the café on the corner. They've got a good wine cellar. They serve pretty okay food, too. I don't know about you, but I could use a drink. Let's talk. But no more fisticuffs, okay?"

Ro sniffled. "What the hell," she agreed despondently. Then, "Oh, crap, I can't go to the café. I don't have any money. Julia cleaned out our bank account. I don't know why."

Oh, brother. I thought I knew why. Thinking guiltily of the five hundreds now reposing in my copy of "Bartlett's Familiar Quotations", among my reference books, I winced. Now I knew: the money had not come from CLAW. It had come from Julia Stevens's and Ro's bank account. Julia was my employer.

"No problem," I told Ro. "It's on me."

ఈ౨

At the café, the three of us took a high-backed booth in a dark, private corner, behind a flourishing ficus tree. Indeed, the place sported a veritable garden of ficus trees, as well as ferns and some pendulous green plants in hanging baskets that I didn't recognize. Botany was not my long suit, but it was certainly pleasant to see such a display of greenery, given that Victoria was beginning its annual slide into the slough of despond called winter.

The café was about half-full, a pleasant buzz of dinnertime conversation in the air. Miranda and Ro took seats across from me in the booth. When our server appeared, Ro ordered a bottle of Labatt's Blue and a plate of poutine — that astonishingly popular dish of French fries, cheese curds and gravy. Ugh. Poutine has risen, improbably, from good old-fashioned *Quebecois* comfort food to the status of Canada's national fare. Both Miranda and I looked askance at the food when it arrived, she ordering a Bushmill's and I a Jameson's.

Ro swigged her beer, swallowing about half the bottle before her face crumpled and she dissolved into tears again. "It's all my fault," she said. "If I'd gone to help with the damned cat, Julia might be alive. But no, I was mad at her, so I didn't go." She took a few more gulps of beer. "She said she was going to text you next, Kieran. I guess she remembered your name from the meeting. Did she?"

"Yeah," I said.

"Did you go help her?"

"I did."

"So you saw her? Monday night?" Ro asked hopefully. " Do you know what happened? How she got into that accident?"

I hesitated, wondering just how much I should tell her. "Not really, Ro. I met her, took the cat, and she drove off." That seemed safe . . . and truthful. The rest of it? Maybe later. Maybe not at all. I'd have to see how things went. Miranda met my eyes and nodded slightly as if in agreement with me.

"If only . . ." Ro began, then fell silent. She finished her beer and motioned our server over for another. The poutine had been, apparently, forgotten. Deservedly, I thought, shuddering.

"Ro, why were you mad at Julia?" I asked.

"We had a fight," she said, shamefacedly. "I got pissed with her and moved out of the place we were sharing. After that first meeting, all Julia talked about was CLAW, CLAW, CLAW. Endlessly. The group really impressed her. But we're students. We're supposed to be going to lectures, writing papers. Not getting caught up in animal activism. Yeah, I like animals, and I'm sorry for the raw deal they've gotten from society, but I sure wouldn't —"

"March? Demonstrate? Throw red paint on fur coats?" I guessed.

"Yeah. Those kinds of things. Extreme things. All that seemed to resonate with Julia."

"How did you two happen to be at the CLAW meeting?"

"We saw a flier at school," Ro said. "That first meeting, a couple of months ago, that was our introduction to CLAW. Julia couldn't wait for the next meeting, the one where they talked about Island Naturals and getting some information they needed to prove they were going back to testing on animals. Then planning some demonstration."

Ro swigged the last of her beer and looked around again for our server, motioning him over. I was a little concerned about her. This was beer number three.

"It was so stupid . . . what Julia came home and told me," she said. "I didn't go to that meeting — I had a paper to write. But she was thrilled that they had a job for her. They assigned her a code name: Shrew. Get it? Mole? Shrew? Like this was some bloody World War Two undercover assignment. Julia loved it, though."

The server came by and Ro started in on her fresh beer. "She just got . . . lost in all that stuff. When I heard about the code name and the job she was supposed to do at Island Naturals, I hit the roof. We had a huge fight. I yelled at her, told her we both had scholarships to protect. We needed to be concentrating on getting As, not skipping class and ignoring essay deadlines. I didn't want to hear any more about CLAW, so I moved out. Now I'm living in some shithole room over a friend's garage." She put her head in her hands.

"I'm such an idiot. We'd been together since the beginning of our freshman year. We were partners. We shared everything. I just didn't get where she was going." She broke off, shredding her beer bottle label. "It was like CLAW had mesmerized her."

"Ro, people change," I said, wanting to tell her something, anything to make this change in Julia understandable. "They discover passions."

Especially young people, But I didn't know how to tell Ro this unpleasant truth without sounding patronizing. Or, God forbid, old. Paths diverged, people parted, hearts were broken.

Ro motioned the server over for another beer.

"Julia became . . . another person," Ro said. "I didn't understand it, but I should have tried harder. I got scared. For myself. For us. Nothing I said mattered. Julia couldn't hear me. She was leaving me behind."

She began to cry again. "I couldn't stand what was happening. I just wanted to run away from it. She needed my help, she called me for help. But I didn't want any part of what CLAW had put her up to. And now she's dead. For something stupid."

Ro's weeping has turned noisy again, and a couple at a nearby table looked at us curiously. Miranda put her arm around her, and Ro, drunk now, put her head on Miranda's shoulder.

"Ro, I want you to hear something," I said. "You might not remember all of it tomorrow, but I'm going to tell you anyhow. Julia didn't die for something stupid. She died for something she believed in. Not something she was doing for CLAW. Something separate. Something important to her. She stepped in, in a desperate, horrible, torturous situation. She made a difference. She saved a life."

Ro looked up at me.

I went on. "How many of us gets to do that? This is who Julia was. She may not even have known this about herself — about her own caring and courage — until she went to Island Naturals. When she rescued the cat, she wasn't CLAW's creature. She was her own person. This was her decision. This was a gift she gave the cat — his life."

Ro looked at me blearily. "But *you* went to help her with the cat. I didn't."

Oh, brother. Was she even hearing me? She was stuck on guilt, stuck on herself. Well, it was late and she was clearly drunk. Maybe I'd done enough talking for tonight.

"I think I'm going to be sick," Ro said. Then, fortunately, she passed out on Miranda's shoulder.

"Giselle had a point," Miranda said. "I think we better put Ro to bed. I have no idea where that friend's shithole room over the garage is located, but your place is just around the corner. Would that be okay?"

"Sure," I said. "You need help?"

Mirada raised her eyebrows. Ro was maybe five feet tall. Possibly she weighed in at ninety pounds. Miranda was easily five ten. "I think I've got this," she said, winking.

"I thought you did," I told her. "I'll get my car."

❧

Aliya met us at the front door. I'd called and asked her to make up the living room couch for an overnight guest. Good lord, was my home becoming a refuge for down-and-out wandering souls? A latter-day version of Emily Carr's "The House Of All Sorts?" Hmm. Her eyes widened as she saw Miranda and Ro, Miranda supporting Ro who staggered along beside her, sobbing fitfully.

"This is Ro," I told Aliya. "She's a U Vic student who has had a bit too much to drink. She's going to crash here. Thanks for making up the couch."

"No problem." She watched Miranda lower Ro to the couch. "What should we do for her?"

I remembered back to my own unwise nights of undergraduate drinking. "I don't think much is required. Let's get her hoodie and shoes off, then cover her up and let her sleep it off."

Ro was horizontal now, snoring softly, and I peeled off her bulky hoodie while Aliya unlaced her sneakers and put them on the floor. She'd be much more comfortable without her sweatshirt and shoes. Underneath her hoodie she had on a gray U Vic T-shirt. It looked a little skimpy and, worried that she might be chilly, I pulled the blankets up around her shoulders. She moaned and rolled over, making a burrito of herself in the covers.

"Oh," Aliya said. "I started coffee."

"You did?" I asked.

"Yes," a voice called from the kitchen. "I asked her to. I think we'll need it."

I turned. It was Connie. Funny, I hadn't noticed her car in the driveway, but it seemed my driveway had recently become a parking lot. Cars belonging to me, Aliya, and Helen, jockeyed daily for space.

"You're back pretty early," I said glancing at my watch. Just after nine. Somehow I thought they'd be plotting all night. "Did the CLAW meeting not go well?"

"Those people," she said, shaking her head. "They seem determined to get themselves arrested. Let's sit. I'll tell you all about it."

CHAPTER 24

IN THE KITCHEN, Aliya and I got mugs, a container of powdered ersatz cream, sugar, and spoons ready. The coffeemaker burbled happily on the counter and I thought, *This is becoming a familiar scene. Nocturnal Plotting With Caffeine: Act Two.*

"Kieran," Aliya said, clearly hesitant, "I wanted to ask you, well, can I talk to you guys? I have an idea that I've been thinking about. I was looking again at the files on the flash drive and something occurred to me. It's crazy and off-the- wall but . . ." She shrugged.

"Sure," I said, mystified. "I'm always open to crazy and off-the-wall. Let's see what Connie has to say first, though."

Aliya, Connie, and Miranda got coffee and took seats at the dining room table. The slumbering Ro was just around the corner in the living room on the couch, and I checked on her, satisfied myself that her snores meant she was okay, then poured coffee for myself and joined the others.

"They're hopeless!" Connie sputtered. "This issue — Island Naturals' adopting animal testing — has become the latest outrage for them. They've caught wind of it somehow and won't let it go. I guess because the company is right here on our doorstep. But I thought they were at the information-gathering stage. Getting Julia hired at Island Naturals was a smart move. I know, I know," she said, raising her hands as if to ward off imaginary blows. "It turned out horribly because Julia intervened to save the cat. But information-gathering is usually good."

Connie took a sip of coffee and continued.

"I hoped they might go down the path that Henry Spira had blazed to bring about change in the animal exploitation world. Peter Singer even wrote a paper about it." She shook her head. "I handed out copies of his paper at one of CLAW's meetings. I guess the points that Singer made such as trying to understand public thinking, setting a number of goals that are achievable, and so on were too tame for them. I should have known. They're ineducable."

"I'm sorry, Connie," Miranda said sadly. "I know you've tried with them. They really should have listened to you. How many other groups have the advantage of learning from someone who actually worked with the man who helped bring Revlon to its knees? But I don't think they'll ever change. From what you've told me, they really are the Sisters of Outrage. They'll not suddenly become reasonable. You can give them all the literature you like, but they'll ignore it. They scored a great PR and media coup when they threw red paint around at The Bay. They seem to want to repeat that." She frowned. "Did they give you any indication of what their plans are for Island Naturals?"

"Nothing specific. Yet," Connie said. "Oh, they talked about various things but couldn't decide. Something dramatic, though. Something that will focus the public's attention on Island Naturals and its backsliding into the hell of the animal testing world." She laughed bitterly. "Or on themselves as champions of animals and whistle-blowers."

"That's not going to help the larger issue, though, is it?" I said. "You'd think they'd use their energies better. They could urge their members to make phone calls or send emails to their MPs in support of the cosmetics bill. And God knows there are plenty of other causes for them to pursue: rodeos, factory farming, pound seizure." I snorted. "But Island Naturals is right here. An oh-so-tempting target."

"I agree with Kieran," Miranda said. "Making a fuss will achieve exactly nothing."

"It was getting tedious," Connie said wearily. "Lots of silly ideas. I got tired of listening. So I left the meeting before they'd decided anything specific. I can't tell you what they're planning. But I can tell you when."

"Oh yeah?" I asked. "When?"

"Saturday night. When no one's around. Apparently they need privacy for whatever shenanigans they have in mind. Julia found out that there are no cameras, no security people. The place makes *shampoo* for heaven's sake! So they'll have a clear field."

Hmmf, I thought. Evidently CLAW didn't know the rabbits were due for their Draize date on Saturday. Fine. I hadn't had time to plan anything in detail, but I'd been thinking that I'd go liberate the rabbits late Friday night. Once all the employees were gone. At least I wouldn't get mixed up with the CLAWs and whatever they intended. I had a few things to arrange first: transportation, cages, food and bedding, places to stash the stolen animals.

"So it looks as though we have to go get the rabbits on Friday night, right?" Miranda said.

"Who's this 'we', girlfriend?" I asked, although privately I was relieved by her use of 'we.'

"Oh, c'mon," she said. "Did you think I'd let you go alone? Connie's going to stay behind at The Sanctuary with her phone on in case we run into trouble."

"Miranda," I said, honestly, "I'm flattered that you want to come along, but, well, it might get dicey."

"Yeah? How much dicier could it be than the rescue we pulled off last year?"

"Well . . ." I equivocated. "You better be sure about how badly you want to be involved. We didn't have to break too many laws when we rounded up Con, Peter, and Stephanie, and liberated the animals. This time it'll be different." I ticked off the likely crimes on my fingers. "Breaking and entering, theft, possibly destruction of private property, definitely trespassing."

"Yeah, I've thought about all that," Miranda said. "My conscience is okay with it. And you do need help. Specifically, a van. Are you going to stash the cagefuls of rabbits in the back of your Karmann Ghia? And for that matter, do you even have any cages? We have a bunch at the Sanctuary."

"I must admit, my planning has been . . . sketchy. In fact, I haven't given it more than five minutes' thought." I hesitated, but only for a few moments. Hell, of course I needed help.

"I'd be happy to have you along. And your cages. And the van. But," I said, "I have to tell you, I'm worried about the van. Can you disguise it somehow? After all, it has The Sanctuary's name on it. The last thing we want is for some night-owl workaholic to remember they saw it going into the parking lot. I don't want the pigeons to come back to roost on you. Figuratively speaking," I said. "Oh hell, you know what I mean."

"I do," she said. "We have an old, beat-up van that we use for dirty jobs. I'm sure it has mud on its license plates. Or will have." She wiggled her eyebrows. "We'll use that. It'll be going incognito."

I looked at her and laughed. "Why, Miz Blake, you're going to enjoy this, aren't you?"

"You bet, Miz Yeats," she said. "Sometimes being on the other side of the law, the cop side, was just too frustrating. Since I met you, I've discovered the simplicity of direct action. Sticking a thumb in the bad guys' eyes, as you would say. If you and I had scratched our heads and thought twice out there in the forest last year, those missing pets would be in research labs now. And the thieves would have gotten away scot free."

"I take your point," I said. "I'm grateful for your help."

Aliya cleared her throat and I suddenly remembered she had something she wanted to talk to us about.

"I'm sorry," I said to her. "You had something you wanted to say."

"Yeah, I do," she said, clearly uncomfortable with three sets of eyes on her. "It's probably crazy . . ."

"Crazy is sometimes good," I said. "Go ahead."

"Well, I was wondering, what would it take to undo all this? To make all this fuss go away — the animal testing at Island Naturals."

"Do you mean returning the company to its former cruelty-free status?" I asked.

"Yeah."

"A time machine!" Connie said, laughing.

"That would be nice," I said. "But I think I see where you're going. We can't pretend the vote and the subsequent plans never happened, but what would it take, in practical terms, to undo the decision? Isn't that what you're asking?"

Aliya nodded.

"Miranda?" I asked. "You have a board of directors. Is it anything like Island Naturals' board? How do you undo a vote?"

Miranda looked thoughtful. "It's not hard. You vote again. It happens all the time. New information comes to the fore. Minds change. You go in a new direction. It's happened to us occasionally. We've had re-votes on several important issues: on declawing, on euthanasia, on what constitutes no-kill."

"So how is that done? The re-vote?"

"Just like any regular vote," she said. "There's a meeting, usually a special meeting. The president calls the board together. The issue is discussed, someone calls for a vote, and people vote."

"I may be a little naïve," I said, "but is this what you're saying? That if enough new information were to come to the fore as you put it, that might change people's minds? And if the Island Naturals' board were to vote again on the same issue, testing on animals, there might be a different outcome?"

"That's what I'm saying," Miranda said. "At least that's how it would happen with The Sanctuary board. True, we're a nonprofit organization, but I suspect Island Naturals is not so different. They're privately held, so there's no shareholder input, or accountability. But there's a problem," she said, looking at Aliya apologetically.

"A problem?" Aliya echoed.

"Well, two problems," Miranda said. "Remember from the board minutes we looked at, Portia was voted off. Philip is president now. I can't see him calling for a new vote. He was the one pushing this. And as I recall, the vote was eight in favor of animal testing and five against. So while in theory what you suggest is possible, Aliya, I can't see how it would succeed in practical terms." She looked up thoughtfully at the ceiling. "Unless . . ."

"Unless . . ." Aliya said eagerly.

"Unless one of the other officers called the board meeting, Portia was voted back in as president, and the eight people who voted for animal testing changed their votes. Or some of the eight anyhow. Enough to form a majority. But why would they? Board members don't get paid, of course, but Philip must have convinced them that this new direction would be good for the company. Financially, that is," she said. "I guess they checked their ethics at the door before that board meeting."

"Yeah," Aliya said sadly. "I see."

"Portia would have to lobby like hell to re-take the company and change minds," Miranda said. "I don't know if she's even interested in doing that. Her feelings might be massively hurt at having been voted off the board of the company her father founded. Hell, she was ganged up on. Philip clearly engineered this to take place at a meeting when she wasn't even in attendance. If it were me, I'd be beyond irked."

"I get it," Aliya said. "It's kind of unlikely. Just thought I'd ask."

"Sounds like you know Portia pretty well," I said to Miranda.

She shrugged. "Pretty well? Yeah, I'd say so. We go back quite a few years."

"Do you know that she *isn't* interested in trying to regain her seat on the board? And getting re-elected president?" I asked.

"No," Miranda said. "I haven't talked to her recently."

"Maybe we could go and chat a bit," I suggested innocently. "After all, I have an expensive coat that should be returned to her."

After Aliya went downstairs to bed, Connie gathered up our mugs and put the dishwasher while Miranda and I sat in the dining room. Ro was still snoring on the couch.

"I know what you're up to," Miranda said.

"You do?" I said, feigning innocence.

"Yeah. You're so transparent. You're trying to get out in front of this impending disaster. You're trying to save hundreds of animals from perishing in Island Naturals' newly decked-out cosmetics testing lab. You want to short-circuit all that animal misery. Have it not happen. Right?"

"Right," I agreed. "An ounce of prevention and all that."

"Kieran, what if Portia isn't interested in putting Humpty Dumpty back together again? What if she just doesn't have the stomach for a board fight. They can get awfully ugly."

"Well, then she isn't and doesn't," I said. "But I'd like to find out."

Miranda looked at me levelly, concern in her blue eyes. "This isn't your fight, Kieran. Getting the rabbits out of the testing lab, that's your fight. That's what you were hired to do. And I'm happy to help you with that. What they'll go through if we don't remove them — it makes me ill. But the rest of it?" She threw her hands in the air. "It's too big. And it's not our fight."

"No?" I said. "To coin a phrase: 'If not us, who? If not now, when?'"

"Omigod, you're quoting Ronald Reagan to me? Or is it Yoda? I never know with you," she said.

"Actually it was Rabbi Hillel," I told her. "But I'm not suggesting we do anything other than talk to Portia. After all, she'll have to be the one to carry the fight to the board, right?"

She looked at me suspiciously. "We'll just talk. Right?"

"Right."

"Okay, I'll go to your office and call her," Miranda said. "It's pretty late, but she's a night person. Or was. I'll see if we can deliver the coat tomorrow. And talk."

"Philistine," I told her as she dug her phone out of a pocket and walked through the dining room toward my office.

"I heard that," she said. "And I still say it's Yoda. Really, Kieran, we can't save them all."

"Yeah, I know," I muttered under my breath. "But we can try."

⁓

Just before midnight, my phone buzzed. Sleepy, I snapped on the light and picked it up. I mentally located the people I loved, about whom I hoped this was not bad news: Zee reading in her armchair with a cup of Dragonwell tea and Willard Gaylin; Trey snuggling with his new bestie, Jeoffry; Connie and Miranda drinking cocoa with kittens; Aliya creating fearsome green dragons for a fantasy book cover; Tris wrapped in her Lion King comforter, dreaming of tall white birds; Lawrence and Max, snoozing in the same bed (Lawrence had confessed this to me). That left . . . who? Jen, of course, and looking at the phone I saw it was indeed Jen.

"What's up?" I asked. "Besides you?"

"Kieran!" she wailed. "Mary Oliver died!"

"Oh, honey," I said. "That was a while ago."

"But I didn't *know* it, Kieran! I was planning to write an essay on her, and I just read it in Wikipedia."

"I'm sorry it was such a shock," I said. "You must be so sad."

Jen said nothing, only sniffled.

"She had a good, long life," I said, trying to make this hurt less. "She worked at something she loved, and people loved her for it."

"The poem you texted me last year when we saw the geese," Jen said. "The one called 'Praying.'"

"Uh-huh," I said.

"Well, I really liked it," Jen said. "So I looked up more of her poems online. I printed out the ones I liked best. Like 'Wild Geese'. Then tonight I went to Wikipedia for more information on her and found out that she *died*." More sniffling. "Kieran, it feels, well, spooky. I can't explain it. Like someone I knew just stopped speaking in the middle of a sentence."

"Tell me your favorite poem," I said.

"That's easy. I like 'Wild Geese' but I like 'The Summer Day' too. The one about the grasshopper."

I wondered which part of the poem spoke to Jen. I hoped it wasn't the line third from the end, which was perhaps the most heartbreaking single line in poetry. Surely not.

"What lines did you like best?" I asked her.

"The lines at the end," she said, "I might not remember them right. But it was a question, something about what we plan to do with our life — I think she called it precious. Maybe wild and precious." Jen was quiet for a minute, then continued.

"When I read those lines," she said, "it was as though she was speaking right to me, like she was in my room with me. It felt so *real*, like she was telling me to think hard about my future. I have thought about it, but I still don't know, Kieran."

I laughed gently. She was only thirteen. "It's okay not to know, Jen. That's what being young is for — finding out."

"Are you sure?"

"I'm sure."

I waited for a minute, then asked, "How are you doing? Still sad?"

"A little. Which poem of hers do you like best, Kieran?"

"Hmm. I think 'Wild Geese.' Say, do you want to read it together?"

"Okay. That would be cool. I've got it right here."

"Let me get it on my iPad. I have to Google it. Okay, got it. Do you want to read, or shall I?" I asked Jen.

"You read, okay? I might cry."

So I read, Jen listened, and we both flew with Mary Oliver's geese.

"Feel better now?" I asked her when we were through.

"Uh-huh," she said. "I'll maybe read a few more poems, then go to sleep. Thanks, Kieran."

I turned off my phone and lay there, thinking of Jen and Mary Oliver and grasshoppers and wild geese and the third to the last line of 'The Summer Day,' the line I hoped Jen had not remembered, about everything dying at last and too soon.

That was too hard a thought for a thirteen-year-old. Hell, it was too hard a thought for an about-to-be-forty-year-old. Sleepy, I turned off my light, and all at once I was somewhere else.

A slender woman stood in a starless night on a bare hilltop. Old in years, she stood nevertheless straight and tall, her eyes keen, her heart still alive to beauty. She was tired, though, so tired. Overhead, nine geese flew in a ragged V against a huge white moon. They angled down toward her, and now they were so close she heard the rasp of their wingbeats. She heard their cries: "Free! Free! Free!" and realized suddenly they had come for her, to offer her a place in their formation, a place in their song, which was a song of belonging, a song of salvation.

She opened her arms and rose to meet them.

FRIDAY

CHAPTER 25

WHAT WAS THAT horrifying noise? I opened one eye, saw the time on my clock radio read 6:30, realized that the bee buzzing in F sharp was my alarm, and whacked it. Why the hell did I need to be awake at six-thirty? Sluggishly the gears of my brain meshed and I remembered: today was Friday. Fridays I had breakfast with Helen, my upstairs tenant. She didn't teach on Fridays, which meant the morning provided a good opportunity for us to socialize and get caught up on each other's activities. Hers were numerous and always interesting, unlike mine, which were few and required editing in order to be shared. When Helen wasn't teaching, she was flying off to one of our distant provinces for a marathon, lunching with her editor in Vancouver, hiking on Saltspring Island, or attending a three-day tai chi workshop in Toronto. I felt like a sluggard by comparison. Walking to the end of the driveway for the newspaper sometimes seemed like a noteworthy event.

I wanted to ask her if she had gotten any feedback on the Pub Talk. I bet she had. Pulling on some clean sweats, I found my socks and sneakers, splashed water on my face, brushed my teeth, ran a comb through my hair, and then I was ready. There was a text on my phone from Miranda that Portia would meet us that afternoon. Good, I thought. The house was quiet — neither Tris nor Aliya was up and about and I tiptoed to the door leading to the stairs and Helen's suite. I'd left a text on Aliya's phone asking her to play den mother to Ro today as the poor kid would likely be hung over from her evening of drinking and still depressed about Julia. If it were me, I'd be in a horrid funk. Most other days I would be available to commiserate and handhold, but I had a full itinerary today, to say the least, and I just couldn't fit Ro in. I hoped Aliya was okay with this.

As I announced myself at the top of the stairs, Helen called out, "Coffee's on in the kitchen!"

"Thank heavens," I said. "I'm in serious need of caffeine. Too many late nights." I took a seat in her cheery kitchen — white-painted cabinetry, buttercup yellow walls, healthy green succulents in pots here and there, two places set for breakfast on a white-painted table. Overhead, a skylight let in the early morning daylight, and somewhere Eric Satie's "Gymnopedies" played softly.

"I have fruit and yogurt," Helen announced. "Improbably, strawberries from that greenhouse operation on the mainland. Bananas from who-knows where. Oh, and scones from the Back Alley Deli. Sound okay?" She looked bright and disgustingly healthy. Today she wore a pale blue long-sleeved T-shirt that said NEWFOUNDLAND MARATHON 2010 on the front in white, and comfy-looking, faded jeans.

"Sounds wonderful," I said. "So tell me about the aftermath of the Pub Talk. My friends and I had to leave. I hope no blows were exchanged."

"Surprisingly, no," Helen said. "The group was pretty much in agreement that cosmetics testing on animals was unethical. Shannon had email addresses for people to send letters supporting the Cosmetics Bill to their MPs, and most folks wanted them.”

“Good,” I said. “I thought Shannon and Howard did great. They were very poised. And very well-informed.”

I ate a little yogurt and wondered if I should tell Helen the dirty rotten truth about Island Naturals. Fooey. No need to hasten to bring bad news. It was better that she find out herself, if and when Island Naturals backslid into the morass of companies that blinded and killed rabbits. But I did want to get her take on Maleck. After all, she *was* a psychologist interested in our sometimes ambivalent relationship with animals.

“I’m involved in a case,” I began, intending to spare her as many of the awful details as I could. “There’s a guy, well he’s a felon and ostensibly the director of a cosmetics testing lab, but in reality he’s an animal torturer . . . oh, crap.” I ended up telling her the whole nasty story: my midnight rendezvous with Julia, the rescue of Jeoffry, the so-called one-car accident, my meeting with Maleck, the dirt Edgar had dug up, and my planned trip to the testing lab.

“Dammit,” I said, “I hadn’t meant to do a podcast about this, just give you some background. Then in a clever appeal to your professional curiosity, I intended to ask if you can help me understand Yvon Maleck’s godawful behavior. This isn’t the first case of animal cruelty that I’ve dealt with, but it’s the first case in which I’ve been personally, hands-on involved. I’ll never forget opening that sack and seeing the little tabby’s eyes.”

Helen looked at me sympathetically over the rim of her coffee mug. “Animal torture . . . it is godawful, and it’s a subject that interests me professionally, too. So you certainly don’t need to apologize, Kieran. I can tell you what I’ve read.” She paused. “You do have some horribly interesting cases, don’t you?”

“I do, don’t I?” I agreed. “And I seem to keep tripping over animal cruelty. It figured in the case that drove me away from the law, and I’m smack up against it again. It’s my *bête noir*, no pun intended.” I ate a few strawberries. “I might as well admit that I’m not interested in animal cruelty as a predictor of assaultiveness. I’m happy to leave the Dark Triad, the Macdonald triad — bed-wetting, fire-starting, and animal cruelty — to law enforcement. I'm more interested in understanding what fuels little boys' desire to harm animals in the first place, what gets warped in their psyches that makes them think it's okay to microwave the family rabbit, or use kittens for target practice."

Helen murmured her assent.

I broke off, ate some slices of banana, then continued. "I think animal cruelty starts considerably earlier than the rabbit-microwaving, though, doesn't it? Doesn't it start with so-called 'common childhood cruelty' inflicted on 'unimportant' life forms — crickets, beetles, grasshoppers, toads, lizards? Then, it seems to me, the cruel behavior, if it's unchecked, just escalates to more 'important' life forms — mice, squirrels, rabbits, cats, dogs. It's as though the crickets and beetles are a rehearsal."

I frowned, then continued. "But what I really don't get is why it starts, this 'common childhood cruelty.' I was hoping you could, well, help me get it. I've begun to have strange metaphysical theories about innate evil, and stranger ones involving dopamine and addiction. I figured it might be time to consult a professional," I said, only half-joking. "Perhaps you could start your meter running."

"Can I help you get it? Hmm." Helen poured more coffee for both of us. "In spite of all my reading on the subject, I'm still not clear on the why of it. It might be one of those questions that has multiple answers."

"Ha," I said. "That reminds me of the line in *The Lord of the Rings*: 'Send not to the elves for counsel, for they shall say both no and yes.'"

Helen stirred her coffee. "I'm sorry this bedevils you, Kieran."

"Me, too," I said. "I'm tempted to just say the animal torturers are evil, but that's lazy thinking. I also don't believe the theory that they lack empathy or do what they do out of a misuse of power." I shook my head. "All those things may be true, but I think there's something else going on with them."

"So what does psychology know about this?" Helen asked. "We're getting there. By that, I mean there have been some studies done and some papers written. What have we learned? Well, we've learned that cruelty to animals is a conduct disorder that is associated with the male sex. We know that." Sensing my impatience, she smiled. "Even though you're consulting a psychologist, why do I sense you want a metaphysical answer?"

I nibbled on my scone and drank some more coffee. "Hell, I don't know. Maybe it's simpler than metaphysics. Or psychology. Maybe it's a question of biology. Maybe this indefinable, reprehensible *something* is carried on the male chromosome. Maybe it's a function of testosterone. I'm struggling here, Helen. All I can say is that the question of why men — and when they're younger, boys — harm animals has consumed a great deal of my thinking since I took this case. I have a pretty good undergrad degree in philosophy but I have to say that it didn't prepare me to think about this issue." I laughed. "I had no idea I would even *want* to think about this issue. So maybe let's get back to psychology and abandon biology and metaphysics. Tell me what you've read that might help me."

"What might help you. Hmm. Okay. It's pretty well established that most animal torturers were themselves tortured. By that I mean that they were beaten or severely punished as children. Close to seventy percent of them. Another factor in the development of an animal torturer is parents' tacit approval of their cruelty. One case I read described a boy who 'shot up' the family farm, went gunning for the ducks and the chickens, and received no punishment from his mother. Another case describes a boy's grandmother recounting with pleasure a boy's killing birds with a whip and with firecrackers."

I shuddered. "Jesus, Helen."

"I don't need to recount more cases," she said. "But this is how these boys grow up — they're beaten, they're humiliated, they're angry, they seize on the weakest thing around to repeat what was done to them. And they're never discouraged from bad behavior. No one tells them it's wrong to kill the chickens or the birds."

"Yeah," I said thinking. "But I want to go back to what you said about the beatings. It seems to me that plenty of kids grow up having been beaten by their parents, but don't turn into animal torturers. What happened in the lives of the kids who did? How were the beatings different?" I wondered.

Helen nodded, listening.

"And why, as adults, do former child animal torturers keep on, well, torturing," I asked. "Do they really just keep on doing it because they like it? Because it gives them a kind of pleasure they can't get anywhere else?" I thought about the German concept, *schadenfreude*. Malicious joy. Interesting that we didn't have a word in our language for this reprehensible feeling.

"In my wilder moments of speculation," I continued, "I ask myself if animal torture isn't a form of addiction, if torturers don't get a huge dopamine hit out of it. Maleck, the animal torturer I referred to earlier, was tried and convicted of felony animal abuse, sentenced to the maximum of five years' imprisonment, and ordered not to have any contact with animals after his release. So what did he do as soon as the prison door creaked open? He took his forged identity, fled across Canada to the far left-hand corner of the map, and got a job with animals. Jesus! And even before the job started, he couldn't resist torturing the warehouse cat. It's damned well incomprehensible. He's like an alcoholic who can't stay off the booze, or the opiod addict who just can't stay clean. Or am I wrong?"

"I don't know, Kieran," Helen said. "Addiction is a difficult thing to understand. It's surely not my field. But here's another way to think about this. It might answer your first question."

"My first question . . . oh yeah, about the beatings."

"Well, think about Maleck as a little boy."

"Must I?" I said.

"Okay, If that's hard for you, think about any animal abuser as a little boy."

"Okay. Better," I said.

"And let's consider the elements of the Dark Triad."

"Bed-wetting, fire-starting, animal abuse."

"Right. Law enforcement finds their predictability useful and tends to give equal weight to each of the elements. But I think they may be wrong. I think there's one that causes the other two." She took a deep breath. "I'll confess to you my off-the-wall theory, formulated one night in a bubble bath." She grinned, although I felt that underneath the grin she was deadly serious.

"I think the determining factor behind assaultiveness is animal cruelty alone. Not a combination of Macdonald's three factors. Or even sadism added onto the triad, as current thinking proposes. And I think animal cruelty is born out of humiliation and rage."

"Go on," I said.

"Think of a boy, a very young boy, maybe three or four or five. He wets the bed. God, the humiliation of it! He's so ashamed, because he's a big boy now. Or so he's told. He doesn't need diapers. And look what he's done. Look at the mess he's made! So his father beats him. More humiliation. The episode is traumatic. So, angry, shamed, and humiliated, he does what? Sets a fire?" She shook her head. "I don't think so. No, I think he turns his humiliation and rage on something close to him, something small and defenseless, something he can dominate and destroy. Maybe this becomes an awful habit, a repetition compulsion, a behavior that he falls back on every time he is beaten and humiliated."

"He repeats what was done to him," I said. "He traumatizes others. A cricket, a grasshopper, a lizard, a mouse. And then a cat." I thought about this for a few moments. "You know, I could almost feel sorry for them. The boys. The men. Almost."

"Almost," Helen agreed.

"But what about the adults who keep on torturing?" I asked. "The defendant in my last case, Owen Mallory, the guy who tortured his girlfriend's dogs to death. He was a grown man, for crap's sake. And Maleck, who just couldn't keep his hands off Jeoffry? They never seem to outgrow this awful behavior."

"I just don't know," Helen said. "Do they have some need that's fulfilled by continuing to torture animals?" She laughed a little. "Perhaps I need to take another bath. Formulate another theory."

"Well, your theory is certainly something to think about," I said finally. "It does provide a 'why' that isn't metaphysical. Or biological. But I still don't completely understand it. The bed-wetters, the beaten boys who become cricket-crushers and cat-maimers. And maybe worse."

"It *is* still a theory," she said.

"You know, maybe this is beyond my intellectual pay grade," I told her. "Maybe it's for people like you to tease out the why of it. And to let the rest of us know."

"Perhaps," she said, smiling. "In the meantime, perhaps it's for people like you to intervene, to remove the Jeoffrys from harm's way. One at a time. To toss a single starfish back into the ocean."

I raised my eyebrows, not sure what she meant.

"The anthropologist Loren Eiseley liked to describe how he once found a beach littered with starfish. He began throwing them back into the ocean until a young man came up beside him and criticized him. 'It's useless. There are too many of them. You can't make a difference,' the young man said. But Eiseley ignored him and picked up a single starfish. 'I can make a difference to this one,' he said, and threw it as far as he could out into the ocean. Perhaps you're a starfish thrower, Kieran."

"Fooey," I said, more than a little embarrassed. "I'm but a humble investigator, Dr. Mikita. Great scones, though. Good strawberries, too. Until next week?"

"Until then," she said.

CHAPTER 26

WHEN I GOT back downstairs, Ro was sitting with her elbows propped on the kitchen table, head in her hands. She was wearing her gray U Vic T-shirt and what I suspected were a pair of Aliya's pajama bottoms, a cheery pink plaid. Her hair stood up in tufts and her face was as pale as the dry-erase board in my office. In short, she looked a fright.

"How are you feeling?" I asked.

"Like crap and like a fool," she said, looking up at me. "I almost punched someone. I got drunk. I cried. I said things."

"Don't worry about the getting drunk," I told her. "We've all been there. We lived through it. As for crying and saying things, well, you've had a terrible loss. You're entitled."

"Thanks for understanding," she said, looking miserable.

"Say, is Aliya around?" I asked, worried about leaving Ro here alone. I had to shower and get on with my day — specifically a meeting with Mac. I had decided to come clean concerning what I knew about Maleck and dump the whole tangled mess in his lap. The Oak Bay Police Department could take things from here. Tax evasion, credit card fraud, felony animal cruelty, a parole violation, possibly manslaughter, possibly murder — someone would have a field day with Maleck's malfeasances.

"Aliya took your daughter to school," Ro said. "She told me to tell you she'll be back in a bit." She chuckled. "Tristan sure is a great little kid. We had a nice chat about egrets and whether trees talk to each other. She brought me toast and coffee."

I laughed. "That kid will talk your ear off. About birds and squirrels and trees and cats . . . and just about anything else if you let her."

"Kieran," Ro said abruptly, "last night. I wasn't completely blasted. I heard a lot of what you guys were talking about. About the cat and Julia. And CLAW. And the animals in the lab."

Oops, I thought. Should have stashed Ro in my office. "Uh-huh," I said.

"I thought this over," she said firmly. "And I've decided. About tonight and Island Naturals. I want to help. I want to come with you."

Somehow I wasn't too surprised at this. If any of us could have a do-over for some reprehensible act in our past, who wouldn't jump at the chance for atonement? But did I want a hot-headed twenty-something assisting me with my planned B & E caper? After all, Miranda would have my back. Hmm.

"Okay —" I started to say.

"Okay?" Ro asked, astonished.

"Let me finish. Okay, I hear you. But I have to think about this. And while I'm thinking, you need to do three things."

Ro grinned. "Like an RPG, right?"

"A what?" I asked, puzzled.

"An RPG. A Role-Playing Game."

Oh, for heaven's sake. "No," I said testily. "Listen to me: you have to have a shower, get dressed, and go to school today."

Ro wilted. "But — "

"No buts," I said sternly. "Go to class. I bet you haven't been to lectures all week. Go. Get notes for what you've missed. Don't fall further behind. Your scholarship is a gift, Ro. Don't screw up. I'm going out in about half an hour. I can drop you at U Vic. Go to class, then go to that shithole room over someone's garage, as you put it. Pack some clothes. Knowing Aliya, she's said you can stay with her downstairs for a bit, right?"

"Right," Ro. "But what about . . . you know . . . later . . . " she trailed off.

"Let's worry about later later. Is your car at that shithole room over the garage?"

Ro looked stricken. "No. I don't have a car. Julia's VW, well, it was legally hers, but we both drove it. It's totaled."

Indeed it was. "Okay, you're carless. So you'll have to take a bus from the campus back here. There's a key under the big flowerpot on the back steps. Let's say we see each other here at say, suppertime."

Ro nodded. "And you'll think about whether or not I can come with you tonight? Promise? You're not just shining me on?"

"I'll think about whether or not you can *help* me," I said. "That's what I can promise. As for coming along?" I shook my head. "I don't know, Ro. That's a biggie and requires lengthy and serious head-scratching. Now, let's get on with things. Showers, coiffures, clean clothes, matching socks, optimistic attitudes. The important things in life, right?"

Ro gave me a quizzical look but wisely didn't argue. "Right," she said.

❧

Mac was waiting for me at a corner table in The Snug — the Oak Bay Beach Hotel's famous pub. On another day we could have eaten outside, but today was gray and iffy, with rain alternately spitting and threatening to spit. Still, through the pub's floor-to-ceiling windows, we had a wonderful view to the east of the little islands just off the coast and farther on, the San Juans, mostly shrouded in fog today.

A fire burned in the fireplace, and the café's dark-timbered ambience was soothing, in contrast to what I'd come here to discuss with Mac.

As I took a seat opposite him at the little table, I reflected that it was probably no accident that the pub had been given the evocative name of The Snug. Here on the island, geologically adrift from Canada's mainland, I believe we islanders crave the experience of snugness, especially in the bleak midwinter. Perhaps not by accident, many of northern Europe's languages express similar longings.

How about *cosag*, meaning cozy? From the Gaelic. It means a small hole you can creep into and indeed, who doesn't long for a *cosag* when the frosty winds make moan? And when the rain and the mizzling damp rise from inlets and fens, don't we yearn for the feeling that the Dutch call *gezelligheid?* Derived from the word for friend, *gezelligheid* describes both physical circumstances — being snug in a warm and homey place surrounded by good friends — and an emotional state of being held and comforted. The Danish *hygge* (coziness) and the Finnish *kodikas* (homelike) have similar connotations. But apparently, it's only we northerners who share these yearnings for warm snugness. I'd taken more than one riffle through the languages of the sunny Mediterranean and not found similar longings.

It was just before noon, and The Snug was only half-full. Now that the year was sliding into winter, and the tourists had abandoned us for Saskatoon and Santa Fe, we locals had the place pretty much to ourselves. And we liked it that way. Mac had ordered our usual Snug fare, consisting of a couple of glasses of Guinness, and the assortment of breads and cheeses called Ploughman's Lunch.

"You're looking tweedy," I told him, commenting on what was evidently a new addition to his hairy blazer collection, a brownish herringbone.

"And isn't it Mary's fault, then?" he said, brushing self-consciously at the front of his jacket. "My wife is intent on getting me in touch with my inner Caledonian. She orders Harris Tweed directly from the Hebrides now and has the bolts of fabric shipped to some poncy haberdasher's shop downtown. I can't say no to her even though the itch factor is, sadly, quite high."

I smiled. There were worse burdens to bear in life than a doting partner.

"She still talks about making haggis for you," he mentioned, peering at me from the thicket of his sandy eyebrows. "She mentions it often. We ought to set a date."

I'm sure I blanched. I never have been able to work up any enthusiasm for the dish: sheep's "pluck" (heart, liver and lungs), minced with onion, oatmeal, suet, spices, and salt, then mixed with stock, cooked, and traditionally served in the animal's stomach. Ai yi. Then, miraculously, I thought of a reason to put *finis* to these invitations for haggis.

"Ah, that might be a bit of a problem," I told him with feigned regret. "You see, Tristan has recruited the household to veganism, of all things, and I'd feel disloyal if I strayed from the path. As much as I'd like to sample Mary's haggis."

"Och, well," he said. "We'd still like to see you for dinner sometime. I'm sure she could manage a meatless dish. Neeps and taties perhaps."

"And I'd love to come for dinner," I said truthfully, although I was certain Mary could concoct something more appetizing than neeps and taties — turnips and potatoes.

The waitress arrived with our Ploughman's Lunch. We'd probably better do business, I thought, taking a sip of Guinness. Dinner plans later.

"So, Mac, did you get my email?" I asked. "Julia Stevens's accident, the VW Bug and the Sequoia, the tortured cat . . ."

"I did," he said. "I read the file with great interest. Your Mr. Maleck has a very checkered distant past. And a very brutal recent one. I can certainly see the potential for several charges in his future. After the proper investigations, of course." He paused. "Would you like to tell me how you happened to cross paths with Mr. Maleck? I sense there's quite a story there."

"There is quite a story, but I can't tell it just yet," I said, thinking of the visit to Island Naturals that still lay before me. I wanted the animals someplace safe before I talked to Mac about everything I knew. I had an odd feeling of unease that I just couldn't shake, a miserable low-level dread like a psychic toothache. Maybe it would dissipate once the rabbits were safely tucked up at Miranda's Sanctuary. I certainly hoped so. "I'd be happy to sit down with you, oh, perhaps tomorrow." After I had time to rearrange the facts of the story to omit the details of upcoming animal theft. I helped myself to cheese and bread.

"Listen, is there any chance you could pick him up for questioning?" I asked. "Maybe just based on the video? It surely is evidence of animal cruelty."

Mac drank some of his Guinness, wiped his moustache with a paper napkin, and smiled. "It's already been done. I'm happy to tell you that Yvon Maleck is currently a guest of the Crown," he said with evident satisfaction.

"Holy smokes, Mac? Do you mean you've taken him into *custody*? So soon? I just sent you the email and the video Wednesday night!"

"I wish Oak Bay were that efficient," he said. "We're still looking at the video and reading the contents of the files you sent us. There's plenty of material there. I can see a plethora of charges. No, a certain Darlene James went to the Saanich station in Sidney on Tuesday afternoon and swore out a complaint against Dr. Maleck. It seems he assaulted her at work and she fears for her safety around him. Saanich arrested him later that day."

I was stunned. Darlene? The Darlene who works at Island Naturals? Meek Darlene? Where on earth had she gotten up the gumption to swear out a complaint? She must have taken seriously my warning her to stay away from Maleck and decided to do something more useful than calling in sick to work. I took off my metaphorical hat to her.

He nodded. "I haven't read the complaint closely, but when I saw your email, I remembered the name from the booking report. There couldn't be two Yvon Malecks. So now that Saanich has him, we'll pay him a visit and question him regarding those other wee offenses you emailed me about — the credit card fraud, the tax evasion, not to mention the parole violation. I'll get Erin to call Quebec and get his trial records faxed over to us. Then she can put in a call to Revenue Canada. Mr. MacLachlan, I think it is." He drank some more beer, wiped his moustache again, and bared his teeth in what was definitely not a smile. "Then we can contemplate current charges. In this jurisdiction, not Quebec. I don't think Dr. Maleck will be breathing free air for a long time. If ever."

"Mac, that's . . ."

To use an overworked phrase, words failed me. A great sense of relief pervaded my being, and I suddenly felt lighter. Buoyed up. Optimistic. I'm usually in touch with my feelings, but I must have put on an emotional back burner my worry about meeting Maleck in the testing lab tonight. Of course my left brain knew that the likelihood of this meeting was small, but still. My right brain recalled the atavistic dread I'd felt when he'd looked at me at Island Naturals. I shuddered. Probably the downside of my overly active imagination. Or too much coffee.

"In custody," I marveled. "You know, I practically witnessed the assault on Darlene. I could give a statement if you'd like."

"Do that," he said. "It might be helpful."

"And in another matter, you might want to tow Maleck's Sequoia to Forensics," I suggested. "It's probably in the Island Naturals' employees' lot. You'll likely find that the red paint on the driver's side door is a match for Julia Stevens' red VW Bug. I did some amateur sleuthing — probably unnecessary — but I got a pretty good look at the Bug. And I got a good look at the Sequoia also. They have matching damage."

"Ah," Mac said. "That's what you wanted to look at in the Forensics' lot the other day when you called me."

"It was," I said.

We drank a little more of our Guinness, ate some more bread and cheese, listened to the logs in the fireplace pop and snap, and watched a trio of cormorants fly low over the bay.

Finally, Mac spoke up. "Would I be wrong if I offered the services of a friend who is offering to pay close attention to his cell phone over the next little while? Say tonight and tomorrow? This friend, well, he senses something brewing."

I laughed. "'Double, double, toil and trouble?' That sort of thing?"

"Perhaps," he said. "Not that this friend doesn't believe the inimitable duo of Miz Yeats, probably accompanied by Miz Blake, can't handle any toil and trouble, but . . ." He left the thought unfinished.

I considered my planned nighttime activities at Island Naturals. CLAW wasn't due to stage a disruption until Saturday. Maleck was cooling his heels in a cell in Sidney. Short of a fiery comet striking Island Naturals, what could go wrong?

"I think things will resolve nicely on their own," I said. "But I'm grateful for the friend's offer nevertheless."

Mac's phone buzzed, and I took this as a sign for a quick exit. I left money on the table for my half of the bill, mouthed a good-bye, and walked out of the pub into the gray afternoon. And straight into a funk.

What?

Maleck was in jail, the rabbits would soon be removed from Island Naturals, my part in this unpleasant business was about to be wrapped up. Why this case of the dismals? I tried to recapture some of the buoyancy of spirit I'd felt when Mac had informed me that Maleck had been arrested, but something — the lowering afternoon sky, the time of year — something was amiss.

Dodging raindrops, I hurried to my car.

CHAPTER 27

M IRANDA WAS WAITING for me in the reception area at The Sanctuary, blue rain jacket in one hand, cell phone held to her ear. She looked elegant: a cream-colored cashmere cable-knit sweater instead of her well-worn RCMP sweatshirt, and fashionable black pants. Clearly Miranda dressed for meetings with Portia. I, on the other hand, the perennial victim of laundry procrastination, could only manage a clean navy turtleneck, a Fair Isle wool vest with lots of blue in the pattern, my second-best pair of brown cords, and hiking boots.

As I carefully closed the outside door behind me, I realized that the reception area was, well, very bloody warm. Connie was dressed for balminess in a short-sleeved green Hawaiian shirt festooned with pink and purple orchids, her exuberant hair tied back with a festive turquoise hank of wool. The cagefuls of abandoned kittens, for whom this Floridian microclimate had evidently been created, were sacked out in tabby, orange, and Siamese heaps in fuzzy beds in their cages. A few blissful moans rose now and then from the heaps, as the kittens snoozed in dreams, unaware of the enormous heating bill three space heaters were undoubtedly creating.

"Toasty," I said to Connie, unzipping my windbreaker. Good lord, the temperature in the reception area must have been approaching eighty. I feared for the staying power of my deodorant.

"Our central heating quit overnight," she said. "Hence the space heaters. I've called the repair service but no one has showed up yet. Hmmf. It was about forty degrees in here this morning. Poor little kittens — we have to keep them warm." She got up from her desk and motioned me into a little storeroom just off the main room. It smelled pleasantly of cat kibble and wood shavings for small animal bedding. Bags of both were piled against one wall.

"What's up?" I asked.

"Just to warn you," Connie said. "Miranda's like a bear with a sore paw. We got turned down for a grant that she was counting on. To say she's aggravated is an understatement. The turndown from the foundation produced a fifteen minute rant about how we need to hire a fundraiser. Anyhow, we really could have used that money. It was for capital improvements, including the damned heating system. I'm afraid we're going to have to buy a new furnace."

"Okay," I said. "Thanks for letting me know."

Guiltily, I realized that I'd never asked Miranda about The Sanctuary's finances. What had I imagined? That financing fell like manna from heaven? A fine friend I was.

"What about tonight?" I asked. "Should I, um, disinvite her from the great animal-nabbing caper?"

"Heavens, no," Connie said. "It will take her mind off the grant turndown. A little animal rescue will improve her mood."

"Well, if you think so," I said.

"Animal rescue always improves my mood," Miranda said, glowering from the doorway. "I'm looking forward to tonight. But right now, we need to go and see Portia. I've been trying to get her on the phone to confirm our meeting. But she's not answering."

"Is that unusual for her?" I asked.

"She's just not very good about answering her cell phone," Miranda said. "So it might not mean anything."

"Why don't we assume we're still on for our meeting and just show up?" I suggested.

"Yeah, I suppose," Miranda said thoughtfully. Then, "Hell, yes. I'm just in a major funk." She walked over to look out the window in the reception area. "I see the rain has let up a little. There's even a patch of blue sky in the east. Let's take the coast road. One of my orca-loving friends called to tell me that J pod's orcas are in the bay. I'd like to see them. Are you driving?"

"Sure thing," I said. "But before we go, here's a piece of good news. Not as inspirational as the orca sighting, but good news still."

"What?" Miranda shrugged into her jacket. "Tell me. I'm positively starved for good news."

"Yvon Maleck is in jail," I said, unable to keep the glee out of my voice.

"No shit, Sherlock!" Miranda exclaimed. When she saw my grin expand, she said, "How the hell did that happen?"

"Our favorite Oak Bay policeperson told me as I was having lunch with him a little earlier."

"MacLeish," Miranda crowed. "That canny old Scot! So he looked at the video! And I'm sure you told him about the Bug and the Sequoia. Maleck's a bloody murderer as well as an animal torturer. Did he pick him up?"

Miranda and Mac had been friends for years. I guessed Mac wouldn't mind her calling him "that canny old Scot".

"No. That is, yes, he's looked at the video, and he got my email about Julia, but Oak Bay didn't have a chance to pick Maleck up. Saanich did. It seems that Darlene James from Island Naturals, the woman Maleck assaulted, got up enough guts to go swear out a complaint against him. Saanich picked him up, oh, late afternoon on Tuesday. Apparently he's cooling his heels in a cell in Sidney."

"Wow," Miranda said. "The opposition is falling like ninepins. Think about it. We don't have to worry about CLAW tonight, nor do we have to worry about the despicable Dr. Maleck lurking in the testing lab. Not that he would have been, but you know what I mean.

This ought to be a walk in the park. Let ourselves in with Julia's key card, load up the rabbits, waltz out."

"Oh, and speaking of waltzing," I said, "a certain little feisty redhead wants to come waltz with us."

"Ro?" Miranda raised her eyebrows.

"Yeah, Ro. She has her reasons, as you might expect. And I wouldn't even consider it but, well, things seem to be falling into place. As you said, no CLAW, no Maleck, no problems. Maybe Ro can drive the van and wait in the parking lot listening to the radio while you and I go fetch the rabbits."

"Hmm," Miranda said after a moment's thought. "I have no problem with that." She shrugged. "It ought to be clear sailing."

"Ought to be," I said. But privately, I wasn't so sure. The best laid plans sometimes *gang aft agley* (translation: go to hell), to quote Robbie Burns, another canny Scot. But what the heck, it never hurt to hope.

❧

Indeed there were orcas. We sat in my car on a steep bluff overlooking the ocean on the way to Uplands and Portia's home. About fifty feet below us, in a little bay, half a dozen triangular black fins cut through the cobalt water. Miranda had brought along binoculars and murmured now and then, finally passing them to me.

We Victorians feel very protective of this little pod of orcas — J pod. Indeed there were only three pods of orcas in the bigger group called J Clan, or the Southern Resident Killer Whales: J pod, K pod, and L pod. These three pods were united through their dialects, or songs, which are quite different from the dialects used by other orca communities, such as the one farther north. The clan we regarded as ours — J Clan — was officially listed as endangered, and these were, arguably, their last days.

"None of those damned whale-sighting boats out on the water today," Miranda remarked. "It's too late in the season. Good. The orcas can eat and navigate in peace."

It was true. As if they didn't face enough problems from polluted water from runoff and the devastation of the salmon runs, they were being loved to death by the tour companies.

"You know," she said, "when I was a kid, my family and I sometimes took the Washington State ferry now and then through the San Juans to Anacortes, then back to Sidney. The crew would halt the ferry whenever a pod of orcas was sighted. I was ten. I really didn't know why we were stopping." She laughed. "I guess I thought there was a traffic jam. Anyhow, it turned out the ferry crew cut the engines whenever orcas were close by to let them echolocate."

I passed the binoculars back to her.

"Now the tour boats motor up as close as they can to let the tourists take pictures. Screw the orcas' need to echolocate. God. It's just business, right? They want to give those tourists from Toronto or Tulsa their money's worth. Oh, they don't mean any harm, they assure us, but all that racket disorients the orcas. Puts them off their hunting. No wonder the pod is starving."

As I watched, one of the orcas breached — rocketed out of the water — showing its white underbelly, then fell back into the blue water with a great rooster-tail of a splash. Endearingly, it had a dark patch under its chin, like a white cat with a secret tabby spot.

"One of these days, probably in our lifetime," she said sadly, "there won't be orcas here at all." Alas, I knew the statistics. There were only twenty-three orcas left in J pod. L pod had thirty-five members and K pod only eighteen. "We're lucky we saw them today, Kieran. Every time I come this way and see them, I consider myself blessed. It's just so awful. Remember Tahlequah?"

"I do," I said. Tahlequah, or J35, excited all of us when she gave birth to the first calf born in the pod in three years. But tragically, he lived only half an hour. Then, in an extravagant display of mourning, Tahlequah carried the lifeless body of her baby on her head for over three weeks, a period of grief never before seen in an orca. She traveled over 1,000 miles, carrying the dead calf with her, only relinquishing it when it began to decompose.

"I do remember it," I said again. "It was so goddammed awful. It was one of the saddest things I've ever heard of."

"Yeah," she said. "Orcas grieve just like we would grieve over a lost child. Their brains are so much like ours — incredibly complex. They feel, well, probably much like we feel. About their children. About many things."

Miranda sniffled, my not-so-tough ex-Mountie friend, tearing up over the tragedy of Tahlequah and her calf. It was a heartbreaking story, and I didn't blame Miranda a bit for weeping.

We sat in silence for a while, then she turned to me. "You know," she said after a moment, "we should bring Tris up here one day, maybe in the spring. I think she should see the orcas. The world we're leaving her — the world right here on the Straits of Juan de Fuca — might well not have a single orca left in it by the time Tris is twenty-five. Oh, maybe somewhere off Iceland, orcas might still swim, and forage, and have calves . . . but right here? Not likely. But one day, when Tris is older, she might look back and remember that she had an orca moment. Like we're having today."

This broke my heart, too, and I said, "You're right, Miranda. Let's do it. She deserves that memory."

"There they go," she said, her binoculars trained on the orcas again. "We won't see them again until spring. I wish them well up north — their winter feeding grounds. At least they'll have peace and quiet. No tourist boats." She put the binoculars down and we watched them swim away.

Our little window of blue sky had closed, and a battalion of pewter-colored clouds was sailing in from the east. A brisk wind had sprung up, making whitecaps on the bay, buffeting my car where we sat parked on the clifftop. And on the heels of the wind came the rain again, bringing fat raindrops to spatter on my windshield.

Miranda said after a while, "Sorry I've been glum. Sometimes I go down the rabbit hole of all the animals we can't save. The orcas, or that mouse in Australia that just went extinct, or the seals that are stranding themselves on the east coast, or the gray whales on the west coast, or the hundreds of species we're inevitably going to lose. Oh, I know that we shouldn't break our hearts mourning them. I know that. It would paralyze us — we would be useless to help the animals right under our noses. Of course, our focus ought to be on saving the animals we can, not mourning the ones we can't help." She sighed. "But God, it's hard to keep that focus sometimes."

I heard the despair in Miranda's voice. And suddenly I realized she was the starfish thrower in Helen Mikita's story about Loren Eisley. Miranda, not me, was the one who figuratively picked starfish up off the beach and threw them back into the ocean. It must weigh terribly on her at times. I tried to think of something to say that would help her.

"Maybe small needy creatures left on your doorstep taped up in cardboard boxes help to bring that focus back," I suggested.

"Yeah, that'll do it. Or ringworm." She managed a small smile. Then she said, "You know, all this talk about saving lives has made me think about Portia again. About what a great, good thing she could do. She could save hundreds of animals from horrible deaths in that damned testing lab. If she would only step up."

"Yeah," she could," I agreed.

"Okay, so what about this," she said. "Five board members voted against Philip's proposal. With a little prodding in the right direction, the five could recruit a few of the others. Allies. There only needs to be two defections from the pro-China crowd to make a majority, and with a re-vote, the China proposal would go down in flames. No more talk of turning the clock back to animal testing here on the island; no more rationalization that the animal suffering to take place will be worth it once the money from China is counted."

"So maybe we need to go tell Portia that," I said. "Just that. That she could rally the troops, as you put it. Gather allies. Sort of like the fellowship of the ring, right?" I winked. "Aragorn, Legoloas, Gimli, Gandalf . . . hmm, weren't there a few others?"

Miranda threw back her head and laughed — a sound I was happy to hear.

"Miz Yeats, you are so weird," she said. "I can always count on you for a cheery literary reference. What the hell. Let's go find out what's up with Portia. Just carry on down the coast road."

 env

Ah, Uplands. Lawns as vast as polo grounds, green as dreams of Ireland. No weed would have the temerity to sprout in these serene, manicured swards. And if one did risk taking up residence, I was certain a vigilant gardener would pounce, yanking it out by its upstart roots. Not only decorum but privacy were the watchwords here. Entire mini-forests hid one vast estate from another, and coyly meandering driveways discouraged exploration.

Portia's house was a black and white half-timbered Tudor-inspired bungalow, one of the smaller mansions on the street. It would probably list for, oh, a mere five or six million, I figured. I followed Miranda's directions, carefully steering my car between copses of rhododendrons and hedges of laurel until we emerged finally onto a circular gravel drive, presided over by one enormous Garry oak.

Poor lonely thing. It should have a grove for company, I thought sadly. Even oaks need friends, and in the case of the Garrys, they need the symbiosis provided by others of their arboreal ilk. They grow nowhere else in Canada, indeed in the world, and just a few hundred remain here on the southern tip of Vancouver Island. But we're seemingly oblivious to the fact that we should be their caretakers. We continue to sacrifice them for freeways, apartment complexes, fast-food restaurants, leaving only a token specimen here and there marooned in asphalt to expiate our guilt. As Joni Mitchell said, we've paved Paradise, and put up a parking lot. I had a couple of Garry oaks in my yard and I fretted over each leaf that fell.

"Yikes," I said to Miranda as I turned off the car's engine. "I probably should have left a trail of breadcrumbs. However will I ever find my way back?"

Miranda shot me a give-me-strength look. "I wonder who's here," she said, indicating the four cars parked in the driveway: a silver Mercedes, a black Lexus, a grey Prius, and a blue Bolt. "None of these is Portia's car. Guess she has company."

A sudden inspiration struck me. "You don't suppose . . ."

"Suppose what?"

"That the cars might belong to Aragorn, Legoloas, Gimli, and Gandalf?"

"What?" she said, mystified. Then, "Dammit . . . I bet Portia rallied the troops. All on her own. We didn't even have to twist her arm. She must have started calling them last night after I talked to her." She turned to me, eyes sparkling. "Those cars might belong to the dissenting board members."

"I bet they do," I said. "That's probably why she has her phone off. Or isn't answering it. There may be a council of war inside."

"Yeah," Miranda said. Then, "Just don't quote any more Tolkien to me. I'm still stunned."

"Sure thing," I said. "Maybe just go to the door, return her coat, and ask for a tiny clue. Then we could sleep soundly knowing the ring is on its way to Mount Doom."

"Kieran!" Miranda said in mock vexation.

"Sorry, I couldn't help myself." I reached into the back seat and handed her Portia's coat, abandoned at the Pub Talk. "Here you go."

Miranda took the coat, which I had folded neatly and put in a plastic bag, and hurried to the front door. I couldn't see what transpired, as we were parked at an angle to the house, so I sat there thinking. Maybe Philip could be reined in. Maybe Portia could be reinstated to the board. Maybe the China deal was not inked yet. As I considered these hopeful possibilities, my phone buzzed.

"Connie?" I said, perplexed, wondering why she was calling me and not Miranda. "We're at Portia's. Miranda's giving her back her coat. We think — "

"Miranda's phone is going to voicemail," Connie said, sounding agitated. I looked on the passenger seat. Sure enough, Miranda had left her phone there. "So I'm calling you," Connie continued. "I just talked with Giselle from CLAW. There's going to be trouble tonight. Come on back and I'll fill you in."

Uh-huh. Just as I'd feared. The best-laid plans *gang aft agley*.

"We're on our way," I told her.

CHAPTER 28

"YOU HAVE to be damned well kidding," Miranda said in exasperation, hanging her rain jacket up on a hook in The Sanctuary's reception area.

"I wish I were," Connie said.

"Rabbit costumes nailed up on the front of Island Naturals? Rabbit masks with the eyeholes circled in red paint? Where in hell would you even get a rabbit costume?" Miranda asked in disbelief. "And they're going to paint the windows red? To simulate blood?" She collapsed heavily on a chair in front of Connie's desk. "And why did they move their timeline up to tonight?"

Connie shrugged. "Giselle didn't say."

"Oh, I can see why they moved their shenanigans up to tonight," I said. "They intend to call the media early Saturday morning. It'll be a story all weekend. Sounds like a reprise of their stunt at The Bay.

They struck first thing in the morning back then," I said. "It got them a hell of a lot of press. And that's what they're after, right?"

"Of course," Connie said glumly. "Though I tried to talk Giselle out of it. The public doesn't need to be outraged over animal testing — most people already are. The anti-fur campaign needed a boost and benefitted from CLAW's antics, but they're not needed here."

"And Giselle called you to . . . ?" I asked.

"To help. Nail up a few costumes. Paint a few windows." Connie shook her head in exasperation. "Of course I told her no. But I'm glad she called me in any event. At least you're prepared. You know CLAW will be there."

"Yeah," I said. "I imagine they'll be working out front. There are big windows there. Perfect for painting. And they'll want to nail up the rabbit costumes there too. It will be very photogenic."

"So how do we avoid them?" Miranda asked.

"We get there first," I said. "Connie? Did Giselle give you any idea when this nonsense will take place?"

Connie nodded. "If I wanted to come along, I was to be at her house in James Bay at nine."

I looked at my watch. "Okay, it's just five. It'll be dark soon. We have time before CLAW gets there. Right now, though, we need to eat and run. Miranda, do you want me to help you load the rabbit cages into that old van you say you have?"

"I already did it," Connie said. "Two folding cages."

"I'm not dressed for this," Miranda said. "I need to change clothes and you'll want to go home and do the same, Kieran. Oh, is Ro still coming along?"

"I don't think she'd let us go without her," I said. "If we're quick, we can get this done ahead of CLAW's hijinks. Same plan — Ro's in charge of the van, we're in charge of the rabbits."

"Okay," Miranda said. "I'll see you two shortly."

I'd called ahead to ask Ro to make me something to eat and to tell her to be dressed in grubby clothes and ready to go when I arrived. I intended to rush inside, grab some food, throw on some old jeans and a dark sweatshirt, then bite my fingernails waiting for Miranda to pick us up. Damn CLAW anyhow. This crack-brained scheme would succeed in getting them news coverage all right, but it would create an unnecessary scandal for Island Naturals. So much for our hopes that Portia could quietly turn things around with the board, cancel the China deal, and have the public none the wiser about the company's near fall from grace.

Parking in the driveway, I hurried inside, mentally rehearsing my apologies to Tris. She'd told me that she and Aliya were cooking tonight, and I was sorry (or was I?) that I'd miss the joint culinary effort.

"Hi, Kieran!" Tris sang out from the kitchen. "Come and see what we're making!"

I dutifully headed into the kitchen and, to my surprise, it smelled wonderful in there — onions, green peppers, some exotic spice I couldn't identify.

"Hot dog, but don't you look a sight?" I teased Tris, who was standing on a small stepstool at the kitchen counter, a yellow flowered apron wound several times around her skinny self.

"Aliya made me wear it," Tris said. "She said all chefs wear aprons." She was spooning something from a bag into a measuring cup, and my traitorous stomach gave a moan of distress. "We're making chili. Vegan of course," she said virtuously.

"Of course," I said, and planted a kiss on the top of Tris's head as I passed through on the way to my bedroom.

"*Kierannn!*" she said, feigning indignation.

"It's a job-related peril for cooks," I said. "They have to put up with being kissed now and then."

"Kieran's right," Aliya said, dumping a handful of chopped something into a pot that was simmering on the stove, winking at me behind Tris's back. "I read it in a job description."

"Well, she didn't kiss *you*," Tris told her. "How come?"

"Because she's not as cute as you are," I said. "Sprout, will you save me some chili? I have to go out. Ro's going with me. We'll miss dinner."

"Oh, both of you?" she said, plainly disappointed. "We could wait for you."

"Nah," I said. "I don't know how long we'll be. It might be late. Leave us some chili? I'll warm up a bowl and bring it into your room when I get back. We can read another chapter in your book together, if you like."

"Okay," Tris said. "That'll be cool." Then, my proclaimed absence clearly forgotten, she turned to Aliya. "Aliya, here's that crumbly veggie stuff. I measured it out."

Ro was hovering in the kitchen doorway and I motioned her to come on into the back of the house with me. She was dressed appropriately for our nighttime activities — faded jeans, scuffed sneakers, black hoodie, and a black baseball cap jammed on her head.

"Did you have time to make me something to eat?" I asked her as I rummaged in my bedroom closet for some old clothes that I wouldn't mind being decorated with rabbit pee. "I'm about fainting."

"Sure," she said. "I used some Tofurky slices and made a couple of sandwiches. I ate one and wrapped up another one for you. It was pretty good, but don't you guys have real food here?"

I heaved a heavy sigh. "Don't start with me, short stuff. We're embarking on the long and winding road of veganism. Sacrifices need to be made."

"Oh," Ro said. "Okay."

In the closet, I found some ancient jeans with a hole in one knee, and an old navy sweatshirt, and quickly changed. After a moment's hesitation, I took my holstered .38 out of my locked gun safe, checked the load, and clipped the gun to the back of my jeans.

"Whoa," Ro said. "A gun. This is serious. I didn't realize — "

"This is just insurance," I said, trying to reassure her. "We probably won't run into trouble that we'll need this for. I'm being overly cautious. After all, how much trouble can six small, furry things cause? Miranda will be here with the van in a jiffy. Let's go wait for her in the hall."

"When will you tell me what I'll be doing?" Ro asked as we walked toward the front door.

"Just as soon as you tell me that you went to school today, attended a lecture, got notes for the days you missed, and are all caught up," I said. "That was our bargain. So did you? Do those things?"

She nodded. "I did. All of them. I went to Professor Goldstein's class. I photocopied a friend's notes. I'm ready for next week."

"Hmmf, okay. By the way, what *are* you studying?" I asked her, looking out the sidelight beside the front door, keeping watch for Miranda.

"Me? Oh, well, nonprofit management. With a minor in art history. The art of our First People. The Haida. The Kwakiutl."

"Nonprofit management," I said. "Sounds dry. But the art history sounds pretty darned interesting. I'll tell you a story about the Group of Seven sometime, if you like."

She brightened. "Yeah? You know something about them?"

"Sure do. I'm not just your garden-variety thug. I have unguessed-at depths."

"I know you do," she said, looking embarrassed. "I've looked at your library." She frowned, clearly wondering what to make of me. But at that moment, Miranda's van turned into the driveway and our cultural discussion was terminated. I took my black leather jacket from the hall tree, put it on, and zipped it up. It felt comforting. A little like armor.

"Kieran?" she asked. "About tonight?"

Yeah, yeah, I thought. Tell the redhead what her role will be. She won't like it, but tell her anyhow.

"We'll be committing a bunch of crimes tonight," I said. "Some breaking, some entering, possibly some property destruction. And definitely a side order of theft. Those will be the charges if we're caught and Island Naturals gets pissy. Even though saving six rabbits from a hideous death in the testing lab is the right thing to do — and what Julia hired me to do when she said 'Don't leave the others behind' — the animals belong technically to Island Naturals. But you won't be doing the actual breaking and entering. Or the theft. That's why you'll be driving the van. I'm trying to minimize your exposure."

"No, Kieran, I want — " Ro protested.

"I don't give a hoot what you want," I said. "This isn't negotiable, Ro. Hell, I'm having second, third, and fourth thoughts about letting you come along at all, let alone drive. But I know you want to help. And I know why. So, driving, well, that's how you can help."

"But Julia *died*," Ro whispered hoarsely. "She was doing something important, something brave. Let me do something brave, Kieran."

Oh, brother. The kid was evidently not going to be satisfied with driving the van and waiting patiently in the parking lot while Miranda and I went in after the rabbits. Too bloody bad.

"Listen up, Ro. This is my show," I said assuming my tough-broad persona. "You do what I tell you to do or you stay here and eat chili with Tris and Aliya. No more discussion. No complaining. Okay?"

"Yeah, okay," Ro said unhappily.

I felt like a worm.

CHAPTER 29

THE CREEPINESS FACTOR of a deserted parking lot at night cannot be overstated. Island Naturals' lot was no exception. An octet of low-intensity sodium vapor lights on tall aluminum poles shed ghostly pools of light onto the asphalt, turning our hands and faces a zombie-apocalypse gray.

"Over there," I said, directing Ro to park in front of the stairs beside the loading bay.

"Wait, Kieran," Miranda said. "Who's here?" She pointed at a big, light-colored SUV at the edge of the lot.

A premonitory shiver ran down my spine and I told myself to get a grip. Just groundless worrying. "Beats me," I said. "Who'd be working on a Friday night? Probably a janitor. But best to check it out."

I told Ro, "Swing over there while we take a look at the car."

As she drove over to the SUV, I noticed three things simultaneously: it was a Toyota Sequoia, it was white, and it had a Quebec license plate.

"Well, shit," I said.

"What?" Miranda asked.

"It's Yvon Maleck's car."

"I thought he was in jail," Miranda said.

"He is," I said. "Let me think for a minute. According to Mac, he was arrested on Tuesday. The cops picked him up here. So his car's probably been in the lot since then. And Mac wants to talk to him in Oak Bay once Saanich is through with him. So . . . that Sequoia may grow old here."

"Okay," Miranda said. "Let's not spook ourselves, then."

I bent forward to tap Ro on the shoulder. "Back in by the stairs. It'll make unloading and loading easier."

"So here's my plan," I told Miranda. "You and I are going to grab the folded rabbit cages, go on up the steps to that little door marked DELIVERIES at the top of the stairs, use Julia's key card to let ourselves in, go down the corridor to the testing lab, open that door with the key card, unfold the cages, load the animals, hurry back here, stash them in the back of the van, and get the hell out of here. I figure fifteen minutes, tops. Sound good to you?"

"Sounds perfect to me."

"Then, let's go," I said.

The first problem was that we couldn't get the damned door marked DELIVERIES open. I swiped the card through the sensor box several times but nothing happened.

"Hell," I muttered, looking back at Miranda who was a black-clad shadow behind me, folded cages in her arms.

"What?" she asked.

"The bloody key card doesn't work. Maybe Island Naturals canceled it." I tried it again, cursed, and Miranda peered over my shoulder.

"Hmm, I don't think that's the problem, Kieran," she said. "There ought to be a red light illuminated on the sensor box. But there isn't. Usually there's a red light on these things that turns green when a card is swiped through the box."

"Maybe no red light just means the alarm system isn't on," I said hopefully.

"Maybe," Miranda said. "But the door should still open. I think it's more likely that the power's off."

"What?" I said. "In the whole building?"

"Maybe not," Miranda said. "Maybe it's just this part of the complex. A bad circuit."

"Well, I guess we'll see when we get in," I said. "Okay, let's try Plan B."

"Which is?"

"The bathroom window. I taped the latch open when Lawrence and I were here a couple of days ago. Just in case we needed an emergency ingress or egress route. It's over there, just to the right of the loading bay. C'mon."

We hurried back down the stairs, past the loading bay, to a spot under the bathroom window. A battered blue dumpster had appeared since I was here last, and it was conveniently situated right where we needed it.

"This'll be a breeze," I said with a lot more confidence than I felt. Dammit, I don't like wrinkles in my plans. "A hop up onto the dumpster, a wriggle through the window, and we'll be in. Never mind the damned deliveries door."

I put my hands on the dumpster and hauled myself up onto its closed lid, then duck-walked over to the window. Standing upright, I found I could reach it easily. I gave it a shove and it opened smoothly. Three cheers for low-tech. And duct tape.

"Okay," I said, "I'm going in." It was a tighter fit than I had thought, but I wriggled through and dropped onto the lavatory counter.

"Miranda," I said, poking my head back out the window. "Pass the cages in to me."

She clambered up onto the dumpster and passed the cages through the window one by one. The feeble light from the parking lot did little to illuminate the interior of the bathroom, and I flipped on the little flashlight I had brought with me, standing the folded cages on the bathroom floor. I looked back at the window: Miranda had pushed it open, and her head and one arm appeared in the opening and then . . . stopped.

"C'mon," I whispered.

"I don't think so," she replied, and for a moment I thought she'd lost her nerve. But she said, "Nope. I can't get my shoulders through. The damned window is too small."

"Fooey," I muttered, my stomach clenching a little in apprehension. "You need to give up that bodybuilding, Miz Blake."

"Ha, ha, Miz Yeats," she said. "I'm certain you have Plan C up your sleeve."

"Sure do," I told her. "How about you take Ro's place in the van? Send her in through the window. She's small. If you brought a flashlight, give it to her. Okay?"

"Gotcha."

In a few minutes, Ro's head of curly red hair — minus her baseball cap — then her shoulders and arms, followed by the rest of her body, snaked in through the window. She hopped down to the floor, brushed off her jeans, and gave me a grin.

"Thanks, Miz Skinny," I said.

"Hey, no problem," she said magnanimously. I sighed. She was positively enjoying this — it was just what she'd wanted. To do something hands-on, to be a real animal rescuer, not a van driver. To do what Julia had done. Something brave. I hoped like hell that carrying a cageful of rabbits would be brave enough for her. Because that's all I had to offer.

Oh, stop fretting, I told myself. Who was I really worried about — Ro, or myself? After all, I'd counted on Miranda having my back. Now, not only was that back untaken-care-of, but I'd have to take care of Ro's, too. But, really, wasn't the hard part over? No one would need to have anyone's back.

"Let's each take a cage," I said. "We'll unfold them in the testing lab. Did Miranda give you a flashlight?"

"Yup," she said, flicking it on.

"Okay," I told her. "We'll just go out and down the hall, jog to the left, then we'll be there."

I let Ro go first, and as the bathroom door closed silently behind me, she paused for a moment, juggling her cage and Miranda's flashlight. As she stood there in the dark hall, the grey metal breaker box on the wall to her right emitted a shower of sparks.

"Shit!" she yelled, dropping her cage. Alarmed, I shone my light on the breaker box. The sparks seemed to have subsided, but I saw that a sullen plume of smoke was rising from the box. And there was an acrid, choking smell in the air.

Ro shone her light on the box also, and before I could urge her not to touch the damned thing, she opened its little grey metal door.

"Omigod," she whispered. "Kieran, there's a fire here! It's fried one of the circuits. Worse yet," she put a hand on the wall beside the box, "the wall's hot." She turned to me. "My dad's an electrician. I used to help him. I know a little bit about this. The fire — it's traveling along the wiring. No telling where it is. Kieran, we need to get out."

I thought about Leroy complaining few days ago about the shoddy wiring here in the renovated storage facility, now the testing lab and offices. Wincing, I remembered the loading bay door crashing down as it overloaded its circuit and tripped the breaker. Maybe something like that had happened today. Who knew? Damn. When we needed to get out, I'd probably have to haul the blasted door up manually by its chain, as Leroy had had to do. Well, I'd deal with that later. As for right now, though, get out? Nope.

"I have a job to do, Ro," I told her. "Just leave your cage and go on back through the bathroom window to the van. I can make two trips with the rabbits. This isn't your show. As I told you back at the house, it's mine."

I could see her dithering. I'm sure she was asking herself if she was as brave as Julia. Had Julia backed down when she'd felt the hot breath of peril breathing down her neck? Hell, no. Could Ro do any less? Should she wimp out and scuttle back to safety? Ro closed her eyes and I could see her gathering up courage from somewhere deep inside.

"No," Ro said. "I want to help. To really help. I meant it. Let's go on."

I wasn't sure what I thought about this, but I nodded. "Grab your cage then. Let's hurry."

CHAPTER 30

IN TOTAL DARKNESS, our flashlights making bright stabs of light ahead of us, we made our way down the hall toward the testing lab door.

"Tell me about this fire-in-the-wall thing," I asked Ro.

"Well, something that drew a lot of power all at once overloaded its circuit. Shoddy wiring in the first place probably," she said critically. "Instead of just tripping the breaker, this time it started a nice little fire in the box. But that had to have happened hours ago. The fire then spread down the crappy wiring, setting whatever wood it came across — joists, beams, two-by-fours — on fire. We don't know how far the fire's spread. My guess is if the wall was hot when I touched it, it's spread quite a ways. This is an old building. And fire's sneaky. You never know."

"So when does this, ah, sneaky fire break out into the halls and offices and so on?" I asked.

"When it gets a nice shot of air," she said. "It will either burn through the walls or . . . I don't know. It's kind of trapped in there, smoldering away. We need to get the rabbits out of here and get out ourselves."

I noticed that she was babbling a little. Poor kid. I couldn't blame her. I felt a little like babbling myself.

"Okay, here we are," I said, as we came to a door marked TESTING: NO UNAUTHORIZED ENTRY. I pulled Julia's key card out of my jacket pocket, swiped it through the sensor box and . . . nothing happened.

"Shit!" I yelled. Because the testing lab sensor box was as dead as the one at the top of the Deliveries staircase. No cheery red light glowed in the darkness, waiting to be turned green by the kiss of Julia's card. What the hell?

"No power," Ro said. "The fire must have fried the wiring all the way along the hall. Or farther."

Feeling a bit frenzied, I rattled the doorknob, just in case. Nope. The lab was locked up as tight as the vault at my local ScotiaBank.

"Kieran," Ro said, her voice breaking a little, "how *will* we get in?" I realized that the kid had been doing a great job of explaining fires-in-the-walls to me in an effort to squelch her panic, but right now she might be a whisker away from having a screaming meemie meltdown. Time for me to step up and solve things. After all, wasn't this what I had been paid five hundred dollars to do? You betcha. And resourceful *was* one of my middle names.

"No problem," I said. "Cover your face."

"What?"

"Do as I say," I told her, drawing my .38. I whacked the glass window in the door as hard as I could with the butt of my gun, hoping I could break it. Nope. Sighing, I put the muzzle of the gun against the sensor box and pulled the trigger. There was a flash, a huge noise . . . but the door still didn't open when I reached in and tried to turn the knob. All I'd done was destroy the sensor box. Wonderful. Well, there was another way in.

"Keep your face covered," I told Ro. "And here, take my flashlight." I angled the muzzle of my gun down, hoping I wouldn't hit anything vital inside the lab, held one arm over my face, and shot the window out of the door. The glass obligingly fell to the floor inside in dozens of tinkling pieces. But before I could tell Ro that we were going to vault agilely through the broken window in the door, the interior of the lab caught fire. Flames shot out of every wall socket, fire burst from wooden cupboards, and I felt, or seemed to feel, a wind ruffle my hair.

"Air," Rowan squeaked. "You just gave the fire the air it needed to break out of the walls. It's drawing air from the hall through the broken window in the door."

"Ah, shit!" I yelled, peeling off my leather jacket and draping it over the ragged edges of the glass in the door's window. The fire was so far limited to the walls of the lab, but as I watched, questing tongues of flame lapped across the floor, seeking anything flammable.

"We'll need to be quick," Ro said unnecessarily.

"What's this 'we?' You're staying out here."

"But — "

"But nothing. Just get those cages unfolded." I clambered through the broken window and Ro passed me the first cage. About two feet by eighteen inches, I hoped it would be big enough for three rabbits. Well, hell, it was going to have to be. For their part, the rabbits were hopping around in their stainless steel cages against the side wall, evidently terrified by the advancing fire. Damn, but they were cute, white with black noses, ears, and paws. I'd never had a rabbit as a pet, and I didn't have the tender goofy feelings for them that I had for cats, but I couldn't imagine anyone dripping caustic liquid into their eyes.

I flashed back to the dream I'd had a few nights ago in which I'd been imprisoned in a box with metal bars, the smell of urine, feces, and despair in my nose, a hot, deadly, crackling *thing* advancing across the floor toward me. Hell, I'd been one of these rabbits in that dream. Well, no time to freak out about it now. I just needed to get them *out*.

Orange tongues of flame were poking eager fingers out from under the big bank of cages, and I sidestepped them, placing the cage Ro had given me on top of a counter in the middle of the floor. Fortunately, the big cages against the wall were unlocked, and I shone my flashlight on one of them, lifting the latch, retrieving a soft, squirming rabbit, and stuffing him into my cage. The bank of stainless steel cages from which I had removed him was, I noticed, as I placed one hand against it, getting very bloody hot. No wonder the rabbits were jumping around.

"One down," I mumbled to myself to cover up my terror. "Two to go."

I repeated the rabbit retrieval twice more, noted that they were pretty uncomfortably packed in their transport cage, mentally apologized to them, and carried the cage over to Ro. We traded cages. She passed the empty one to me, and I passed the cageful of squished rabbits to her where she waited in hall on the other side of the door.

I repeated the rabbit retrieval and was just securing the door on the rabbits' cage when a fearful banging came from the back wall of the lab. What the hell? I shone my flashlight back there and saw a door with a window in it, similar to the entry door on the other side of the lab. An office? And who was making the banging? I made sure the rabbits were okay in their crowded cage on the counter, and took two steps toward the office, shining my light on the window.

"For God's sake!" I yelled. Because framed in the window was Yvon Maleck, frantically attempting to break the glass with a heavy book, and having as little luck as I'd had trying to bash in the hall window with the butt of my .38. I shone my light down on the useless sensor box by the doorknob, and understood. What rotten timing for poor Maleck — he'd evidently posted bond, slipped through Mac's fingers, and here he was, collecting whatever he needed prior to disappearing. He must have come in early, gotten caught in his office when the power went out, and was now well and truly trapped. Why the hell did his office have a sensor lock on it anyhow, I wondered. Was Island Naturals' super secret formula for mint toothpaste stashed in there?

"Help me!" he yelled. I almost laughed.

I remembered the video Julia had taken of Maleck leering at Jeoffry as he tortured him, remembered the sound of Maleck slapping Darlene, and thought, *Oh yeah? Help you?* I remembered, too, with hot shame my own funk as I'd faced him in the supply cupboard —

frightened by the gleeful, cruel, and completely alien thing that looked out of his eyes. Well, how about it, I asked myself. Was I going to help him? Turn this monster back out into the world? He'd only end up working in some animal testing lab somewhere else in Canada, torturing more small, defenseless things, more "others" in the guise of product testing, destroying them for the *schadenfreude* it brought him. I'd already drawn my gun, I realized, thinking of shooting out the office window and freeing whoever was trapped in there. But that was before I'd recognized Maleck.

Put your gun away, a vindictive little voice inside me whispered. *Leave him here. Let him burn. No one will know.*

"Kieran!" Ro called to me, "c'mon! There's fire down the hall now!"

I shouted at Maleck to get back, motioning him to stand away from the window. When he was clear, I shot out the glass. Flames leaped from electrical outlets on the wall of his office, catching a bookcase and a row of books on fire, and I heard him yell. I found that I didn't give a damn.

Holstering my gun, I passed the cageful of rabbits out to Ro, hoisted myself back through the window in the door, grabbed the cage, and ran with her down the hall, around the corner, and straight into an orange river of fire dotted here and there with islands of unburned floor.

"Kieran, we can't —" Ro screamed.

"Oh yes, we can," I told her. "Just keep running!"

CHAPTER 31

S WIFT AS CHEETAS, nimble as springboks, terrified as two warehouse mice with Vlad on their heels, we ran for the loading bay door. The soles of Ro's sneakers were smoking and one leg of my jeans was charred, but we made it. Almost home free. Almost safe. Fresh air and freedom were just on the other side of that demon roll-up door.

"Oh, fuck," Ro moaned, falling back against the door. "How do we get *this* open?"

"I have to haul the damned thing up by its chain," I said, handing her my cage of rabbits, forcing myself to be calm. "When the opening's big enough, slide the cages out and slide yourself out after them. There's a concrete ledge — it's, oh, ten feet wide. There's plenty of room for you. With any luck, Miranda will be there waiting. Then you two can get the rabbits loaded into the van."

"What about you?" Ro said.

"I'll be right behind you," I told her. Never mind that I had no idea how I would simultaneously hang onto the chain to keep the door up and get myself out onto the concrete ledge. I'd looked around for the screwdriver that Leroy had put into the chain to hold it up days ago, but it was nowhere to be seen. "Ready?"

Ro put the rabbit cages on the floor, knelt beside them, and nodded.

I leaped as high as I could, caught the chain, and dangled from it, two feet off the floor. I was hoping that my hundred and forty-eight pounds would be enough to persuade the door to move, and for a moment, I panicked. Because nothing was happening. Oh, behind us in the hall plenty was happening — a huge blast told me that something — chemicals in the testing lab, cleaning supplies, God only knew what — had caught fire and exploded. And the wooden door to the bathroom was now engulfed in flames. I cursed, because the bathroom had been my ace in the hole. If I couldn't get this damned metal door up, I had intended to take us back out the bathroom window. Getting the cages through might have been a problem, but hell, we could have removed the rabbits one by one, tossed the cages to Miranda, and re-caged them outside. Doing so would have been more time-consuming than just scooting out under the loading bay door, which was why it wasn't my first choice, but now that option was gone. Now, our lives literally depended on this miserable, heavy, capricious door.

"Move, you bastard!" I cursed, kicking it, the chain wrapped around my hands. As if to taunt me, the door rose a tantalizing trifle. I looked down. Ro was shining her flashlight on the bottom of the door, giving me enough light to see a pair of hands reaching through the opening from outside. Miranda. Thank God.

"Just a little more, Kieran!" Miranda called to me.

I kicked the damned door again, cursed some more, and it rose maybe another meager six inches. Would it be enough or would I dangle here forever, kicking the door and cursing, as Ro and the rabbits roasted? Then, looking down, I saw Ro sliding the rabbit cages out under the door, Miranda reaching in for them, and Ro snaking out headfirst through the opening.

"Kieran, c'mon!" Ro yelled.

Crap, yes, Kieran, c'mon, I gibbered to myself. I realized I had one last effort in me, and as I kicked the door and it rose another few inches, the chain slipped through my hands. I fell to the floor, expecting the door to come crashing down as it had for Leroy, but it didn't. It just . . . hung there. Omigod. Was the opening big enough for me? And if I thought it was, did I have the guts to roll out through it? I lay on the floor for a moment, looking out to the starry night sky and said a silent *Fuck it!* With a total-body shudder, I rolled out.

And then, miraculously, I was outside on the loading dock. Scrambling to my hands and knees, I was preparing to jump down and join Miranda and Ro in the van when the door rattled behind me. What? I turned . . . just in time to see Yvon Maleck's head and shoulders come through the opening. He was face down, scrabbling along, trying to pull himself forward with hands and elbows.

"Maleck!" I yelled. "Be careful of the door! Don't touch it!"

He ignored me, flipping over onto his back, squirming. Then he put both hands on the door and pushed, squirming a little more . . . a little more . . . and I heard the chain rattle as it slipped. I knew what was coming next.

"No!" I yelled as the door fell, pinning him just above his waist. He shrieked in agony, pounding on the door, pushing against it. But it was stuck, and he was stuck beneath it. Panting in pain, he looked at me, eyes desperate.

"Help me!" he screamed, a reprise of his plea in the testing lab. "The fire! It was right behind me . . . I can feel it on my feet now!"

I was sure he could, because even from where I knelt, I could feel it radiating through the metal of the door — a great, hot, hulking *presence*. Scrambling to my feet, I grabbed the bottom of the door and heaved with all my strength. But it didn't budge one iota. Maleck reached entreatingly for my hands, and I took his, pulling backward as hard as I could. Nothing. He screamed again, and I wasn't sure if it was from the weight of the door across his midsection, or the fire at his feet.

"Do something!" he shouted. "Oh, God, my feet! Anything!"

I suddenly realized that I was not going to be able to free him. It was as though he was held in the jaws of an enormous beast. But wasn't this karma? After all, how many beasts had he dispatched, laughing at their pain, their cries, their despair? Reveling in them? And here he was at the end, caught in the metal jaws of an ineluctable horror, crying out in his own pain, begging for release. Against my will, I felt a spasm of compassion for him, an incomprehensible being driven to torture animals, bound forever in a hell of his own making, the only joy he knew caused by the pain of others. Had those others come round, finally, for justice? Or was I a romantic fool?

"Listen to me," I said urgently, taking my gun from its holster, kneeling beside him. "I can't get you out. But my .38 has three shots left in it. Take it. You don't have to burn to death."

I laid my gun on his chest and closed one of his hands around it. He was weeping and I wasn't sure how much he understood. But all at once he opened his eyes and I saw comprehension in them.

"You do it," he begged. "Please."

"No," I told him. "I can't." Or was it *won't?*

He took my gun and, weeping, held it up in front of his face. I was about to say something else when with a demonic squeal of metal, the loading bay door bulged outward. I put up an arm to shield my face as a tsunami of flame burst from the door, the force of the blast lifting me off my feet and hurling me backward. I flew . . . and with me flew pieces of the metal door as it tore itself apart. I was aware that one piece struck me in the head, but curiously there was no pain, and it seemed to me that I rose toward the stars like a drowning swimmer buoyed by a friendly wave, like a soul seeking heaven, up, up, up, into the night sky, bemused and unafraid. And just before I fell to earth, I recalled that I might have heard the crack of a gunshot a few moments earlier, but I wasn't certain.

I was never certain.

SATURDAY

CHAPTER 32

I WAS A pair of ragged claws scuttling across the floor of silent seas. Above me was water the hue of swimming pools so brilliant it hurt my eyes. Below me was a rippled sandy ocean bottom. A huge black sting ray circled appraisingly above me and I became terrified of his stinger, which trailed behind him like a threat. Suddenly the bottom fell out of the sea and I slid into a smooth-sided well that ate the sunlight, and as I slipped down the sides, a horde of giant chittering ants with mandibles like scythes clashed their jaws, eager to strip my skin from my bones.

"Kieran!" someone said urgently, shaking me. "You were moaning."

I came awake, opening my eyes.

Where was I? On the couch in my living room, wrapped in a comforter.

What day was it? Saturday. I was sure it couldn't still be Friday, so it must be Saturday.

And no one was asking, but I had a headache the size of Saskatchewan.

"Miranda," I said. "Thank God. There were ants . . ."

"She's awake," a worried small voice said. "But maybe her head's hurting. Should she have another pill? I could get her some water."

I became aware of a small person in jeans and a black T- shirt with a goldfinch and the words BIRD NERD on it in yellow, sitting at the end of the couch, holding one of my sock-clad feet. Lamplight made a nimbus of her golden hair. Lamplight? Was it that late?

I wiggled my toes and Tris grinned.

"No more pills, Sprout," I said, raising tentative fingers to my head, finding an alarmingly large bandage just above my left temple. "If they're a morphine derivative, I'm allergic to them. They make me hallucinate. You know, see things that aren't there. I'd take a Tylenol though."

"Aliya!" Tris called. "Kieran's awake. She says she wants a Tylenol."

"C'mon out here, Tris," a voice I recognized as Aliya's replied from the kitchen. "She and Miranda need to talk. We'll get her a Tylenol in a minute."

I sat up, slowly, in case my head became detached from my body and floated away.

"Ro, the rabbits?" I asked.

"The rabbits are stuffing themselves with rabbit chow, alfalfa hay, and half a carrot each back at The Sanctuary," Miranda said, ticking things off on her fingers. "Apart from them, the gang's all here. Ro's downstairs on Aliya's futon. She's nursing burns on the bottoms of her feet, but she's otherwise all right. Lawrence and Max are with her — they're playing Scrabble. At least Lawrence and Ro are. Connie's helping Aliya make dinner. Tris, as you can see, was holding vigil and fretting, but she's okay now that you're awake. Oh, and Jen and Zee are due any minute."

What on earth were Jen and Zee due for? I evidently had some serious holes in my memory. I'd ask Miranda about that later, but there were other things I wanted to know first. "Island Naturals? Did it burn down?"

Miranda shook her head. "Nope. Just that firetrap storage building that Island Naturals had renovated to house the testing lab. The fire department was able to keep the fire contained. I talked to Portia this morning." She grinned. "She says it won't be rebuilt. No rabbits will ever die there."

"No?"

"No. She's in charge again. The board voted her back in. And put the kibosh on the idea of taking a step backwards into cosmetics testing on animals here on the island. Ditto for allowing it to happen in China. Portia explained to them what it would really mean. Apparently when she described the Draize test, they were very upset. And very ashamed. And," Miranda said, "she lectured the board on doing business with China. Why the hell should they, she said, when China is holding two of Canada's citizens on bogus espionage charges? Not to mention that China celebrates that damned dog and cat meat festival every year. As well, she pointed out that our fentanyl problem can be directly traced to China, which is doing nothing about stemming the tide of greenies which seem to be produced by every other Chinese guy with a chemistry set and a pill press. This information has been in the news seemingly every other day. But in case the board members missed it, she enlightened them, she told me."

"Wow. What lit a fire under her?" I asked.

"She said it was coming to the Pub Talk. It was her road-to-Damascus moment."

"Hmmf," I said. "And Philip?"

"Is no longer on the board. The deal with China hadn't been finalized, so when he was voted off —"

"— he was no longer able to negotiate," I said. "Neatly done." I was silent for a moment, thinking. "You know, I'm not complaining, but the end of the Island Naturals affair reminds me a little of the last scene of a Shakespearean comedy. Order is restored, villains get their come-uppance, star-crossed lovers couple up, and everyone sings 'Kumbaya.'"

"Well, not everyone," Miranda said.

"What do you mean?".

"Maleck died, you know," she said. "In the fire on the loading dock."

"I figured he might," I said. "I just couldn't pull him out. I hope he didn't burn, though." I looked up at her. "No one should die like that."

"Hmm," Miranda said.

After a moment, I added. "I gave him my gun, Miranda."

"Oh," she said, surprised, raising her eyebrows. "Well. That would have been a better death. If he used it."

"If he used it," I agreed.

"That was compassionate," she said. "I don't know if I could have been that compassionate."

I remembered Maleck pleading with me to kill him, and wondered what Miranda would think of my refusal. How compassionate had I really been in the end?

"I don't want to sound cruel," she said, "but maybe he got . . ."

"His just deserts?" I said.

She nodded.

"Yeah, maybe," I said. "People usually don't. But, you know, Maleck's death, how he brought it upon himself, how he fled across Canada, changing his name, trying to escape justice, well, it reminds me of something I read once. It's from an ancient Mesopotamian tale. I have a headache so I might not remember all of it, but I think I can recall the main points."

"There was a merchant in Baghdad, I think, who sent his servant to market to buy provisions. In a little while the servant came back, white and trembling, and said, 'Master, just now when I was in the marketplace I was jostled by someone in the crowd and when I turned, I saw it was Death that jostled me. He looked at me and made a threatening gesture. And now, I'm very frightened. Please lend me your horse, and I will ride away from this city and avoid my fate. I will go to Samarra and there Death will not find me'. So the merchant lent him his horse, and the servant fled the city. Then the merchant went down to the marketplace, and when he saw Death standing in the crowd, he came up to him and said, 'Why did you make a threatening gesture to my servant when you saw him this morning?' 'That was not a threatening gesture,' Death said, 'it was only a start of surprise. I was astonished to see him in Baghdad, for I had an appointment with him tonight in Samarra.'"

"Ah," said Miranda.

"Ah," I replied.

We sat in silence. I thought about Maleck, and death, and just deserts. My head hurt. Maybe I didn't need to think about him anymore.

"Kieran!" Tris said, bounding in from the hall, "Jen and Zee are here for dinner. They have Trey. And they have another cat with them. Is it Trey's buddy? The one you were talking about?"

"Another cat?" I winked at Miranda behind Tris's back. "Well, I guess it must be Trey's buddy. Better have them come in here," I told Tris, who danced out the front door.

"Something's not clicking in my brain," I told Miranda. "Did I invite guests for dinner?"

She looked at me shrewdly. "Yes. Well, I did it for you. When you were being stitched up, you told me that you wanted people to come for a *Samhnagen* dinner and asked me to call them. Remember?"

"No."

She frowned. "Hmm. Well, the hospital said you might have holes in your memory."

The hospital? I didn't remember a thing about it. That was probably just as well.

"Holes," I said. "Wonderful. Well, help me fake this, okay?"

"Sure thing."

"Look!" Tris said, as Jen led Jeoffry into the living room on one lead and Zee led Trey in on another. Both cats, I noted, had matching red harnasses.

Trey, for his part seemed a whole different cat. Gone was the downcast, furtive, miserable creature he had been for the weeks following Vlad's departure. Every now and then he trilled, rubbed his head against Jeoffry's, and gave the smaller cat an avuncular lick on an ear. He had become . . . Uncle Trey. He had a purpose in life.

Jeoffry, now that he was on his feet and I could get a good look at him, was a beauty, a dramatically marked brown tabby with probably some Bengal in his lineage. As he looked around with wide golden eyes, my heart contracted a little. How much could he really see?

"Trey's friend . . . Kieran, he looks a little like Wild Thing," Tris said, excited.

Wild Thing had been one of the missing cats Tris, Miranda, and I had rescued on my last case. I knew Tris had become very fond of the little Bengal, but he'd been promised to Jen. I smiled, though, because I thought I knew what Zee and Jen were engineering here.

"Yeah, he does, doesn't he?" I agreed.

"This guy's name is Jeoffry," Jen told Tris, eyes wide innocence. "He needs a home. We've come to, well, talk to you and Kieran about that."

"Hmm," I said, giving Jen a meaningful look. "Subtle is not one of your middle names, Jen Lau."

Jen had the good grace to look guilty, smoothing down the front of her black MEAT IS MURDER sweatshirt. Ah, the moral certitude of the young.

"Couldn't *we* give him a home?" Tris said, bending down and gathering both cats into her arms. "Jeoffry could come and live with us. I love him already. And he *is* Trey's friend."

"How's his eyesight?" I asked Zee.

She waggled one hand. "About fifty percent, I'd say."

"And what about you?" I asked. "As I recall, you were getting pretty fond of the little guy."

Zee looked regretful. "I was. But you can see what happened. Fate intervened. Jeoffry and Trey, well . . ."

"Are having a bromance," I supplied.

"Exactly," she said.

"I've been double-teamed, haven't I?" I said. "You and Jen."

Zee smiled inscrutably.

Tris looked up at me, her arms full of cats. "Kieran?"

"Well, friends shouldn't be separated," I told Tris. "So I guess he better move in with us. Do you know he's famous?"

"Famous?"

"Yeah. There was a poem written about him, oh, hundreds of years ago. Written by a man named Christopher Smart. People thought he was crazy — even put him in an institution for the mad. But he sure wrote a great poem. Here's part of it, if I've got it right:

'For I will consider my cat Jeoffry:
For there is nothing sweeter than his peace when at rest;
For there is nothing brisker than his life when in motion;
For every house is incompleat wthout him,
And a blessing is lacking in the spirit.'"

"Wow," Tris said. "A poem about Jeoffry." The she frowned. "Are there any poems about Trey? I don't want him to feel left out."

"I'm sure we can find one or two," I told her, laughing. "We'll look later."

Satisfied, Tris put the cats down.

"Zee," I said, "why don't you and Jen talk to Tris about what Jeoffry's going to need. And maybe set him up in Tris's room for the time being . . . kibble bowl, water dish, litterpan, comfy bed. I have to go outside for a bit."

Zee looked at me strangely, but nodded. I motioned for Miranda to come with me out onto the enclosed back porch, Vlad's previous kingdom, where I rummaged in a drawer, found what I wanted, and put it in a pocket of my jeans.

"Are you okay?" she asked. "You're sure about Jeoffry? I could take him to The Sanctuary. We have several adopters with blind cats. One in particular I know would be very good with him. Adding another to her household would be no problem."

"He's not completely blind," I explained, leading the way to my backyard, leaving the door open behind us. "You heard what Zee said. He's regained maybe fifty percent of his eyesight. Who's to say it won't keep improving? And he and Trey have bonded, according to her. So I think . . . yeah, we'll try him out here."

We stood on the porch steps looking up at the sky. It was a clear, cold night now that the past few days' storm system had passed, and the stars shone like chips of diamonds tossed on an expanse of dark velvet.

"This is nice," Miranda said, plainly curious, "but —"

"But what the hell are we doing out here on my back steps in the middle of the night, freezing our hindquarters off?"

"Yeah," she said, laughing, "something like that."

"We're going to light a *Samnhagen* fire. Bet you've never done that before."

She looked at me appraisingly. "Are you *sure* you feel okay? You want to light another fire? After, well, you know . . ."

"Yeah, I'm sure. And yeah, I feel okay. Help me rake these leaves out away from the house. I pushed them back here under the eaves a couple of days ago to keep them dry."

In a few minutes, we had a sizeable pile of leaves in the center of the yard, well away from the house and the apple trees.

I explained, "This is a ceremony. A kind of ritual. A throwback to my Irish ancestors. Like the extra place I asked Tris to set at the table." I frowned. "At least I think I asked her to do that. Did I?"

"You did," Miranda said.

"So, the extra place is a symbol. A place for the dead to join us for one last meal before they go to the shadowlands. Tonight the extra place can stand for, oh, anyone we've lost. My ancestors did this — the extra place at the table, the fire — every *Samnhagen*. Just before winter." I looked over at Miranda. "Is this creeping you out?"

She shook her head. "No. It's a little odd, but . . . no."

"I promised my grandmother Aiofe that I would light a *Samnhagen* fire for her after she died, and I never did," I said. "So this one is for her."

I passed Miranda one of the books of matches I had brought from the house.

"Let's light it up, Miz Blake. We need to get this done before the Oak Bay Fire Department comes."

"Indeed, Miz Yeats. Let's do it."

One of us on each side of the pile, we struck matches and tossed them into the leaves, where they caught instantly.

"Now what?" Miranda asked, sensing I was waiting for something.

"Now we wait," I told her.

"For . . ." she asked.

"We'll know when it happens," I said.

The fire grew until the entire pile of leaves was burning, flames turning Miranda's face a ruddy orange. For several long moments, the fire lit up half the back yard, sending a dazzle of light high into the night sky. I raised my face to the sickle moon, trying to follow the path of the sparks. How high did they rise, I wondered. Would they be high enough to reach the wandering spirits of the dead? Aiofe . . . would she come?

The fire began to burn down a little, and a brisk wind from the sea came scudding across the yard, twisting smoke and sparks together into fantastic shapes. One last flurry of light leaped high into the night air, an explosion of reddish gold motes like a school of copper minnows darting through dark seas, and from the house behind us came a resounding *whump*.

Miranda jumped. "The wind," she said, clearing her throat. "Just the wind."

I looked over at the closed back door of my house and smiled.

We stood there for another moment and then she asked, "Are you disappointed?"

"What?"

"Are you disappointed? Because, you know, nothing happened."

"No," I said, "I'm not disappointed."

"Good," she said, teeth chattering.

"C'mon," I told her. "Let's go in. We're freezing and I have a guest to take care of."

Puzzled, she looked at me, then nodded. "Oh yes. Jeoffry. Your new cat."

I smiled, not wanting to confound her with too much truth.

"Right," I said. "Him, too."

AUTHOR'S NOTE

Although this book is a work of fiction, it is a fact that animals still perish needlessly and cruelly in cosmetics' companies testing labs. Thirty-seven countries including the European Union and most of Asia have gone "cruelty-free", meaning rabbits are no longer dying for their citizens' next dates. Incredibly, the United States has not followed suit. Canada is on the cusp of passing its cosmetics bill, and by the time this book is published, may well have done so. Kudos to Canada.

What can ordinary people do about this reprehensible situation? As I described in my book, **look for the leaping bunny** symbol on personal care products. Purchase them. Let your dollars serve your ethics. You can be certain that any product bearing this symbol has never blinded a rabbit. Next, contact the companies who do not qualify for the leaping bunny symbol and urge them to stop testing on animals. Last, do not throw your money away donating to spurious campaigns advertised by the huge alphabet organizations.

Here are a couple of resources. The first is the nonprofit organization in Canada that has shepherded the cosmetics bill along for decades. The second is the website for the international nonprofit that administers the Leaping Bunny Program. You can check out your personal care products there.

Animal Alliance of Canada
#101 - 221 Broadview Avenue
Toronto, Ontario M4M 2G3
Canada
www.animalalliance.ca

Coalition for Consumer Information on Cosmetics (CCIC)
www.leapingbunny.org

To My Readers

I hope you enjoyed reading "Sacrificed: A Kieran Yeats Mystery."

And if you did like it, I'd be enormously grateful if you would go to "Sacrificed's" book page at Amazon and write a short review. Just tell the world if you liked the book and would recommend it to others. That's all. It would be tremendously helpful. In these brand-new days of indie publishing, Amazon reviews help boost authors' sales immensely. We have no big marketing department at a traditional publishing house to boost our sales — we rely on word of mouth, so to speak. I'm relying on you to spread the word.

Thank you in advance for this favor.

And if you like, you can head on over to my website and get on my email list to be notified of upcoming books. Or simply shoot me off an email letting me know that you liked my book. I'd love to hear from you.

Linda J Wright
www.lindajwright.com
lindajwright@mail.com

TTTTT